Amanda's Young Men

He looked at her feet and raised an eyebrow. 'You have a very small foot, madam. Our highest heels are six inches tall. You'd be balancing on the tips of your toes in them. Are you sure . . . ?'

'Try me.'

He measured her foot with the delicate touch of a spider. 'One moment, madam.'

The shoe he brought to her was a plain classic pump in metallic bronze, with six-inch steel-tipped heels that were as slender and vicious as nails. He knelt and used his palm to push up on the blunted spike to press the shoe's heel on to Amanda's foot. Amanda bore down, forcing his right hand lower and lower, until its back was flat on the floor, and trapped. Then she put just a little weight on it, indenting the flesh of his palm.

Paul looked up at her face with both pain and lust in his eyes.

'Now the other shoe,' she said.

'I . . .'

'You'll manage.'

'Yes, madam.' Awkwardly, he worked her foot into the second shoe, one-handed, until a third of her heel was in it. He set his palm beneath its spike and looked up again, his deep-brown eyes silently pleading.

By the same author:

Wild Card

Amanda's Young Men
Madeline Moore

BL

This book is a work of fiction.
In real life, make sure you practise safe, sane
and consensual sex.

Published by Black Lace 2008

2 4 6 8 10 9 7 5 3 1

First published in Great Britain in 2008 by
Black Lace
Virgin Books
Thames Wharf Studios,
Rainville Road
London, W6 9HA

www.rbooks.co.uk

Addresses for companies within The Random House Group Limited can be found at:
www.randomhouse.co.uk/offices.htm

The Random House Group Limited Reg. No. 954009

A CIP catalogue record for this book
is available from the British Library

ISBN 9780352341914

The Random House Group Limited supports The Forest Stewardship Council [FSC], the
leading international forest certification organisation. All our titles that are printed on
Greenpeace approved FSC certified paper carry the FSC logo.
Our paper procurement policy can be found at www.rbooks.co.uk/environments

Typeset by Palimpsest Book Production Limited,
Grangemouth, Stirlingshire

Printed and bound in Great Britain by
CPI Bookmarque, Croydon, CR0 4TD

1

The young road worker rotated his lollipop sign from 'Slow' to 'Stop'. Amanda could have sneaked by him legitimately, but she chose to slam on her brakes and stop within five feet of the skinny lad. Under his hardhat, his face was young and smooth. He couldn't have been more than eighteen or nineteen. Perhaps he was a student working through his summer vacation. He was tanned and bare-chested, with a circle of wiry dark hair around each small hard nipple. There were a few straggly hairs in the middle of his chest. His underwear rose an inch higher than his sagging tool belt and baggy work pants. A bead of sweat trickled from his armpit and ran down his ribcage. Amanda powered her window down and sucked in a long deep breath but all she got to taste was hot tar and dust. A thin straight line of hair descended vertically from the teen's navel to disappear under his waistband. Amanda's imagination followed it.

In contrast to the hirsute bear of a man who was attacking a slab of concrete with a jackhammer ten feet further on, the boy didn't look old enough or tough enough for hard labour. Amanda wondered whether the rougher and older men ever took advantage of the softer, vulnerable youth. Perhaps they sometimes took him into one of those portable canvas things that road workers use and passed him around like a bottle of cheap booze – made him suck them off, or forced him to bend over a sawhorse and take their big thick dicks all the way up his tight young bum.

An experience like that could confuse an impressionable young man; maybe even make him doubt his masculinity. What he needed to reassure him was a mature but sexy older woman to take him in hand, or in her mouth ... a lascivious woman, one with no agenda of her own, except of course for an overwhelming need for a good, hard ...

A car's horn blared behind her. The lad she'd been fantasising about was waving at her to get a move on. His sign had already twirled from 'Stop' to 'Slow'. Amanda put her Lexus into drive and cruised through the construction zone with no more than a few quick glances at the big bronzed, sweaty labourers.

'Brutes,' she muttered, and meant it as a compliment.

By the time she'd made a left on to Argos Road, a right on to Jason Way and pulled into the driveway of number 247, home, her fantasy included both the lean boy *and* the bearman, which made for an interesting but slightly uncomfortable scenario.

If Amanda had been anything other than just plain horny in her youth, she'd tended to be sexually submissive. Even now, when she daydreamed about older men, like her own husband, Roger, she was consistently at least a little subservient. But when she thought about sex with men who were younger than her, much younger, she was always in charge. Fantasising about both at once felt awkward, which was making it, happily, even more exciting.

What to do? She was squirming on her buttery leather seat and definitely needy. Amanda had two choices. She could either take a waterproof toy to her bath, or repair with a vibrator or just her flying fingers to bed. Those counted as just one choice – masturbation – not two. Or ... she could stretch it out for hours by turning it into a seduction-of-Roger scenario. If she could just get Roger to come home at a reasonable hour for once, she knew she could entice him. The latter choice would be preferable but the poor man had been working an awful lot of late nights recently. Money, money, money.

Amanda jangled the charm bracelet on her wrist, as he'd told her to do when she got impatient with him. The charms spelt 'H-I-G-H M-A-I-N-T-E-N-A-N-C-E', which was a lot of charms considering the bracelet was 18K gold. It had been his gift for their first anniversary. Point taken.

As soon as she got inside, she phoned Roger's office. 'Darling? T-bone steaks tonight, on the barbecue, OK?'

'Lovely, I'll do my best.' He sounded happy, as always, to hear from her.

'Do you know about what time you'll be getting home? I want to make it a specially nice night as I've barely seen you all week.' She cooed the words into the phone.

His voice rumbled low as he asked, 'Specially nice?'

'You know exactly what I mean,' she purred.

'I sure do. In that case, expect me at seven, OK?'

'The steaks will be ready, and so will I. Seven will be fine. If anything happens to delay you ...'

'It won't. I won't let it.' He paused. 'I've missed you, sweet-heart.'

'Me too.'

She hung up, already tingling with anticipation. When she'd married an older man, her girlfriends had warned her that her love-life would suffer. Maybe she didn't get it as often as she might have liked but, when she did, Roger's loving was very *thorough*. He knew her inside and out, body and mind. She tingled with excitement. Damn, it would be great to have company when she climaxed for a change.

It wasn't Roger's fault that she was over-sexed; anyway she hadn't always been this way. Much as Amanda had enjoyed sex in her twenties, it was only when she'd hit her thirties that she'd started to really need it. Maybe, as a young woman, she'd been too wrapped up in romantic dreams to coolly consider the quality of the love-making. She'd had some duds.

Marriage, a corral for many wives, had turned out to be a wide-open prairie for Amanda. With, of course, only one stud-horse to play with. A studhorse that might soon be put out to pasture?

Amanda banished the traitorous thought and set to work on the meal. Most women her age would have been happy with the kind of love-making she enjoyed once every three or four weeks. In any case, that and her once-a-day self-satisfying routine kept her perfectly content. Perhaps not 'perfectly', but pretty content. Sort of content? Content-ish?

Marginally dissatisfied?

Damn that young road worker, with his seductively lean chest and his tempting trail of belly-hair!

Amanda got the steaks out, seasoned them, prepared two large baking potatoes, mixed a Greek salad, opened a bottle of Bull's Blood to let it breathe and went upstairs. For her, this was when the love-making really began – with her elaborate preparation ritual. From the moment she dropped her day clothes into the laundry hamper and made her way, deliciously naked, into the bathroom, she was making love to Roger, even though he wasn't there and wouldn't be for another couple of hours.

She poured sandalwood and vanilla oils into her steaming tub, for Roger. The Jacuzzi jets drummed against her skin, awakening her senses, for Roger. It was for him that she rinsed and twirled a facecloth into a tight spiral so that she could delve into her most intimate places. It was to please Roger that she waxed her pubes and pumiced her elbows and feet. It was because she was saving her lust for him that she only allowed the bubbling stream from a jet to flutter her pussy lips for a few minutes, instead of letting the thrumming delight take her all the way.

When Amanda felt that she was positively glowing with cleanliness and steaming with lust, she climbed out of the tub and went into the shower stall for an intense rinse and to wash her hair. Roger loved her multi-streaked blond mop. 'Coarse-cut marmalade,' he called it.

Once she'd dried and moisturised her body, she remained naked, all the more to enjoy the primping and pampering. Roger loved her narcissism; he encouraged it. And this, she knew, was why. If they hadn't been together so long, and if she was just a little younger and not his first and only spouse, she could be considered a trophy wife. Amanda preened.

After blow-drying and fluffing her chin-length mane, she expertly dusted her eyelids with violet shadow and applied two coats of waterproof mascara. From among dozens she chose a cherry lipstick and matching nail varnish. Her lips got three coats and her nails, both finger and toe, got two.

It was time to decide what to wear. Amanda visualised her walk-in closet in her mind, though it was only a few feet away. Now that she was over thirty she was supposed to exercise her memory in order to keep her mind alert, and this was much more fun than reciting poetry by heart.

They'd be eating on the patio beside the pool. The woven cedar fence around it was twelve feet high, so she needn't worry about looking 'decent'. Truthfully, Amanda was in the mood for tall stiletto pumps, sheer black hose, a constricting waspie and a velvet choker, but somehow those didn't seem right for an al fresco meal. Nude but for strappy sandals was a tempting possibility, but if she greeted Roger totally bare he wouldn't wait to eat. Roger would need his protein for the evening's events and it was always best for his blood sugar if he ate at regular times. Anyway, she liked to make him wait, getting hornier and hornier, until he erupted into action.

She had several bikinis, two of them too skimpy to be worn in public but perfect for a private party, but they didn't quite match her mood and it wasn't like she was planning on swimming, waterproof mascara or no. Now that she'd abandoned the 'elegant bordello' look, she fancied going for 'total slut'.

Then she saw it in her mind's eye, way in the back of the walk-in, tucked in with a few remnants from her past that she'd been too sentimental to get rid of. A rummage though her actual closet uncovered an outfit she hadn't worn since she was fifteen and had (almost) forgotten she owned – a faded denim mini and a matching bomber jacket. They'd been put away when her parents forbade her to wear them. They'd said the outfit made her look cheap. That made it perfect for the look she sought.

Amanda managed to zip the skirt, although it was just a tiny bit tighter now. The jacket wouldn't do up. In fact, it wouldn't even come close. That was fine. When she posed in the skirt, well, it might have been considered scandalously short way back then, but ...

As she didn't care about ruining it, she hacked four inches off with a pair of shears. Now, *that* was short. When she bent over, two pink half-moons of her bum were exposed. Roger was in for a major treat.

Amanda chose a pair of raffia slip-on wedgies with half-inch platforms and four-inch heels from her collection of 122 pairs of footwear. She revelled in the combined advantages of being married to the owner of 31 shoe stores and having sample-sized feet. Amanda hadn't spent a penny on shoes in over eight years. The shame was Roger's chain never stocked the same styles that he brought home for her. He'd told her, more than once, that they were just too extreme for Forsythe Footwear's conservative clientele. Even plain pumps were rejected if their heels were more than three inches high. Amanda doubted Roger's judgement on that, but he was adamant and, after all, his family had been 'in shoes' for three generations, so he had to know what he was talking about.

It was shoes that had brought them together. They'd met right here in their home town of Toronto, at the Bata Shoe Museum, when both had admired a pair of sparkling Louis XV rococo pumps. His interest in selling shoes and hers in wearing them had led to a whirlwind courtship and a vigorous honeymoon. The vigour was sporadic, now, but that had more to do with his being overworked and distracted than with any real waning of lust.

But not tonight!

Amanda paused long enough to rub another helping of creamy lotion into the smooth skin of her delicate little feet before slipping on the wedgies and making her way downstairs. In her sexually expectant state, even the simple act of descending was titillating. With each step she took, a cool little breeze sneaked up her skirt and tantalised her naked sex, reminding her that she was a very naughty girl. Oh boy!

Amanda had just dropped the seasoned steaks on the grill and started the microwave when she heard the front door open. She called out, 'You've just time for a very quick shower, darling. Your robe's hanging behind the bathroom door. We'll be informal, so that's all you need.'

'I can take a hint,' he shouted back.

Amanda moved back and forth, between the patio and the kitchen, anticipation putting a swing into every step. She tended to the steaks. The microwave pinged. She took out the potatoes, split them and added sour cream and chopped chives. By the time she'd poured the wine and set a bowl of strawberries in cream on the table, Roger was with her.

'Yummy,' he said.

'The steaks are just the way you like them.'

'Not the steaks – you.' His fingers lifted one side of her loosely hanging jacket aside to fully expose her breast. 'Dessert?'

She nodded towards the bowl she'd prepared. 'Strawberries and cream.'

'Your creamy skin and your strawberry nipples?'

She slapped his hand down playfully. 'No, silly. Real strawberries and cream.'

'If you're good,' he whispered in her ear, 'I'll let you be my bowl.'

'I'll be good,' she replied. She batted her lashes and gave him a coy look. 'I'll be *very* good.'

He slid into the other side of the long rustic picnic table. Amanda joined him, opposite.

'Lovely view,' he said.

'Eat your supper.' She pushed his wineglass towards him.

Roger cut and ate his steak by instinct, it seemed. The entire time, his eyes were on her deep cleavage. Flattery like that deserves to be rewarded. Amanda pulled her feet out of her wedgies and stretched her legs out to set her soles on Roger's bare insteps.

'Nice feet,' he said.

'Thank you.' She ran the toes of her right foot up behind his left calf. His back arched a fraction in appreciation. The sole of her left foot caressed its way up his left shin. With her feet between his knees, she pressed to each side, spreading his legs.

Roger licked his lips.

Amanda had to hitch her bottom forwards on her seat to reach as both of her feet crept up Roger's thigh, parting his robe as they went.

'So soft,' he sighed. 'Silken skin!'

Her right big toe burrowed gently under and between Roger's balls, and wriggled. He put his fork down. His mouth went slack. Amanda's left foot joined her right, squirming into the hot pocket beneath his impressively large scrotum. 'Nice?' she asked.

'Mm.'

'How about this?' Her feet retreated a few inches, soles turned in, so that she could stroke them up both sides of his erection. It was quite a rush, being able to get him so excited using only her most distant extremities, which she considered her least sexual parts, her pretty little feet.

Roger leant back and shifted forwards on his seat before swigging his wine.

The ball of her left foot pressed his shaft into the hollow of her right foot's arch and worked up and down, up and down. Amanda watched Roger's face. He gave up on the last of his steak and gripped the edge of the table. His eyes hooded and lost focus. Amanda's stroking accelerated. A tiny frown appeared between Roger's eyes. His face took on an intense look. He sucked in a breath . . .

And Amanda stopped.

Roger grunted.

'I could keep this up until you squirt all over my toes, if you like,' she offered.

He cleared his throat. 'Tempting, but don't. I want to make love to you properly, Amanda.'

She raised an eyebrow. 'You do? Why's that?'

'Because you're the sexiest little minx any man could ever wish for, and you damn well know it, don't you?'

'It's nice to hear. How do you want to make love to me? Tell me, darling. I love it when you talk dirty.' Her toes gripped his shaft again, just for the pleasure of feeling its heat and satiny texture.

'Missionary, doggy, sideways, hard and fast, deep and slow, loving and like a crazy animal – and you'd better stop what you're doing right now or I'll come.'

'All that, for little me?' she teased. Releasing him, she climbed up on to her bench seat. Very slowly, she lifted her skirt the few inches it took to expose her naked mound. 'Is this what you want?'

His voice squeaked as he said, 'You know it.'

'And this? She turned and bent over stiff-legged to show him her bottom.

'Amanda!'

She turned again and pouted at him. 'And my mouth? There once was a time when you loved to use my mouth.'

'Amanda, I adore your mouth.'

'You like to fuck it, don't you?'

'And kiss it,' he defended.

'Both are good.' She looked at his plate. 'Are you going to take long with that?'

'Not another minute.'

He stood up and wrapped his arms around Amanda's naked thighs.

She squealed, 'Unhand me, you brute!'

Roger faked a Victorian melodrama laugh. 'Too late, me pretty. You're in me power now!'

'Oh no!'

He carried her to the other end of the table and laid her on it, on her back. The wood was brutally hard. Somehow, that made being crushed on to it even sexier. Roger captured Amanda's mouth with his and kissed her until she started to tremble. When he released Amanda, her high spirits had been subsumed by a weightier emotion – desire.

She looked up at him, her lids half-lowered over her bright baby-blues. 'What are you going to do to me, you monster?'

'This!' He lifted her heels and pressed them wide apart, obscenely exposing her to his admiring gaze. Holding her in place, Roger bent his face down to his wife's sweet sex.

'Oh, God, Roger, please ...' she moaned.

'Mm.' The tip of his tongue ran up from the pucker between her bottom's cheeks, across her taut perineum and up to the slick nether lips that practically quivered in anticipation. 'Yummy!' His tongue squirmed into her.

Amanda held her breath, wanting to ask him to lap higher but not wanting to hurry him. It wouldn't have done her any good, anyway. He, just like her, loved to tease.

His tongue worked from side to side. Roger had often told her how much he loved to consume her juices and, though it had been a while since he'd paid her that compliment, he didn't seem to have lost his taste for her. His hands moved, crossing her ankles above her head so that one hand could hold her like that. What was he doing, reaching sideways? Oh yes – the strawberries and cream.

Amanda felt something very cool touch the delicate tissues that lined her sex. It withdrew, to be replaced by his tongue. That was new! He'd never put cream inside her, to eat, before. So, old dogs *can* learn new tricks.

Then the cream was being daubed on her little button. Yes! And something was probing inside her. From the feel of it, a very large strawberry was being worked in and out of her. It was strange; the rough berry's texture, the cool smoothness of cream, her hot velveteen inner walls yielding to the shape of the fruit. Once Roger had established a rhythm with the strawberry he was pushing in and out of her, his lips closed on her cream-coated clit. He sucked and lapped and flicked it, making her more and more excited and still it went on and on and ...

And he stopped.

'Don't stop!'

'Say please?'

'Please?'

'Beg for it!'

'I'm begging. Let me climax, please, Roger. I can come again, after. You know that! *Please.*' Some irrational part of her honestly feared he'd stop, now, and keep her from the locked and loaded orgasm in her gut.

'In that case ...' His licking resumed.

Amanda felt his fingertips curl up behind her pubic bone and massage her G-spot. She practically sobbed with relief. 'Yes, Roger,' she gasped. The orgasm launched without further delay. 'Yes, yes, yes ... Yes!'

Her legs tried to flail but Roger held fast, trapping the deep contractions inside her, or so it seemed. She groaned with each spasm. Relief mixed with satiation; it was so damn good to orgasm by his hands rather than her own. So goddamn good. Only when the last aftershock had shuddered through her did he release her ankles. She collapsed, as if sun and sex had melted her bones.

'You're the best, baby,' she crooned, eyes half-closed. 'The very best.'

'Thank you.' He loomed over her and bit into the strawberry that had been inside her. 'Want a taste?'

She nodded dreamily.

He put the berry to her lips. 'That looks sexy – the way your lips work on that strawberry,' he said.

'Let me up and I'll show you something even sexier.'

Roger released her.

'Your turn to get on to the table,' she announced. Amanda stood, only slightly unsteady on her feet. The melting bliss of a moment earlier was gone and, more than she'd ever wanted anything in her life, or so it felt at that moment, she wanted it back.

'OK.' He sat, knees wide.

'Lie back.' She put her small hand to his big chest and pushed lightly. He fell back. His robe parted so that only the tie ran across his belly. She pulled the knot apart and the robe fell completely open. She observed his body as an artist might observe a blank canvas. Amanda placed a strawberry in his navel. She dabbed two dollops of cream on to his nipples, snow on his two dark little peaks. Amanda smiled at him, wanting to make him ask.

Roger shook his head slightly, smiling back. He wouldn't try to rush her any more than she'd tried to rush him.

Amanda took a big scoop of cream in her fingers and slathered it up and down his rigid shaft.

'Ahhhh. That's nice,' he said. He seemed to relax a little against the hard table.

'I love cream,' she told him. 'Yours is my favourite, but this'll do for now.' She took him in hand, two fingers holding him delicately at his base while she ran her tongue up the length of him in one long slow slurp.

Roger's hips twitched up at her.

Her lips closed over the head. It was usually hot in her mouth, feeling as if it had a fever, but the cream cooled it and made it slippery. She nodded, just a little, rubbing his crown against her hard palate, knowing how much he liked that. His moan didn't surprise her. Amanda's free hand found the strawberries and cream. Her fingers searched for a big berry. When she found one, she scooped up more cream on it and applied it gently to the tight knot of Roger's rear passage. He'd never allowed her to penetrate him there, but he did enjoy having the sensitive ring of muscle tantalised.

Rotating the berry and applying just a tiny bit of pressure, Amanda began to work him with her mouth in earnest, lips smacking, tongue lapping, head bobbing, fingers gripping, all progressively harder, until he was hitting the back of her throat with each thrust.

Roger blurted, 'No – stop!'

Amanda stopped. She raised her head.

'Stop.' He groaned.

'But I like it when you come in my mouth.' She smiled, her lips loose and wet.

'I know, but not yet, my darling-slut.' Roger rolled off the table, and shrugged off his robe, his naked body thick and powerful, his chest matted with dark hair, his manhood smooth and hard, rising from a thatch of crinkly pubic hair. 'Here you go!' He heaved her up bodily and perched her on the table's very edge, so that her pussy was just beyond it. Amanda leant back on straight arms. Roger's left hand lifted her minuscule skirt out of the way. His right steered his smooth rigid shaft to the parted lips. His hips pushed and he sank deep into her.

The thrust seemed to extend from his tip right into the dark pit of her belly. Amanda's groan was deep, as if he'd forced it from her with the weight of his push.

'I love it when you do me like this, Roger. Go slow, please, make it last.' She shuddered. Her jacket slipped halfway off her shoulders.

Taking the hint, he leant over her and took her nipple between his lips.

She arched her back. 'Oh yes, yes. Suck hard, please. Bite me.' She felt his teeth, gripping hard enough to send electric shocks from her nipple to her clit, gentle enough to do no harm.

His head drew back, elongating her breast, before he released it. Roger's hands cupped the cheeks of her bottom and lifted. She wrapped her arms around his neck and Roger stood, taking her clear of the table. Her legs folded around his hips. He jerked, throwing her upwards a few inches, and met her descent with an upwards thrust of his hips.

Older man? Yes, he was, but not so old he couldn't make love to her free-standing. Obviously showing off, Roger strode around the patio and poolside. Each step was translated into a thrust into Amanda. She writhed, impaled on his pole. With his hips under the backs of her knees, she was able to grind her clit against his pubic bone. Her second orgasm hit, sudden and hard. She rode him through the contractions, then straight into another paroxysm that rocked her with pleasure.

Roger's body stiffened. 'Christ,' he hissed. He stood stock still, his fingers gripping her bum hard as he flooded her insides.

'Christ!'

He was bruising her now, his grip was so tight. She clung to him, clenching hard with her pelvic muscles as if to milk him of every last drop. 'You're incredible,' she murmured when he'd stopped swearing. She gave him another experimental squeeze.

Roger couldn't reply. He was still spurting. He staggered a couple of feet and toppled them both into the pool. They came up spluttering and laughing.

'Enough?' he asked. He trod water and leant to kiss her.

'God, yes, for a while, anyway,' Amanda said. She was utterly sated. Amanda thanked her lucky stars that she'd married a man who, although he might be older than she, was still as strong as the proverbial bull.

Ten days later, Amanda got a call from the police. Roger had been found, naked, alone and dead, in a motel that rented by the hour. It looked like a heart attack.

2

They all arrived on the same day: the insurance cheque, the
brass urn with Roger's ashes, his watch, his bunch of keys, his
wallet and his prized hi-tech paper-thin multi-function cell
phone. Amanda laid them in a row on the dining-room table.
This was it, the sum total of a man's life. They'd had no children
so this was all that was left of him. Amanda wished she could
cry like an ordinary widow, but she couldn't. Roger had died
cheating on her and that complicated everything, especially her
grief.

So. She had a life to live. It had been a month. She couldn't
grieve but she'd gone through the other stages: denial, anger,
guilt and so on. The guilt had been the hardest to deal with.
She'd read that it was quite common for newly bereaved
people to experience extreme lust, and that it was perfectly
natural – a genetic response. In her case she had every right
to bring herself off, as she had on those many, many nights
when she'd been left alone while Roger 'worked' late. Even
so, she'd denied herself any form of release because she knew,
if she gave in and masturbated, she wouldn't make it halfway
through before she'd be sideswiped by hate, first for Roger
and then for herself. Even her guilt was complicated.

Now she had his remains in front of her, in her power. Now
it was time to move on. Since the day of their wedding,
Amanda had devoted herself to Roger. Her world had shrunk
to him, home, shopping, a special event here or there and a
few friends who, she now realised, had been more his friends

than theirs. At this point she had two choices: she could take shelter in a cocoon, just 'live' and do what amounted to nothing – or she could go out there, face the world, be dynamic and adventurous.

It wasn't a hard decision to make. Out there, in the real world, there were men, energetic young men practically vibrating with lust. All these years, it seemed, Roger had been tomcatting around while she'd stayed true to him, except in her vivid imagination. But now she took off her wedding and engagement rings and, with them, all the restraints that marriage had imposed.

Amanda had a lot of catching up to do, just to even the score, so she'd better get started.

First, she dug a hole under Roger's favourite apple tree and poured his ashes into it. That was the end of him. Next, she changed into a businesslike black suit and took her million-dollar cheque to the bank.

Mr Sorensen, the bank manager, offered his condolences even as he drooled over the size of her deposit. 'Nice to get rid of that overdraft, right, Mrs Garland, even though . . .' He spluttered to a halt.

'Overdraft? What overdraft?'

'Your husband's account – his line of credit.'

'Why on earth did Roger need an overdraft?' she asked. Amanda wondered just how generous her husband had been to his various bimbos.

'I'm not sure why,' Sorensen continued, 'but Mr Garland hadn't deposited a company cheque in over eighteen months. The line of credit is what he – you – were living on.'

Damn it, how many secrets had Roger had? Amanda cut the interview short and stormed off to Forsythe Footwear's offices on the tenth floor of the Rackstaff Building. She had Roger's keys. She'd inherited his shares, his controlling shares. Those, both the keys and the shares, added up to *power*. She'd never had power before, except the power of love that she'd thought she'd had over Roger.

Amanda marched up to the pretty little pink-haired receptionist and looked straight into her pale-green eyes. 'I want to see the chief accountant, now,' Amanda said, feeling as if sparks were crackling between her fingertips.

'The Chief Financial Officer? Mr Eggerdon? Who shall I say is calling?'

'Your boss, Ms Amanda Garland, widow of the late lamented Roger Garland, that's who!'

It was immensely satisfying to watch the girl's face flush to match her outrageous hair. The call was placed with trembling fingers.

An hour later, Amanda was feeling somewhat mollified but still worried. Eggerdon, a pleasant but owlish little man, had seemed delighted to have Amanda take over the frayed reins of Forsythe Footwear. It seemed that the company had been bleeding money for years. Not only hadn't Roger drawn a salary for the past eighteen months, but he'd been pumping money in. No, Eggerdon had no idea where the funds had come from. Now, with the five-million-dollar insurance that the company had had on Roger, it could stay afloat for two or even three more years but eventual ruin was inevitable, unless some miracle turned its fortunes around.

Eggerdon offered to calculate the back salary owed to Roger and draw a cheque for Amanda. She declined. There was no way she was going to let the company her husband had slaved for all his life go under! Poor Roger – the bastard! It was disconcerting how one minute Amanda mourned the man, the next she hated him. There was only one cure that she could think of – get another man, or two, or three, and have steamy sex with them as many times as it took to get her back to her senses.

3

Apart from the one tailored black suit and the two pairs of old
jeans that she wore for gardening, Amanda's wardrobe could
be divided into two categories. She had stay-at-home things,
ranging from pretty and cute to downright erotic, and she had
'formal' – gowns and dresses for entertaining or being enter-
tained, for cocktail parties or for dancing or the theatre. There
was no way she could launch her new career as a dynamic
businesswoman in any of the clothes she already owned.
Fortunately, after paying off that overdraft, she still had nine
hundred thousand dollars and change.

Amanda went shopping.

Chez Chic was showing a new collection, Dernier Cri,
which Amanda fell in love with. Both the skirts and the
pants were high waisted, coming up to just below her bust.
The skirts came in two lengths: to just above the knee and
down to the ankle. The jackets were in a narrow-sleeved
boxy style, almost Chanel, but abbreviated, just meeting the
skirts. Alternatively, there were bolero tops, minimalised to
the point that they were almost shrugs. Everything was very
fitted. The fabrics were either stretchy and bias cut or clinging
silk knit jersey. The pants' cuffs flared slightly. The hems of
the skirts were very narrow – so restricting it would have
been impossible to walk in them if it hadn't been for the side
slits that were adjustable, fastening with Velcro, press-studs
or invisible zippers.

Amanda liked the idea of being able to decide exactly how

much leg she'd show, and of having the option to increase or decrease her exposure at whim. Since her spending was an investment, not an extravagance, she bought a dozen outfits, mainly in plain black but with a couple in pin-stripe charcoal and one in dove grey, with a pale-pink chalk-stripe.

Her next stop was Coquette, for tops and hose. The stockings she had at home were almost all black, Roger's preference. Black hose would be too much with most of those severe suits, so she bought three pairs of Dim stay-ups in flesh tones and six in gunmetal grey. Amanda found some turtleneck sweaters in silk and in knitted jersey, and purchased a half-dozen of each in a variety of colours. Her new suits called for blouses as well, so she added a couple of white ones in waffle poplin and three more in plain crisp linen before breaking down and splurging on one in each of black and white chiffon and another black turtleneck, but in see-through stretchy net. None of those tops could very well be worn to the office but she just couldn't resist them. Nor would any man she allowed to see her in them.

Roger would have loved those last items. He'd doted on anything that her skin showed through and the black net turtleneck exposed more than it concealed while the chiffon blouses were as transparent as the smoke from an autumn bonfire.

Fuck him! Some other man was about to get the benefit, just as soon as she found a suitable candidate. 'Some other men' and 'candidates' she amended.

High on retail therapy, she also bought three dresses that she had no possible excuses for, except that they looked sexy. Her final purchases were a Gucci briefcase, a Mont Blanc fountain pen and a pristine pad of linen-finish paper.

On the following Monday, Amanda dressed as an executive

for the first time. She chose a long black skirt, slit adjusted to knee height, a white linen blouse and a black jacket. At nine in the morning, she hip-swayed her way into the reception area of Forsythe Footwear, showing boldness but feeling a total fraud. Perhaps she'd fooled old Eggerdon into thinking she could just sail in and turn the company around but she couldn't fool herself. She could, however, reinvent herself. Perhaps she could reinvent Forsythe Footwear at the same time. Which was right now.

'Good morning,' she told the doll-faced candyfloss-haired receptionist. 'Where's my office?'

'Your office?'

'The one my husband, Mr Garland, used when he was alive. I'm taking over.'

'Oh! This way, Ms Garland I'm – um – Nola.' Unaccountably, the girl's voice dropped to a whisper when she spoke her own name. She fluttered out from behind her desk. Her flared skirt couldn't have been as much as a foot long from its low-ride waistband to its flirty hem. Her legs were very attractive. Apparently, Amanda was going to have stiff competition in the leg-show department.

That was a ridiculous thought! She wasn't in any sort of competition, especially not with a girl who couldn't be a day over 25, if that.

Amanda followed Nola into an office that had a plate-glass wall that looked out into the reception area. Thank goodness, the wall had vertical blinds. Amanda certainly didn't want to be on display as she worked, doing ... Well, she'd find out what she'd be doing, in due course. Her dead husband's office held a black leather couch, a credenza that ran the length of one wall and that was inlaid with black leather, and three matching chairs. All three were large but the one behind his desk was by far the biggest.

Roger's desk was long and wide and also inlaid with black leather. It was equipped with a phone, a pen-holder and the sleek screen, mouse and keyboard of a computer, and three silver framed photographs. When Nola left her alone, Amanda hung up her jacket and turned on the computer. The screen asked for a password. She tried her own name. It was accepted. This was no time to wonder for the thousandth time how a man who used his wife's name as a password and kept not one or two but *three* framed photos of her on his desk ended up dead in a sleazy motel, but she did anyway. Who had he been with when he died?

It took her about an hour to find her way around the various programmes. Most of what she discovered were reports and summaries. It seemed that all of the shops were overstocked despite steadily falling sales. Most of them were spending far too much on their payrolls, according to the targets someone, likely Eggerdon, had set.

The company's problems were obvious – low sales, high inventory, high payrolls. The solutions?

Amanda sat back and tapped her new pen on her teeth. Roger had likely been looking for answers for months, or years. What were the chances she'd find one instantly? Perhaps Roger had left notes? She tugged open the narrow middle drawer of the desk and found some small change, a clear plastic ruler and a couple of twisted paperclips. The big bottom right drawer had alphabetised hanging files, which she flipped through fairly quickly. As far as she could tell, there was nothing of particular interest to be found there. Top right? It was locked. Amanda fished Roger's keys from her briefcase and found one that worked.

The first thing that caught her eye was a little bulging velvet bag. When she pulled the drawstring loose and dumped the contents on to the desk, a dozen gold charms, many with precious stones set in them, gleamed up at her. She poked them with her fingertip. There was a little Christmas tree and – her eyes welled at the sight of it – the number 25, with what had to be a diamond flashing above it. A couple of tears trickled down her cheeks as she scooped up the rest of the charms and dumped them back into the bag. He might have been cheating on her but he'd obviously had no intention of ever leaving her. That had to mean something! She held the anniversary charm up to her bracelet; she'd been wearing it for so long it had become a part of her and she'd practically ceased to notice it years ago. Roger. Maybe she should just forgive his indiscretions and focus on the love they'd shared as husband and wife.

Amanda added the anniversary charm to the bag and placed it back into the drawer, back on top of some glossy pages that looked as if they'd been torn from magazines. Curious, fully expecting to find illustrations of footwear, Amanda scooped them up and put them on the desk.

Oh! Oh no! Oh, Roger!

The girl in the first picture that Amanda saw was certainly wearing shoes – shoes with heels that had to be five or maybe six inches high – but those, and hose, were *all* she was wearing. She was posed bent over the padded arm of a sofa, with her bare bottom high, and blotched crimson.

Damn him! Not only had Roger cheated on her, but he'd also been reading kinky magazines. Amanda wouldn't have minded if he'd brought them home and been honest about his predilection – perhaps shared it with her – but to hide it, to keep it in a locked drawer, that was too much! She'd never suspected he had a taste for spanking. If he'd asked her, she'd have let him. He should have known that. She'd never refused him any submissive act or sexual pleasure; in fact, she'd given him the clear green light to bugger her bottom and he'd been the one to balk.

The next picture was a cartoon of a girl dressed as a secretary, over the knee of a man in a three-piece suit. Amanda guessed he was supposed to be her boss. Her skirt was up around her waist; her panties dangled from one ankle. The man was spanking her.

Amanda looked closer. There was a caption that looked as if it was handwritten. It *was* handwritten. 'Us, later?'

Trembling with fury, Amanda leafed through the rest of the pile. The pictures seemed evenly divided between spanking fetish and bondage, with titles like *Februs*, *Fessee* and *Hogtied*. There was a picture of a woman wearing nothing but an incredibly tight corset. She was hanging by ropes that were tied around her ankles and wrists. Someone had scribbled under it, 'The suspense is killing her.' Most of the notes were in the form of suggestions rather than poor jokes. 'I'd like to try this' appeared frequently, as did 'Fancy me this way?' and the like.

'Damn it, Roger!' she barked at the photo of the two of them he kept on his desk – this one taken on a friend's yacht. 'If you weren't already dead I'd kill you myself.'

She was so angry her outburst failed to make her laugh. Roger had been one kinky son-of-a-bitch and, worse, he hadn't shared his fetishes with her. It's bad enough a man cheats, but, when he does things with another woman, or other *women* that he didn't do with his wife, even though she'd have willingly tried them, that's total betrayal.

Boiling mad, Amanda ripped the pages in half, then in half again, but tearing through them another time was beyond her fingers' strength so she dropped them in a waste basket.

Oops! They'd be found there. She retrieved them and put them in her briefcase to get rid of later. But she had to do something to make Roger pay. She fumbled at the jewellery that jangled at her wrist, releasing the lobster claw catch and letting the gold bracelet fall on top of the torn pages. Damn Roger! Amanda scooped up the bracelet and dropped it into the velvet bag with the other charms. Let it never see light again! She'd replace it with a Cartier watch and not notice its absence a bit.

Somewhat mollified, Amanda got up and opened her office's blinds. That girl, Nola, was talking on the phone. Nola had a desk, with drawers, even if not as big as Roger's. Eggerdon had to have a desk with drawers. Come to that, so did everyone here. What if they all held secrets? Perhaps the answer to Forsythe Footwear's problems was hidden in someone else's desk drawer. Amanda decided to find out.

4

At five after five, Nola poked her fluffy pink head into Amanda's office. 'Anything I can get for you, Ms Garland? We're closing up now?'

'No thanks. I'm fine.' Amanda turned back to the computer screen she was pretending to be working at, having finished a thorough investigation of Roger's paper files ages ago. She watched Nola leave. That big window on to the reception area was useful. By peering between the slats of the blinds, she was able to watch everyone leave, even if she didn't know their names or what most of them did, and not be seen herself. Eventually, Eggerdon switched the lights off and locked the door behind him, leaving Amanda alone. She gave him twenty minutes to come back for something he might have forgotten and then turned the lights back on.

Her first bit of spying was in Nola's desk. The girl was the only good-looking female Amanda had seen there so far, so, if Roger had been screwing an employee, she was the most likely candidate.

Yes! Bingo! In the little bitch's bottom drawer, under the innocent copies of *Vogue* and *Bazaar* were issues of *Janus*, *Hogtied* and *Fetishette*, some of which had pages missing – pages that had obviously been annotated with obscene invitations and slipped to Nola's lover, Amanda's husband! The little whore liked to be tied up and spanked, did she! Amanda would like to tie her up and spank her, all right, but she'd guarantee the slut certainly wouldn't enjoy it, not the way Amanda would lay on the beating!

Amanda sat in the trollop's chair for a few minutes to cool off before she checked the other desks. When her breathing was steady and her pulse had stopped racing, she went to Eggerdon's office. His desk was big and ornate, not old enough to be an antique, but getting there. His shelves were crammed with binders and accounting manuals. Amanda opened a few but found nothing of interest. Like Roger's files, it would take some time to go through Eggerdon's paperwork. She decided to move on.

The next office door had a brass plate: 'Sophie Sharpe, VP Purchasing'. Inside, it looked almost unoccupied, with nothing personal anywhere and nothing on or in the desk but a pristine blotter.

Two hours later, the only dark secrets she'd discovered were a yellow rubber duck with a moustache drawn on its bill, a packet of Peek Freans Shortcake and half a box of Quality Street.

Amanda decided to take a break so she returned to Nola's bottom drawer in the hope of learning she-didn't-know-what from those kinky magazines.

No sooner had her fingers closed on the glossy pile than a pleasant but stern baritone asked, 'What do you think you're doing?'

Amanda let the magazines drop back into the drawer and turned, managing to nudge the drawer closed with her knee as she did so. The voice belonged to a very large man in a dark-blue uniform that had 'security' emblazoned on its jacket's breast pocket. He had to be well over six foot, with a neck that was wider than his head and sloping shoulders that were twice as wide as his waist. His face was kind of craggy but it was softened by the almost contained amusement that danced in his hazel eyes.

'I asked you what you were doing,' he said. 'Don't tell me that's your desk because I happen to know that it isn't.'

'I-I . . .' She couldn't very well explain that she was searching her own employees' desks, could she? Amanda tried, 'I haven't stolen anything, honest.' She felt herself blush at the lie. She'd never been able to resist the brazil-nut-shaped Quality Street chocolates that came wrapped in shiny purple paper and she still had one in her mouth.

The man's eyes narrowed. 'I'll have to verify that.'

'Verify?' Amanda chewed and swallowed the candy.

'That you haven't stolen anything. I'll have to search you – unless you'd rather I called the police?'

Amanda swallowed again. Playing dumb, she asked, 'Search me?'

'Assume the position.'

She gave him another blank look while she considered how she felt about having her body searched by this large powerful man. On the whole, she decided, she fancied the prospect.

'Hands on the desk, feet back and spread wide,' he ordered.

'Oh.' Amanda tried to spread her feet but her narrow skirt kept her knees pretty well clamped together. She reached down, found the tab of the invisible zipper and tugged upwards. When she reached the top of her thigh she paused, thought for a second, then continued all the way up to her waist. The look on the man's face told her that he understood why she'd exposed so much more of herself than obeying his order demanded. Amanda glanced back and down at his crotch but there was no visible reaction there – yet.

That amounted to a challenge!

She turned to face the desk, flattened her palms on it and

shuffled back, feet far apart, to make a bridge of her body. Her skirt fell open along the slit, baring her left leg from her high-heeled pump to the rounded softness of her hip. Amanda silently thanked the impulse that had moved her to pull on a minute thong that morning.

The security man squatted behind her and put his big hands on her ankles. It was the first time any man other than Roger had touched her in an intimate way for over eight years. Not knowing his name made the contact more thrilling, more in keeping with her darker fantasies. His palms slid up her legs – over the fabric of her skirt on the right, rasping over the sheer nylon of her stocking on her left.

Then over the naked skin of her left thigh.

Amanda shivered. She sucked her tummy in. The intrusive, violating hands continued higher, over her hips and waist, upper body, shoulders and arms. She held her breath. Muscular arms wrapped around her. Those searching hands cupped her breasts through the linen of her blouse and compressed them.

His voice, breathy and in her ear, said, 'You could be an industrial spy. You might have a tiny camera concealed some-where about your person. I'm going to have to search your body cavities.'

Amanda bit her lip. She could bring an instant end to this humiliation with a few words and the production of her ID. Perversely, she didn't want to. The irony was she was taking advantage of this man by letting him believe that he was taking advantage of her. That made it fair, didn't it? Or, at least, it made it fun.

His fingers fumbled with the button at her waist. Her skirt was whipped aside, leaving her sex to the dubious protection of a minuscule thong.

'Maintain the position,' he growled. His broad hand half-turned her face. 'Open wide.'

Two thick fingers slid between her parted lips. They pressed down on her tongue, then moved it from side to side as he probed into the pouches of her cheeks. Her tongue was lifted so that he could explore beneath it. Amanda felt like an animal that was being inspected by a potential purchaser. His touch was so impersonal she felt sullied – and that was deliciously thrilling.

His fingers left her mouth. Amanda braced herself. He eased the damp crotch of her thong aside. Those invasive fingers parted the lips of her pussy. She held her breath. Her thighs tensed. The tips of two of his fingers were just inside her, then they eased deeper. She felt his knuckles pressing her lips, spreading them wider. He pushed up, to both sides, then down. His fingers curled up behind her pubic bone and palpitated her G-spot.

'You're very wet,' he commented.

Amanda swallowed hard and said nothing.

He explored, not roughly but very firmly, as if he was determined to memorise every sensitive crevice and fold of her. 'There's just one last place you might be hiding something,' he crooned into her ear.

Amanda froze. She hadn't thought of that. Roger had never shown any interest in her there. In that one respect, she was still a virgin.

Her sphincter knotted at his touch.

'It'll be easier on you if you relax.'

She tried, but it was hard. The pad of his thumb rimmed her delicately. It was slick with her own juices. It pressed. Somehow, she forced herself to loosen. The thumb probed. The odd sensation made her groan.

'That didn't hurt,' he told her.

He was right. It didn't hurt exactly. Her discomfort was more emotional than physical. It was so intrusive.

He pushed, opening her, forcing that thick strong thumb up inside her, into the tight hot forbidden passage. Surrendering to some depraved impulse, Amanda pushed back at it, impaling herself deeper.

There was admiration in his voice when he said, 'You randy little slut!'

Meekly, she replied, 'I have no choice. I have to do anything you tell me to. I have to submit to anything you want to do to me. Absolutely *anything*.'

He chuckled. 'That's right, you do.' His left hand flattened on Amanda's tummy, holding her steady. His right spread, his thumb pushing deeper into her bum, two fingers penetrating her pussy. No longer pretending to search her, he pumped into her rhythmically, stretching her, forcing two and then three fingers deeper and deeper, filling her.

Amanda squirmed back at him, meeting thrust with push, riding the degradation as much as she rode the hardness and strength. His fingers and thumb closed, clamping on the thin membrane that divided her rectum from her vagina. Now each push seemed to move her insides. Amanda had never felt so helpless, so vulnerable. A finger of the hand on her tummy found her thickened clit and punished it.

Through gritted teeth, he told her, 'Come for me, bitch! Cover my fingers with your hot cream. Let me feel your insides shudder.'

The lewd words triggered her. Amanda's shuddering climax seemed to start somewhere behind her navel and radiate outwards until she felt it tingle in her toes, her fingertips, even her forehead. With each convulsion it gathered force, until it seemed the orgasm might actually rip her apart. Guttural sounds spilt from her lips. She knocked her head back against his chest. Christ, it was a climax that had been a long time coming and, now that it was here, seemed to go on and on until she half-feared it might never stop. Finally the furious tide began to ebb and, as it did, her strength drained away. If he hadn't held her and lowered her to her knees, she would have collapsed.

When her vision cleared, he was perched on the very edge of Nola's desk, legs spread, stiff and extended.

'Somebody hasn't been properly taken care of in a while,' he commented.

Amanda was too grateful to bother denying it. She grinned foolishly.

'I'm not done with you,' he told her, and pulled the zipper of his fly down.

'I understand.' The words came out in a meek whisper.

He freed his manhood from his fly. It jutted above her face, thick and throbbing, its head already wet. Amanda sat up, inhaled the sweet muskiness and parted her lips. A broad hand covered the back of her head. Resistance, had she wanted to resist, would have been pointless. He was big all over, a hundred times stronger than she, a great alpha male in contrast to her trembling puny female self. It was utterly thrilling. He drew her forwards. His glistening knob pushed her lips apart. Amanda sucked a deep breath, readying herself. His hand compelled her to take the head, then the shaft, pressing her tongue down and burrowing into her mouth until he butted against the back of her throat. Amanda relaxed her gag reflex, something she was happily very good at. He was so big, so smooth, so hard ... So overwhelming!

His grip changed. He took her head between his hands, hands that swamped it, and pushed it away until his cock's head was only just inside her lips, and pulled in again. Slowly at first, but with an accelerating rhythm, the big stranger, she almost thought, 'fucked her face' – but that wasn't accurate. He was *masturbating* himself with her mouth.

The wetness of her mouth and the pistoning combined to make obscene noises that she felt as much as heard.

And then he stiffened.

Amanda waited for what seemed an eternity before the delicious hot flood filled her mouth.

When he recovered, he said, 'You did good. I hate it when my women choke.'

Amanda probably should have been shocked, but she wasn't. The comment amused her and, God help her, made her preen. She giggled.

A crooked smile crossed his lips. 'We haven't introduced ourselves properly, have we? My name's Trevor. I work for the building – security.'

'I'm Amanda, Amanda Garland. I own Forsythe Footwear.'

'You kidding me?'

'No.'

He grimaced. 'You had me fooled, huh? I'm not complaining, though. Er – are you? Complaining?'

Amanda swiped the back of her hand across her mouth. She shook her head.

The big man zipped up. He mock-saluted. 'Ms Garland, anything I can do for you, any time, you just whistle.'

'I don't think I could manage to pucker up right now, but I'll be sure to remember your kind offer, Trevor.'

5

The next day, Amanda didn't get to the office until after lunch. She'd worked late the day before, after all. She managed to smile and say good afternoon to Nola, although it hurt her face. Amanda ordered, 'Black coffee and a mineral water with a lemon wedge, please.'

The girl was small, like Amanda, but much less shapely. What on earth had possessed Roger to make love to the little bitch? Was it her age? Was that how it was with men, to prefer a young chit to a mature woman?

Amanda grinned to herself. Perhaps that was it – a preference for 'young stuff'. That's what *she* had a fancy for, after all. The security guard, Trevor, was younger than she was, but not by much. He was close enough to her own age that she'd been able to accept a submissive role, just as if he'd been older than she was. The uniform had likely helped.

He'd been fun, but the next man she made it with was going to be much younger, she promised herself. Any age over 'legal' would do. But she wasn't going to find a boy-toy in Forsythe Footwear's offices. She had to get out and about.

It was then that she realised she was approaching the company's problems from entirely the wrong end. Everything, the overstaffing, overstocking and the low sales, all originated in one place, or rather, in 31 places – the cash registers of the shops. That's where she should be looking for answers.

Nola breezed in with a tray.

'You can take that back to the cafeteria,' Amanda told her. 'I'm going out.'

The sour look on Nola's face was a joy to behold.

Amanda knew, from her explorations on Roger's PC, that the shop that was losing the least was the one in the heart of the business district, so she decided to start there. Unfortunately, she had no sense of direction and the city's core seemed to be all one-way streets that headed the wrong way. It was getting near to closing time by the time she found it, and then she had to park on the top level of a concrete honeycomb, which made her even later.

This branch of Forsythe Footwear was sandwiched between a trendy young women's clothing store and an internet café. It only had about fifteen feet of frontage, two five-foot windows flanking a five-foot-wide, twenty-foot-deep entranceway. To Amanda's mind, the window displays were far too cluttered and the cartoonish beach scene backdrops were clunky and old fashioned. And this was the shop with the best performance?

Surreptitiously checking her reflection in the window, Amanda parted the slit in her skirt to just above the lacy top of her gunmetal stocking. If she was going to subtly probe the shop's staff for information, it'd be as well to offer them some distraction.

Inside, the shop went straight back for about forty feet before opening up into a circular space with a circular outward-facing bench seat wrapped around a truncated leather cone in the centre. A rather attractive tall thin girl with wavy blond hair and wide-set soft-grey eyes was at the cash register, putting a smart thirty-ish woman's purchase into a plastic bag. Further back, a slender young man with a floppy cowlick of pale-brown hair was fitting a pump on to the foot of a woman who looked to be a well-preserved fifty, but was still dressed as she likely had as a teen, in a very short pleated skirt and a fuzzy angora sweater.

The young blonde asked Amanda, 'May I help you?'

'Is that the manager down there?'

'Yes, madam, he is. I'm the assistant manager, if I can help?'

'No offence, but I'd like the manager to take care of me.'

The look that crossed the blonde's face told Amanda that she was used to older women preferring to have a young man kneel at their feet. 'No problem, madam. He'll be right with you.' Calling down the shop, she asked, 'Rupert, it's five after six. Should I lock up?'

Rupert glanced back. His eyes were the very pale-blue of Alpine lake water. Amanda almost shivered. She had a weakness for pale-blue peepers – the same colour as hers but an entirely different hue.

He said, 'Go ahead, Meg, and then go on home. I can manage.'

'Thanks.' The blonde granted Amanda a smile that was just this side of a smirk.

Instead of dropping her eyes, Amanda gave it right back to her, along with a nonchalant little shrug. If the blonde was saying, 'He gets this all the time,' then Amanda was saying, 'So do I, honey. So do I.'

As she took her purse from behind the counter, the blonde started singing 'Lady Marmalade'. Neither woman actually giggled but Amanda had to press her lips together to keep hers to herself. It seemed she'd just experienced a sort of sisterhood, some kind of liberated or at least liberating moment unlike any she'd ever experienced before.

The front door locked behind the departing blonde. Amanda tossed her mane and turned her attention to the business at hand. 'Am I keeping you late?'

Rupert's face lifted. For a moment Amanda's newfound

resolve wavered; he still had baby fat in his cheeks, giving him a moon face that melted her heart. He looked at Amanda's Manolo Blahnik knock-offs first and then his pale-blue gaze travelled slowly up the long gleaming metallic sliver of nylon-sheathed leg that showed through the slit in her skirt, over her svelte hips, slender waist and plump breasts, to her face. The tip of his tongue slipped from between his lush red lips, as if he meant to lick them, then darted back out of sight. His eyes widened with the effort of recapturing a businesslike expression, but when he spoke the delivery was smooth. 'I'll be delighted to take care of you, madam, if you don't mind waiting a few moments.'

'I'll browse until you're free.'

Amanda put a little swing into her hips as she strolled past Rupert and his customer. The older woman twitched the foot that was cradled in his hands. Amanda supposed it was to draw Rupert's attention back to her.

While pretending to look at the displays, Amanda checked out the young shoe-man. His shirt had narrow vertical red and white stripes, with a pure-white collar. His tie matched the red in his shirt. He was quite the dandy! Rupert was remarkably young to be a manager. She thought he might be about twenty – a very good age for a boy-toy. What a wicked woman she'd become! Still, didn't most young men fantasise about being taught how to make love by mature experienced women? He looked very innocent – the kind of boy who hadn't been pleasured by very many girls' mouths, if any. A boy who'd probably really appreciate the oral skills she'd honed on her damned cheating husband over the years of their marriage. And she'd teach him how to please girls. His lips were so red she would have sworn he was wearing lipstick even though her practised eye told her he wasn't. He had a milky-white complexion.

She frowned down at the ankle boot she held in her hand. What was it she'd been considering when his gorgeousness had distracted her? Yes. It was clear that seducing the lad would be nothing but an act of the purest altruism.

Amanda moved on to the holiday footwear. While she inspected the fake rope sole of a rather ugly casual flat (what had happened to the real thing? Espadrilles?), she mapped out her final moves in her mind. Her plan – for the debauching of Rupert – was perfectly formed by the time his customer was back in her own shoes.

Amanda dropped her jacket and bag on the circular bench and sat down beside her things. She pressed her knees together and turned her ankles to her right, in the classic pose of the lady. Plucking daintily at her skirt, she arranged it so that it covered her legs but so that the slightest movement would uncover her right one. Then she sat very still.

Moments later, Rupert's customer left without buying anything. When he'd locked the door behind her, Amanda said, 'I hope I didn't cost you a sale.' She crossed her ankles where they were pressed together above her pumps. The slight movement made the slit of her skirt part to her knees.

'No problem. She's in once a week, regularly. She only buys anything about every other month.'

'Perhaps she just likes the attention.'

He grinned. 'Could be.'

'Or just to show off her legs.'

'We get that, sometimes,' he admitted.

'Older women?'

'All ages. You'd be surprised.'

'No, I wouldn't – a good-looking young man like you.'

He grinned broadly. 'Gee, thanks!'

Amanda felt another twinge of conscience. Gee? Surely, if he was managing a shoe store, the lad must at least be legal?

Amanda twitched her right knee. Her skirt parted as far as the top of her stocking. Rupert's eyes followed it.

'Er – how may I help you?' he asked.

'Shoes. Something pretty – something very sexy.'

'Pumps? Sandals? Any particular colour? What sort of heels do you like?'

'Anything nice. It's not that I *need* new shoes, but a woman can't have too many pairs, can she?'

Rupert pulled a stool over and picked up a measuring stick. 'I'll just check your size.'

Amanda lifted her right foot to let him remove her open-toed black and white hound's tooth check pump. He eased her foot from her shoe reverently, his fingers curled into her arch, his thumb gentle on her instep.

After he'd measured, he looked up and asked her, 'Did you know that you are a perfect "sample" size?'

'Am I? Is that good?'

'It's the size that looks best in a shoe. Plus, since we often get one-off samples shipped in, it means I have more stylish, um, styles to offer you. You're in luck!'

'That sounds like fun, but aren't I keeping you? Don't you have a date or something you'd rather be doing?'

'Rather than fitting shoes on to the elegant feet of a beautiful woman? I can't think of anything I'd rather be doing.'

'Your parents aren't expecting you home?'

He laughed. 'I live alone,' he said. 'All alone.'

Amanda batted her eyelashes at him. 'Why, I do believe you're flirting with me, young man.'

He turned crimson. 'I didn't mean any offence.'

'None taken.' She paused. 'Shoes?'

He stood and turned away quickly, but not so quickly that she couldn't see the erection bulging in his pants. Rupert was gone through a bead-curtained doorway for a few minutes before returning with three shoeboxes. He tried a kitten-heeled halter sandal on her. It suited her. Amanda lifted up her left foot to try the other shoe on. There was no doubt about it, he was subtly caressing her feet as he worked. She stood and tried a few steps.

'I'll take these.'

'Thank you, madam. Will there be anything else?'

'I never buy just one pair of shoes at a time. What else have you got to show me?'

'Oh – lots. As I said, we get a lot of samples and they are almost always in your size.'

Amanda rejected the other two styles he'd brought. Rupert gathered their boxes and stood up. 'I'll be right back, with more.'

'Wouldn't it save time if I came with you and picked out the ones I want to try on?'

'Sorry, madam, but it's company policy. Customers aren't allowed in the stacks.'

Amanda pouted. 'That's a shame. I love the smell of leather and I bet the back room is redolent with it. The scent of leather ... affects me. Smells can, you know – pheromones.'

'A-affects you?'

Good boy! He was reading between the lines.

Amanda said, 'No one need know. We're all alone. No one can see us. It's very private, isn't it? I won't tell anyone what we get up to if you won't.'

Rupert glanced around nervously, as if he expected his district supervisor to pop out of a shoebox. 'It can't hurt, can it?'

'Might be fun,' she encouraged.

In the stacks, the aisles between the shelves were no more than three feet wide. They could hardly help bumping hips from time to time. Amanda had had no idea, up till that very moment, that the thrills and chills of her youth were still accessible, but every time their bodies connected she shivered inwardly. 'So, where do you keep all these samples?'

'Different shelves, in with other similar styles.'

'Makes sense. What that up there?' She pointed to the larger slightly battered boxes that were crammed into the space between the tops of the shelves and the ceiling.

Rupert pulled a sour face. 'Winter boots.'

'Already?'

'Last year's, and some from the year before.'

'Didn't you have a sale at the end of the season?'

'Too little, too late. Company rules. I'm allowed to reduce them by ten per cent, but not till March. By then, no one wants them at any price.'

'What would you do with them, if you were allowed?' Amanda leant back against one wall of shelves and lifted her right foot to set its toe on the lowest shelf opposite. Her skirt parted like curtains.

'Seasonal merchandise?' Rupert asked. 'Once it's obvious that a style isn't going to sell, I'd slash the price in half. Two or three weeks before each season ended, I'd do the same with everything that's seasonal, regardless of how well it was selling. That way, I'd free up shelf space and budget ready for the new styles.'

'Interesting.'

Amanda lifted her right foot two shelves higher. Her skirt parted further, enough to show a provocative triangle of alabaster thigh above the lacy top of her stocking. She looked Rupert full in his face, then pointedly down to the leg display she was giving him, telling him without words that the show was deliberate.

'Tell me more about how you'd run this store, if it was up to you.'

Rupert cleared his throat and moved a little closer, as if her thigh was magnetic and he was a piece of steel. 'I wouldn't – er – I wouldn't buy styles that I couldn't sell quickly, like nurses' shoes or old . . .' He cleared his throat again. By the look on his face, he couldn't believe his luck and wasn't sure how to handle the situation.

Amanda took care of that. She took his hand and placed it on the bare inside of her thigh. He gulped. She guided his fingers, moving their tips in tight little circles over her taut skin.

'I . . .' he started.

Amanda touched his lips with the fingers of her free hand, hushing him. 'Talk later – after.'

She steered his fingertips a fraction higher with each circle they made. The panties she'd put on that morning were pale-green lace, boy-cut, with wide legs. His fingertips stroked up under the dainty garment and brushed against her naked puffy nether lips. Rupert sucked a deep breath. Amanda pressed on his hand, palpitating her labia with his fingertips.

'That's nice,' she whispered. 'Now try this.' She pulled his fingers out from under her panties and folded all but his index one into his palm. With her finger on the back of his, she guided him to where the lace covered the soft pearl-button-like bump of her clitoris. She used her own finger to make his scratch over its lace-mantled head. It was her turn to shiver. 'Keep doing that, just like that, very gently.'

'I'll do whatever you tell me to,' he said, his voice husky.

'Good boy.' Amanda unbuttoned her blouse and spread it wide.

Rupert's eyes widened at the sight of her plump rosy-nippled breasts. His free hand lifted to touch them but Amanda intercepted it. 'Do as I tell you, *when* I tell you, and not until.'

'Yes . . .' He trailed off.

'You may call me Ms Amanda.'

'Yes, Ms Amanda.'

Amanda rolled her left nipple gently, just to see the hunger in his eyes. She, too, was suffering. The gentle through-the-lace scratching on her joy button made her desperate for more direct stimulation, but ...

What the hell! She was in charge. Why wait?

She put her hand on the top of Rupert's head and pushed down. 'Move my panties aside. Put your tongue to work.'

'I've never ...'

He'd never gone down on a girl? How delicious! She'd had many experiences in her life but this was one she'd either never experienced, or experienced so long ago she held no memory of it. She was about to be serviced by a young and virgin tongue. Just the thought of it had her dripping with anticipation and that made it even better. His first taste was going to be a really wet one. Amanda decided that, if he performed well, she'd reward him amply.

She said, 'Lick my pussy lips first, long and slow, from where they join at the bottom right up to my –' she almost said 'joy button' but stopped herself in time '– my clit.'

He obeyed and had the instinct to give an extra little flick of his tongue when he reached her sensitive polyp.

'Good boy. Now grip it between your lips and lap at it with the tip of your tongue. Start slowly and then go faster and faster until I climax.'

'Climax?' he asked.

'That's right and, when I do, I expect you to suck all my juices out. You are going to do that, right?'

'Right –'

'No teeth! Just – that's right, lips and tongue ... just your lips and tongue, Rudolf.'

'Rup –' he mumbled.

'Of course. Rupert. Just like that, Rupert, you've got it now, keep that up, don't vary the rhythm yet, just ... mmhmm ... just exactly like that.' Amanda stopped talking and focused on the sensations. What he lacked in expertise he certainly made up for in enthusiasm. He was good at following direction, which was a thrill, and it seemed that she was good at giving it, which was, perhaps, an even greater thrill.

When his licking started to really get to her, Amanda gripped his hair in both hands, the better to grind his upturned face against her sex. Her hips gyrated. The lad followed her clit, licking frantically. She pressed herself down on his mouth. Her hands clenched into fists but if his scalp hurt he made no sign. Lucky for him, too, because nothing was allowed to get between her and the orgasm that was curled like a snake in the pit of her belly and now, right freaking now, uncoiled at lightning speed. It struck at her clit, again and then again, delivering not poisonous venom but a pleasure potion that nonetheless might be fatal.

'God!' Amanda's stocking feet arched, her toes curled. Sweet venom coursed through her veins, more like lightning, now, than any sort of liquid. It shot out the tips of her toes and her fingertips and exploded out of the top of her goddam head. 'Fuck!'

Amanda's hold on Rupert's hair loosened but she held his head in place until the last shudder left her and she was able to stand without leaning. She pulled him erect. He was grinning. His face glistened with her juices.

'How did I do?' he asked.

She allowed him a 'good boy'.

He clutched himself through his pants and groaned pointedly.

'I'll take care of that,' she told him. 'This way.'

They were only visible from the shop's windows for the four feet they crossed from leaving the stacks to being hidden behind the bench seat around the leather cone. If anyone had seen them, well, they both seemed fully dressed. No one could have seen Rupert's painfully confined erection or that she had her sopping panties balled in her fist.

Amanda dropped the wet panties on to her purse. 'Up on the bench, standing, facing me,' she ordered. When he was up, with his crotch on a level with Amanda's face, she added, 'Lean back. Spread your arms to the sides and hold on to the leather. Good. Now don't move until I tell you.'

And there he was, like a sacrificial offering, leaning back slightly, presenting the cylindrical bulge in his trousers to her. Amanda paused to savour the moment. She had a young man's package ready and willing to be unwrapped. All she had to do was ...

She slowly tugged down on the tab of Rupert's zipper, prolonging the moment. He made a little noise in his throat. Using both hands, she spread his open fly wide. Amanda leant a little closer and inhaled his burnt-spice aroma. Her mouth watered. With her left hand holding his fly open, she slipped the fingers of her right into his pants. There was dampness. Poor boy! She fumbled around but couldn't find a slit. He had to be wearing bikini briefs. Well, the best way to deal with those is to pull them down by the waistband. Amanda tugged. Hot flesh warmed the backs of her fingers. She wrapped her hand around the boy's shaft and worked it out to jut up into the air right before her eyes.

It was longer than Roger's had been, but not so thick, with paper-white skin, except for a purple dome that was shaped like an oversized, lop-sided, blunt arrowhead. There was a single dewdrop in its eye. Amanda touched the back of her hand to the underside of Rupert's shaft. It resisted and didn't wobble.

He groaned.

'Be patient!' Her right hand delved again. She worked his briefs even lower, cupped his balls in her hand and drew them out carefully. 'That's better.' They were compact, the skin tight and smooth, nothing like the large leathery bag her late husband had proudly possessed. A surge of tenderness for the innocent youth made Amanda hesitate. She shook it off. But she handled him carefully, as if his 'jewels' really were jewels. Taking her time, she arranged them to dangle prettily.

'Ms Amanda . . .'

'Shush!' She scratched behind his sac. His manhood twitched. Amanda made a fist around it. Looking up into Rupert's eyes, she drew the purple dome closer and closer to her parted lips. 'You want me to?'

'Yessss!'

'Then ask for it.'

'Please?'

'Ask properly. What is it you want me to do?'

'Suck . . .' His hips jerked.

'I told you to keep still. Now, what is it you want? You want me to put your nice stiff cock into my mouth, is that it? If so, say it, and don't forget to say "please".'

'Please would you put my cock into your mouth, Ms Amanda. Please?'

'That's better.' She parted her lips and closed the gap between her mouth and his feverish flesh. Her lower lip touched it.

Rupert mewed. 'What do I do?' he blurted.

Again, a surge of tenderness almost undid her. So sweet, this eager young man. So new. 'Enjoy,' she whispered.

Amanda's head moved half an inch. The flat of her tongue laved across his helmet. The poor lad's thighs trembled. She took a little more, so that his head passed between her lips. She closed them around it. Amanda was very aware that this was the first time he'd been held captive by a woman's lips, the first time he'd experienced the warmth and wetness of a woman's mouth around his manhood. She held him like that until he sighed so deeply she felt it as much as heard it. He was ready.

Amanda's tongue swirled around the head once clockwise, once counter clockwise. She tried to squirm the tip of her tongue into the eye of her prize.

Rupert gasped and made a noise as if he was about to speak but he swallowed his words. Out of the corners of her eyes, Amanda could see his fingers scrabbling at the leather he leant against. Should she take pity on him? But teasing him was such fun.

She relaxed her mouth and lapped up the vein under the shaft slowly, from its base to its head and then took it fully back into her mouth, but deeper this time. Good God, it felt fine, the bulk of it, the strength, the heat, the flavour. Amanda turned her head, moving him into her cheek. Being very careful not to let him feel her teeth, she polished his knob. Her mouth was watering but some of the wet was from him seeping. She straightened again and pushed forwards. His helmet slid across her tongue until it butted against the back of her throat. Amanda had excellent control over her gag reflex but, when a knob touched her there, it always made her salivate copiously.

She released him. Rupert sighed another full-body sigh. The tenderness she'd felt towards him moments earlier was gone. Instead, she felt a mischievous urge to shock him. Amanda drew back very slowly. A long silvery strand of her spit mixed with his precome stretched from his knob to her lower lip. She sucked it in, breaking it, and then spat directly on to his purple dome before lunging, taking him in deep again.

Rupert emitted a strangled gasp. Good. She was playing him like a violin. Likely he was very close to his climax. Men of his age could come often, as she remembered. There were all sorts of things she could do to him before he was drained. He really was her toy. She'd take full advantage of that. Amanda slurped fully off him again and pulled his right arm down.

'Jerk off for me, Rupert. Show me how you masturbate.'

He paused. Amanda frowned up at him. Lust overcame his shyness. He took his shaft between his fingers and his thumb and started to pump. It couldn't have taken more than a minute before his face twisted and turned red. He groaned, long and low. Amanda snatched up her panties just in time to catch the fountain of cream.

'My souvenir,' she told him. 'Now let's get you nice and stiff again.' She took him into her mouth again, very gently, and coaxed him back to full erection. It took all of two minutes. She had a fleeting memory of Roger resting after his orgasm, mourning the loss of his ability to do what this boy had just done – spring back into action without so much as a pause for a drink of water. She'd comforted Roger, cooing that it didn't matter, not a bit. Amanda giggled. Actually, it mattered a whole helluva lot.

'Now sit down,' she commanded.

Once Rupert was seated on the leather bench, Amanda pulled her skirt aside, straddled him and squatted, lowering herself until she could feel his wet smooth tip rub her naked nether lips. 'Want to fuck?'

He nodded.

Amanda sank down his shaft. The much-missed sensation of emptiness being displaced by rigid male flesh made her knees weak. Goodbye, old man, hello, boy-toy. Her faithless female parts practically purred a warm welcome. She wriggled a little to enjoy the feel of it. 'I'm going to fuck you now. After you've filled me with your hot cream –' she paused in expectation of his shocked gasp, which he emitted as if on cue '– I'm going to suck you up and off again.'

Her hips gyrated. 'You'll like that, won't you – creaming in my mouth. And then we'll have a nice little chat. You can tell me more about the shoe business.' She jerked her hips and his rubbery dome bumped her G-spot – heaven. 'After that, I'll teach you a few positions you've never tried before and I'll show you how to finger a girl properly. All you have to remember, Rupert, is that Ms Amanda is in charge. Got that?'

'Ms Amanda's in charge.'

'Good boy.' Amanda angled her body to press the top of his shaft against her bud and slowly writhed herself into a frenzy and then jerked into another gut-wrenching, immensely satisfying climax. Then it was his turn, then hers again. And on it went, until her knees and her hips ached and she was so swollen between her thighs it would hurt to cross her legs. And his rod was red and so tender that he gasped at even the gentlest touch. And, once more, their noises were a mix of pain and pleasure and their orgasms insubstantial but welcome, somehow necessary, all the same.

It was close to midnight when Amanda dropped some money next to the cash register to pay for her shoes and let herself out of the shop, leaving Rupert asleep on the bench with a silly grin on his young face and his shrivelled cock limp against his thigh.

6

Amanda spent most of the next few days on her office PC, comparing purchases with sales and making copious notes. The remainder of her time was spent consulting with Mrs Carrey, of the Human Resources department. When she felt sufficiently grounded in the business, she buzzed Purchasing and asked if Mr Dumphries, the manager of that department, could spare her an hour. A whiney voice told her that Mr Dumphries wouldn't be in until ten, or maybe even eleven.

Amanda went down two floors to Purchasing. The whiney voice belonged to Pat, an overweight redheaded youngster with acne and an attitude.

'Where is Mr Dumphries?'

'Not here.'

'I can see that. Why isn't he here?'

'He don't come in early.'

'Really? By whose authority?'

'Ms Sharpe's. She's the VP of Purchasing.'

'Where's she?'

'She's away.' The girl scratched absently behind her ear.

'Is she? Away where?'

'Holiday.'

'Due back?'

'A week from next Monday.' Possibly the redhead hadn't stood still for this long in a while, or perhaps the barrage of questions was getting to her. At any rate, she shifted her weight back and forth, from left hip to right, while they talked.

'So who's in charge of Purchasing right now?'

'I am.'

'I see.' Amanda turned to leave but almost tripped over an open carton that was filled with magazines. More kinky porn? She picked up the top one. It wasn't a porn magazine but what looked like a shoe-trade journal. She couldn't tell much more because it was in German. 'Who do these belong to?'

'No one. That stuff was Paul's, Paul Carter's, but he ain't here no more. I was gonna, like, dump them?'

'He quit?'

'Mr Dumphries, like, fired him?'

'What for?'

The girl leant forwards conspiratorially. In a whisper, she hissed, 'Forgery.'

At last, Amanda felt she was on the track of a crime. 'What did he forge?'

'An order. Mr Dumphries placed an order for fifteen cases of some shoe. Paul Carter changed the one into a four for forty-five cases.'

'Why on earth did he do that?'

'Well, him and Dumphries had had a big fight. Carter wanted to order lots of the style but Dumphries wasn't going for it, so Carter increased the order, like, by forging, you know, faking the number.'

Amanda perched on the edge of a desk, intrigued. 'This shoe, did it sell well?'

'What? Oh sure. Sold out all forty-five cases in about three weeks, it so happens. All the shops wanted more but it were, like, too late.'

'So this Carter person was right about the shoe, then.'

'I know. But that wasn't the point, Dumphries said. He said, like, Paul was dishonest. So he had to go. Dumphries was really pissed off.'

'Because Carter forged, or because he was right?'

The girl shrugged.

'Deliver this carton up to my office, please. I'd like to take a look at these magazines.'

'I don't do deliveries.' The girl actually laughed out loud. 'Do I look like I'm dressed to carry stuff around?

'I see. What's your name?'

'Pat Hughes.'

'Well, Pat Hughes, you may take the rest of the week off.'

'Cool!' Belatedly, the girl asked, 'Who are you, anyway?'

'I am Amanda Garland, the owner of Forsythe Footwear. On Monday, report to Mrs Carrey. She'll have your severance papers and final pay waiting for you.'

'What?' The girl's mouth hung open.

'You're fired.' Amanda felt a tingle of pleasure as she abused her power for the first time. Anyway, the girl was a dud. If the redhead was taking the hit not only on her own behalf but on behalf of all the obnoxious teens who had ever given Amanda lousy service over the years, at the cinema, in shops, at the counters of take-out restaurants, well, so be it.

'You can't do that!'

'I just did.'

Amanda lugged the carton up to her office herself. It didn't just contain shoe magazines from around the world but also scores of sheets of paper covered with numbers and graphs and notes in some sort of code. As best she could make out, they were someone's – Paul Carter's, she presumed – attempts to forecast shoe styles. Considering his row with Dumphries, it looked like he'd succeeded in one instance, at least.

Amanda buzzed Nola. 'Nola, we used to have a man with us, a Paul Carter. Can you find out who he's working for now?'

'Certainly, Ms Garland. Ms Garland?'

'Yes?'

'He was nice, really smart. I was sort of sorry to see him go.' It was the first time Nola had initiated conversation.

'Good looking?'

Nola giggled. 'A real dish, if you like 'em that young!'

'How young?'

'Oh, he'd only be about twenty, I think.'

Amanda smiled. Her world was filling up with potential toy-boys.

At one, Nola brought Amanda a tray with a Caesar salad and a mineral water with lemon wedge. Apparently, she had a memory inside that fluffy head of hers. The way the girl swished in, she was begging to be looked at.

'New skirt?' Amanda asked.

'Do you like it?'

It was in grey flannel, fitted and a few inches longer than Nola usually wore, but with a six-inch slit up each side. Amanda thought that perhaps it was some sort of homage to the skirts she herself wore.

'Very nice,' she said, and meant it. The girl had remarkably attractive legs.

Nola reddened with pleasure. 'I'm so glad you like it, Ms Garland. You always dress so nice, so it's a real compliment.' Her face clouded. 'You're really nice, and smart, too. Not at all like I expected Rog – Mr Garland's wife to be ...' She dried up.

'How did you picture me?'

'I don't know. I'd seen pictures of you, of course, but I thought you'd be dumb. Self-centred and dumb. But what did I know?' Now that she'd started talking again, the poor pink-haired girl clearly couldn't stop. She babbled on, 'If I'd known you were so great, I never would've ...'

'Never would have what?'

'Nothing.' Nola stood frozen to the spot. 'I have to go,' she finally mumbled, and retreated much more clumsily than she'd entered.

Amanda grinned. Hm! That was very close to an apology for screwing Roger, an apology Amanda had a mind to accept. She was starting to like the little upstart. Nola of the pink hair had had the nerve to imagine *her*, Mrs Roger Garland, as dumb. It amused Amanda. And it couldn't have been Nola in that motel room. Amanda had checked the time sheets. Nola had been behind her desk that morning. It seemed that Roger had fooled around with a number of women and girls. Nola couldn't be entirely blamed for Roger's unfaithfulness.

She opened the locked drawer and fingered the bag of gold charms. Roger had been a complicated man, clearly in love with her yet happily unfaithful. Or perhaps all men were like that.

Maybe it had been power that had made him cheat. Amanda had happily seduced both Trevor, the building's security guard, and Rupert, her own employee, directly or indirectly – *and* she planned to screw this Paul Carter, a young man she hadn't even met yet. Any of them might have a girlfriend or a wife. Roger's death had certainly liberated her, if its having turned her into a conscienceless libertine counted.

It was three o'clock when Dumphries, a suitably dumpy little man with a wart between his eyes and a comb-over, bustled into her office. 'What happened to my Pat?'

'I fired her.'

'Why?'

'She was obnoxious.'

'What?'

'Sit down. I want to talk to you.'

'But – Pat ...'

'We can discuss her later ... if it's still relevant.'

The tone of her voice deflated him, and he sank into a visitors' chair. 'What is it?'

'Style number F 102340.'

He frowned. 'Women's black oxford with a good solid built-in arch support. From Ogilvy & Fitch. Excellent shoe.'

'How many pairs have we bought so far this year?' Amanda asked the question in a silky voice.

'I'm not sure. I'd have to check.'

'I already did. Just short of two thousand pairs.'

'Oh?'

'And how many pairs have we sold?'

'That's not my department.'

'Purchasing isn't concerned about sales? Interesting. Very well, I'll tell you. One hundred and eighty-three pairs, as of close of business last week.'

'As I said, it's a good shoe. We must be stockpiling. It's the sort of shoe that's never out of style.'

'Or in it,' Amanda purred. 'And last year, we – *you* – bought just over three thousand pairs. We sold fewer than four hundred. At this rate, in ten more years it'll be the only shoe we stock.'

Dumphries crossed his arms. 'I don't make purchasing decisions. Ms Sharpe decides what we buy.'

'I'm glad you brought that up, Mr Dumphries. What is it, exactly, that you *do* do, apart from come in late, take long lunches and leave early?'

He sat up sharply and wagged his finger at her. 'I'll have you know –'

'What? Tell me what the process is – the ordering.'

'Well, Ms Sharpe tells me what shoes to buy and in what quantity. I pass her instructions on to my assistant – Pat.

She makes up the order forms and brings them to me for signature.'

'So all you do is pass instructions on and sign order forms? And without looking at what you sign, I hear.'

'Now see here!'

'No, Mr Dumphries, I've wasted quite enough time on you. You're fifty-eight, almost fifty-nine, right? You can retire at sixty. I've checked with Human Resources. The cheapest way to get rid of you is to continue to pay you for the next fourteen months, but please don't bother to come in. You won't be welcomed.'

He stood up, spluttering. 'I'll be talking to Ms Sharpe about this!'

'And so will I. You have twenty-five minutes to clear your desk, or Security will escort you from the premises. Goodbye, Mr Dumphries!'

7

Spikes was a much larger shop than any of Forsythe Footwear's. It had about sixty feet of frontage and rose for three tall floors. Its façade was pale-pink reflective glass, trimmed with heavy black chains. The motif was continued inside, with pink mirrors, pink faux-suede seating and displays that were made from black chains that had had their links welded together to make sinuous shapes. Handbags hung from thin black chains, twirling decoratively at eye-level.

Amanda tottered in like a geisha in a black slub-silk jersey skirt that hobbled her ankles and clung to her thighs, a ruffled white chiffon blouse and a short boxy jacket that was fastened by three frogs, leaving a two-inch gap that offered a tantalising hint of her thinly veiled cleavage.

The staff wore uniforms, black skirts with pink blouses or black pants with pink shirts. Happily for Amanda's purposes, they also wore name tags – pink writing on black. When the only male server on that floor asked if he could help Amanda, and she'd checked his tag, she asked him where the higher-heeled shoes were displayed.

He looked down at Amanda's restricted legs, then at the staircase that rose from the middle of the floor, and grinned. 'Upstairs, madam. Shall I have someone bring a selection down for you?'

'No thanks.' Amanda stooped and teased the Velcro fastening on her skirt apart high enough to display four inches of her naked thigh above the top of her stocking. The salesman was still gawking when Amanda was halfway up the flight.

The stairway had been designed for exhibitionists and voyeurs. It was open on both sides and had treads but no risers. It was impossible for anyone in a skirt to climb them without offering an 'upskirt' show to those below. Amanda supposed that the assumption was that women who wore heels higher than the relatively conservative three- and four-inch ones displayed on the lower level had to have exhibitionistic streaks. Clever.

The downside of having a husband in the shoe business, she now realised, was never visiting shoe stores. Amanda's life with Roger had been incredibly isolated and she'd been oblivious to it. It had happened gently, over time, like a light snowfall, one flake following another. Without noticing, she'd been buried. And Amanda had a pretty good idea why. Roger had made damn sure she wasn't tempted, as he'd been, fearing that she'd succumb, as he damn well had!

Amanda paused before she reached the top, turned and gave the young man who'd directed her a big slow smile. He was tempting, no doubt about it, and just the right age – which was to say, young. Amanda flounced up the remaining three steps. But he wasn't the one she was after, not today.

There was only one person serving up there, so he had to be Paul Carter. Once more, Amanda pretended to browse as she watched a shoe salesman, who she planned to seduce, at his work. She was becoming quite the Mata Hari!

In contrast to baby-faced Rupert, Paul had a gaunt look, almost lupine, with prominent cheekbones and large wild eyes. His lips, though not as generous or raspberry red as Rupert's, were just as alluring. His dark spiky hair looked as if he'd just got out of bed – a look that he most likely spent an hour achieving each morning.

Paul went down on one knee to fit shoes to his customer's feet. When he pushed a shoe on, he did so by pressing up on the tip of its heel with the palm of his hand. Perhaps the girl he was serving didn't interpret that idiosyncrasy, but Amanda did. Now she knew exactly how she was going to enslave him.

When the girl left and Paul turned to Amanda, she told him, 'I want to try on the highest-heeled pump you have.'

He looked at her feet and raised an eyebrow. 'You have a very small foot, madam. Our highest heels are six inches tall. You'd be balancing on the tips of your toes in them. Are you sure ...?'

'Try me.'

He measured her foot with the delicate touch of a spider. 'One moment, madam.'

The shoe he brought to her was a plain classic pump in metallic bronze, with six-inch steel-tipped heels that were as slender and vicious as nails. He knelt and used his palm to push up on the blunted spike to press the shoe's heel on to Amanda's foot. Amanda bore down, forcing his right hand lower and lower, until its back was flat on the floor, and trapped. Then she put just a little weight on it, indenting the flesh of his palm.

Paul looked up at her face with both pain and lust in his eyes.

'Now the other shoe,' she said.

'I ...'

'You'll manage.'

'Yes, madam.' Awkwardly, he worked her foot into the second shoe, one-handed, until a third of her heel was in it. He set his palm beneath its spike and looked up again, his deep-brown eyes silently pleading.

Amanda knew exactly what he wanted. She forced his left hand down and trapped it beside its mate.

'Madam?'

'Paul Carter, right?'

'Er – yes. That's me.'

'You left your research behind at Forsythe Footwear.'

Puzzled, he said, 'They wouldn't let me back in to collect it.'

'I have it. I'll return it to you tonight.' She dug into her purse. 'Here's my business card. My home address is written on the back. Be there, tonight, eight o'clock, for dinner.' She slipped her card into the breast pocket of his pink shirt and pressed her heels down harder, for emphasis.

'Yes, madam.'

'You may call me Ms Amanda.'

'Yes, Ms Amanda.'

'Don't be late. Oh – and I'll take these shoes.'

On her way home, Amanda remembered that she had nothing to go with bronze, so she made a detour to Coquette. There she found an ankle-length stretch liquid-metal gown in bronze with a halter top. The salesgirl warned Amanda that it would be impossible to wear anything under it – which suited her purposes just fine.

8

Amanda's new dress, or, rather, the body it clung to, seemed to render Paul speechless. It lived up to the name of its fabric – liquid metal. She looked as if she'd been dipped into molten bronze. It peaked where her nipples jutted, dimpled into her navel and flowed faithfully across the subtle swell of her mound. If she had pubic hair, it would have shown through.

She'd planned everything. Her dress was stunningly sexy and chic enough to intimidate a callow youth. The menu would appeal to a young man's taste buds but was still more sophisticated than she imagined he'd be used to. Everything she thought she might need at any point in the evening was in place.

Paul had arrived in a charcoal-grey two-piece suit, smelling of a decent cologne and bearing pink roses. Obviously, he was hoping to 'get lucky' but uncertain that he would. After the little scene at Spikes, he had to be horny but nervous. He was on Amanda's hook, ready to be reeled in.

She served cream of carrot soup with coriander. At her prompting, Paul explained his system for forecasting fashion trends. It was remarkably simple. He kept track of new styles as they emerged and charted their progress. If a trend started one year in Paris, and reappeared there the following year but also showed in Milan and New York, for instance, Paul was pretty sure it would explode across the fashion capitals of the world in the third year before beginning to peter out. He claimed that his system worked seven times out of eight. The eighth time, he recommended slashing the price and clearing the style out at cost, echoing Rupert's opinion.

Amanda poured them a glass of Bull's Blood each and dished up sirloin tips in a burgundy sauce, with Pommes Duchess and white asparagus tips. 'That shoe that got you fired,' she said, 'weren't you taking quite a risk?'

'I was so frustrated, Ms Amanda. It wasn't the first time Dumphries had underordered a sure winner.'

'Tell me.'

'There were many, but for instance, last summer, there was a Q-number, a flat canvas slip-on that came in five colours, cute and inexpensive. I wanted to order two hundred and fifty cases. It was made in China, so we only had one shot at it.'

'How many did Dumphries buy?'

'Thirty-one cases, one for each shop. Worse, when the shop managers saw it in the catalogue, they all wanted multiple cases, from five, I believe, to thirty.' His face writhed in disgust. 'One store sold out in two days. The last pair in the whole chain went within a month.'

'What was his reasoning?'

'Company policy. Stock up on "standards" and then buy the minimum numbers of each of a wide range of styles. Take no chances.'

'Standards like?' she asked.

'All that Ogilvy & Fitch crap. Old lady shoes. Nurses' shoes. House slippers, for Christ's sake!'

'You really love elegant shoes, don't you, Paul?'

He looked at his plate. 'I don't know about "love", Ms Amanda.'

'Oh? I thought you shared my passion.'

'Well ...'

'You like the shoes you sold me today, don't you, Paul?'

He blushed and nodded.

'I'm wearing them now.'

He whispered, 'I know.'

'Is it that you love both shoes and women, especially *together*?'

Paul nodded again.

'And here I am, a desirable woman who is wearing sexy shoes.'

Yet another nod.

'Do you want me, Paul?'

'Want you?'

'Do you want to fuck me?'

His confusion was delicious. Paul stammered and stuttered, nodded and shook his head, turned deep pink and just about managed to get out a sound that had to be a 'Yes'.

'Then follow me, and do exactly as I tell you. If you obey my every word, I promise you a sexual experience far beyond anything you've ever dreamt of.'

He made a strangled sound in his throat.

Amanda continued, 'Absolute obedience, right, Paul?'

'Yes, Ms Amanda.'

'Good boy. You're learning.'

She led him into the living room and sat herself down on the wide deep black leather couch. Paul went to sit beside her.

Sternly, she told him, 'I didn't say you could sit.'

He jerked upright. 'Sorry, Ms Amanda.'

Amanda pulled her dress up above her knees and arranged its hem across the tops of her thighs. 'Get undressed.'

'What?'

'You heard me – strip off. I want to see you naked.'

'I ...'

'Do it.'

Clumsily but swiftly, Paul stripped down to his bikini under-wear – very skimpy with a leopard print. It barely contained his growing erection. A wet patch betrayed the extent of his arousal. Amanda concealed a grin. Yes, Paul *had* been hoping to get lucky. Well, he was going to, but far beyond anything such an innocent lad could possibly expect.

'Lose the briefs.'

He paused for a second, took a deep breath and skinned his underwear down. When he straightened, it was instantly obvious that, while parts of him were still those of a youth, other parts were all man. His impressive manhood bobbed before him, rising from a thin patch of straight black hair. Paul's hands moved as if he wanted to shield himself but he fought the impulse. He had a runner's body, with long lean muscles, not bulky ones like Roger had had. Lower on his chest, she could see his ribs, but his hairless pectorals were hard shelves. His belly was slightly hollowed but nicely ridged. No hair there, either.

Amanda licked her lips. 'Kneel at my feet. Take my shoes off.'

Reverently, he obeyed. If he feared having his hand pinned down by her heel again, he didn't show it. But they'd already played that game and Amanda had no desire to repeat herself.

'Now, take my right stocking off – just the right one, and be careful not to put a run in it.'

His fingers trembled. He bit his lower lip in concentration. The 'cling' at the top of her stocking seemed to confuse him at first but, once he got the hang of it, he folded the lacy band over, then over again, slowly working his way down Amanda's long leg, over her trim ankle and off her delicate little foot.

'You may kiss my toes.'

His lips pursed and touched the little toe of her left foot.

'You may suck and lick.' She lay back and luxuriated in the warm slithery wet sensations. As she'd suspected, he was good at it, either by experience or imagination she couldn't say, although if pressed to guess she'd pick the latter. God bless these inexperienced boys with their pockets of untapped talent. They were gold.

Amanda was tingling all over when she'd had enough. 'Stand up,' she commanded. 'Hands out, wrists together.'

Without standing, Amanda wrapped her stocking in a figure eight around his wrists and tied a firm knot. 'Put the head of your cock here.' She drew her left foot up on to the couch and pointed to her nylon-sheathed right knee.

It was difficult for the poor lad, but Amanda's emerging philosophy decreed that it was good for a boy to work for his treats. He had to cling to the back of the couch with both bound hands, kneel on one knee on the couch and splay his other leg wide, foot to the floor, and arch his back. Amanda didn't help him.

When his dark-pink glistening knob was in position, Amanda crossed her left leg over it, trapping it in the soft naked hollow behind her knee. 'Fuck me there,' she ordered.

After a dozen or so swivelling thrusts, he seemed to get the hang of it and began to speed up.

Amanda reached behind her neck and undid the tie of her halter. The dress slithered down to her waist.

Paul stared at her naked breasts. He missed a beat. She cupped her right breast, compressed it to extrude her nipple a little and pulled his head down. 'Suck on my nipple. Suck it hard and deep. Make me feel it.'

He obeyed but his position, bent over, working his hips at an awkward angle and clinging desperately to the back of the couch, led to the inevitable. He tumbled to the floor.

'You aren't very good at that, are you?' Amanda allowed a trace of displeasure to show in her voice.

He looked up at her, his expression heartbreakingly contrite. 'Sorry, Ms Amanda.'

'We'll try something easier.'

'Thank you, Ms Amanda.'

Inspired by the instructions Trevor had given her, Amanda said, 'Kneel on the floor facing the couch, hands on it but knees back a bit and spread wide.'

Amanda stood, sucked her tummy in and wriggled her hips. Her dress hissed to the floor.

Paul knee-walked himself into position

Amanda pulled a tube of 'tingling personal lubricant' and a package of latex surgical gloves from under a cushion. Behind Paul's back, where he couldn't see her, Amanda pushed the six-inch heel of one of her shoes into a latex glove and into its index finger, before putting a pair of the stretchy gloves on to her hands.

'Here,' she said, 'suck on this.' She set the other shoe on the cushion in front of his face, its heel towards his mouth.

Obediently, Paul took the metal spike between his lips and began to suck.

'And maintain the position,' she instructed.

He jerked when she squeezed cold lube along the full hot quivering length of his shaft. Amanda felt as if she was radiating. It was – and wasn't – the familiar glow of lust. It was all that, and more. It was the *power*. It elevated her. She had a toy, a living breathing toy, totally in her command. She was a puppeteer, with a human puppet. Whatever she wanted to do to it, she could. Whatever she fancied it doing to her, it would.

With absolutely no consideration for Paul's pleasure, though he doubtless enjoyed her touch, she explored his length with her oily latex-covered fingertips. Its shape wasn't round in cross-section, but more like a slightly squished circle, with a thick ridge running up its underside. Its head was bulbous and hard, even harder than its shaft. With it resting gently on her palm, she could feel its pulse.

Paul moaned.

Moving with deliberate slowness, intending to make it maddening for the boy, Amanda caressed him from his fine black pubic hair to the very tip of his shaft, ending with a gloss of her slippery palm over its head.

Paul was rigid and quivering, drooling around the heel he held between his lips.

One-handed, Amanda squeezed more lube on to her free hand's sheathed index finger. Paul had tight hard buns. It had to be all the deep knee-bends his work demanded. She worked her hand edgewise between his cheeks and found the clenched knot of his bottom with her finger's tip.

Paul shuddered and made a questioning sound, which Amanda ignored. She ringed his anus, spreading lube, and then squeezed more on to the rubber-shielded tip of her shoe's spiked heel.

'There, there. This won't hurt, not much anyway. Be brave. Just relax. Amanda will make it nice for you, Paul.'

With infinite care, Amanda pressed the covered spike against the pin-hole pucker of his anus. A fraction of an inch at a time, the invader sank into his flesh. 'Tell me if it's terrible,' she said.

Paul went stiff and held his breath. As Amanda slowly impaled him, she stroked his manhood with an increasingly firm grip, picking up the pace each time. The muscles in his back twitched. His neck knotted. He had to be in emotional turmoil. Did he love or hate being buggered by the heel of one of the shoes he doted on? Likely, both.

'Breathe,' she commanded.

He did as he was told, his breath a ragged panting sound that further charged the air between them. If he was tortured by what the hand holding the shoe was doing to him, it was obvious he loved what the other hand was up to.

When two or so inches of the spike were embedded in Paul's bum, Amanda relented and tugged it gradually back out, until only its tip was still inside him, and then pushed it back in again.

It wasn't easy, maintaining one rhythm with the hand that was jerking him off and another with the one that was buggering him but Amanda didn't have to keep it up for long. It was so much fun, kicking off a night of passion by showing her new lover just how expertly she could bring him off, knowing there'd be umpteen more orgasms for him, and plenty for her, before the night was through. This wastefulness was positively decadent, and she loved it.

Paul arched, dropped the shoe from his mouth, gurgled and climaxed. She just managed to catch his ejaculate in a wet-wipe and spare her couch.

Amanda slipped the slim heel free of his body, and gave him a count of ten to recover. 'Sit on the edge of the couch. Spread your legs and lie back. Put your hands behind your neck and keep them there.'

Warily, but without protest, Paul did as he was told. Amanda had to grin. His face was crimson and he was doing his best to avoid her eyes but, at the same time, his gaze was avid on her naked and voluptuous figure. Maybe he'd seen the bare bodies of a girl or two of his own age, but, just as young bodies possess a certain quality that they lose as they mature, so do mature bodies gain different earthier attributes that are equally or even more sexually attractive. Or so Amanda's philosophy decreed.

Amanda knelt between his thighs. His balls, like Rupert's, were tight and close to his body, two almost hairless perfect gemstones encased in a sac of the thinnest, smoothest leather. She handled them with care, arranging his scrotum to hang nicely over the edge of the couch. The rest of his lovely young package lay limp on his thigh. She blew on its head. It twitched and rose a fraction. Her left hand took its base and lifted it. Even that slight attention engorged his flesh. Her right hand cupped his balls, with its index finger's tip lower, in gently palpitating contact with his anus's ring.

Amanda dipped her head. As her lips stretched over Paul's knob, he gasped. She didn't take him deep. It was her lips and tongue, slobbering and deliberately making wet noises, that brought him to full straining erection. She rose swiftly and knelt on the sofa astride Paul's thighs. Still holding his shaft, she lowered herself until its dome was snuggled between her pussy's bare lips.

Paul's eyes clouded with lust. Holding his gaze, she sank, teasing herself and savouring each throbbing inch as it sank into her. When she was sitting on him, her lips stretched around his base, she ground down, gaining an extra inch, and rotated, stirring her own insides on the stiff rod that impaled her.

'I'm going to fuck you,' she growled. 'I'm going to get myself off on your hard young cock and it doesn't matter to me whether you come or not. This is for *me*. You understand?'

He nodded.

Amanda took a fistful of his hair in her left hand and twisted it. Paul winced but said nothing. Forcing herself down, Amanda bumped and twitched and squirmed until her clit was trapped between her pubic bone and his. She slow humped, masturbating herself on his captive flesh. The thumb and forefinger of her still latexed right hand clamped on his left nipple and firmly rotated it. Paul winced.

Now that she had two hand-grips, Amanda cut loose, twisting her hips and riding him, hard and fast. It must have been good for him, too good, because he groaned, humped up and collapsed.

'Don't you dare go soft on me,' she ordered, and gave his nipple a cruel wrench.

Perhaps it was the sudden pain, for the flesh that she'd felt start to soften inside her recovered its rigidity. Incredible! She was truly using him just as she'd use a sex toy, pushing his buttons to make him perform exactly as she required. Inspired by her newfound power, Amanda rode Paul harder, faster, pounding her pubic mound down on him, exulting in every sensation. He kept the pace, thrusting up to meet her, matching her wildness with his own. Sweat dripped from her forehead on to his cheek. His tongue instantly stretched to capture the droplet. He closed his eyes, as if to savour the flavour. And it was this, this gentle unexpected wordless declaration of adoration in the midst of their ferocious coupling, that tipped her into a climax so deep, so complete, it made her howl.

An hour later, while she sat with her legs splayed open, Paul's head between her thighs with her pussy's lips spread over his face and his tongue straining to penetrate her succulent depths, Amanda languidly asked, 'What if Forsythe's somehow got rid of ninety per cent of its current inventory, or more? Got any ideas how it could be restocked, quickly, with good styles?'

He nodded, which felt quite nice.

'In that case, tomorrow, you will give two weeks' notice to Spikes. You're back with Forsythe Footwear, in Dumphries's old position, but better paid. Does that make you happy?'

He turned his head to answer her, speaking into the crease between her hip and her torso. 'That's wonderful, but what about Sophie Sharpe?'

'Leave her to me.' She wriggled free of his glistening face. 'Now we're going to try it with me kneeling on the footstool, with my hands on the floor, and you fucking my pussy from behind. You'll like that,' she promised

And he did.

9

'That's right,' Amanda said into the phone, 'as quickly as you can, put everything on sale, half off. The worst styles and everything from last year, make that seventy-five per cent. I want you down to bare shelves by the end of next month.' Amanda ticked off the nineteenth shop on her list and started to dial again.

A tall handsome ebony-haired woman who looked to be in her well-preserved late forties crashed into Amanda's office. 'What the hell do you think you're doing?'

Amanda looked up with as mild an expression on her face as she could manage. 'You must be Sophie Sharpe. How was your holiday?'

'You fired my entire staff, and now you're selling our inventory off at a loss? What are you up to?'

'Running my company, that's what I'm up to.'

'I'm VP of Purchasing.'

'For now.'

'Bitch!'

'Yes, that's true. And?'

'And – it *isn't* your company.'

'No? I inherited fifty-five per cent. That's close enough.'

'No you didn't. Check your stock certificates. Roger sold a block to me shortly before he died. You own *forty-five* per cent. I own ten per cent. The shareholders are fed up with us losing money. Next shareholders' meeting, you'll be forced out. I'll be appointed CEO.'

Amanda swallowed the lump that had formed in her suddenly dry throat. 'Regardless, until the shareholders' meeting, I'm in charge. You may leave my office.'

'If you weren't a recent widow . . .' Sophie took a deep breath. 'Mrs Garland, I'm off right now for a series of meetings with some of our most important out-of-town suppliers. We'll continue this the day after tomorrow.'

Amanda started to say, 'No we won't,' but Sophie Sharpe had already stormed out.

When Amanda checked Roger's safety deposit box, there *were* certificates for only forty-five per cent of the company's stock in it. Roger must have sold the other ten per cent in order to keep Forsythe's running. Damn!

Amanda squared her shoulders. What choice did she have? All she could do was continue with her risky plan and hope that it somehow worked well enough to save her. She had four weeks and a few days in which to perform a retail miracle.

10

A movement beyond the plate-glass wall of her office made Amanda look up. A straw-haired, fresh-faced youngster was setting a couple of books that were secured in a leather strap on top of a battered backpack that he'd put on the bench seat outside. Amanda licked her lips. He had the sort of willowy physique that reminded her of private schoolboys in cricket whites, the clicks of bats on balls and triumphant cries of 'Zat!' He was dressed in grey flannels and a blue blazer, supporting her guess. Unless she was sorely mistaken, he was of legal age, but not by very much.

What on earth was he doing in her company's offices?

She went closer to the window. His books had their spines towards her. Despite the leather strap, she was able to read the titles: they were copies of *The Complete Dramatic Works of Christopher Marlowe*, and *Tea and Sympathy* by Robert Anderson. Heady fare for such a pretty young man, mused Amanda. He couldn't be one of her employees, so who was he, besides eye-candy for Amanda?

The lad had gone up to the reception desk and seemed to be waiting for Nola to finish a phone call. Amanda hurried out to intercept him before the yummy treat disappeared. She'd never find a younger boy to seduce and she wasn't about to let this one escape.

She got to Nola's desk and raised a questioning eyebrow.

Nola explained, 'Ms Garland, this is Tom Sharpe, Sophie

Sharpe's son. He got back from a school – sorry, college – trip early and was hoping his mother would give him a ride home. I told him that Ms Sharpe was off on a business trip.'

Amanda took a deep breath, in case Tom hadn't noticed that her bolero jacket gaped wide and that, although her tailored linen blouse was opaque, it was stretched taut over her braless breasts. The direction of his eyes told her that he *had* noticed.

'Poor Tom,' she cooed. 'We can't leave you stranded now, can we?' She glanced at her new platinum Cartier watch. 'It's a bit too early for lunch, but there's a nice buffet brunch just around the corner. I'll bet you're hungry. Why don't I treat you to something to eat and then drive you home?'

The boy blushed and stammered, 'Thank you, Ms Garland. That'd be way cool.'

Amanda told Nola, 'I'll be gone for the rest of the day, if anyone wants me.'

Nola looked at Tom, then at Amanda, and back to Tom. In a perfectly even voice, she said, 'I know you'll take good care of Sophie's little boy, Ms Garland. He'll be in good hands with you.'

Tom blurted an angry, 'Little boy!'

'Everything's relative, Tom,' Nola said. 'No offence, sweetie.'

Amanda gave the girl a look that promised repercussions later and hurried Tom out of the reception area. 'I see that you're reading Marlowe. Fascinating. Tell me all ...'

At the Big Bite Buffet, Amanda picked at a salad and half-listened to Tom's 'scholarly' conclusions about Christopher Marlowe having faked his own death in a tavern brawl – he was a theatrical, after all – and changing his name to William Shakespeare. Mainly, she ate him with her eyes. His skin was glowing and clear, with no trace of acne or of facial hair. He had big soft-brown eyes, not much of a nose, and the rosebud mouth of a petulant little girl.

Sex with him, she decided, would be halfway to a Sapphic experience. And that wasn't at all an unpleasant thought.

While Amanda toyed with a chef's salad and some bite-sized pieces of assorted seafood, he consumed a heaping plateful of scrambled eggs, sausages, rashers of bacon, slices of rare roast beef and a pile of toast and then went back for more. His only dietary concession to his androgynous looks was a wedge of spinach quiche.

When his discourse on Marlowe finally dried up, Amanda said, 'I see that you are also reading *Tea and Sympathy.* Is that in your course?'

Amanda had dabbled in acting before she'd met Roger; afterwards, she'd participated in community theatre until, somewhere along the way, she'd given it up. But she'd had enough experience exploring character to learn how to interpret facial expressions. Tom glanced at Amanda's chest, then his eyes quickly turned up and to his left, while his lips pursed and his brow creased. He might as well have said, 'I see the goodies that I want and now I'm plotting exactly how I'm going to get my greedy little hands on them.'

His face cleared. With his eyes on his plate, he murmured, 'I'm reading it for my own interest, Ms Garland.'

To make it easier for him, Amanda prompted, 'Your college – are there girls there?'

He shook his head.

'That must be difficult, and confusing. It's only natural that in an all-male environment there'd be some boys you might admire and others you'd feel protective towards. Add that to – um – the physical changes a young man goes through, and it's amazing you don't all worry about your masculinity.'

Tom blurted, 'Oh, I don't have any doubts.'

Amanda waited patiently for him to catch on to the game she was offering to play with him. 'None at all?' She let a little disappointment creep into her voice.

'Well ...' His face brightened – too much to be a natural reaction. 'So you think it's OK to have doubts?'

'Entirely natural. Girls go through exactly the same, at all-girl schools. I know because I went to one.' This was true, although, in fact, while other girls might have had doubts, Amanda had been totally boy-crazy all through her school years.

It took Tom a minute to absorb the implications of what she was saying. His eyes narrowed. 'They do?' he asked. He glanced down at his copy of *Tea and Sympathy*, as if waiting for it to prompt him. Slyly, he asked, 'You seem like a very wise woman, Ms Garland. What advice would you give to a young man who might have some of those sorts of doubts?'

Amanda grinned. She patted his hand and leant in close, to whisper, 'Get laid, Tom. Try some pussy. See if you like it.'

'G-get laid?' he squeaked. 'Pussy?'

Amanda nodded. 'Find a hot girl and fuck her senseless, Tom. That's the way to tell.'

Her bluntness really threw him! For a moment Amanda wondered if she'd overplayed her hand. He glanced around wildly, as if trying to locate the exit. But he stayed put. Still, it took Tom a long minute to respond. 'But that's not so easy, Ms Garland. And I don't think I'd know how, not to do it right, I mean. In sex-ed we were taught about ... doing it, but just the basics – putting it in and condoms and so on. There has to be a lot more to it than that. I've never even kissed a girl, not properly, you know ...'

'Tongues?' Amanda raised an eyebrow.

Tom was really laying on the 'innocent' a bit thick, but that was OK. They were heading in the right direction.

'Right – tongues. I don't know how to do that.'

'A good-looking man like you? Amazing.' She stood up and put some money into the folder their bill had arrived in. 'Come on. This isn't very private. I'll drive you to your home and we can talk some more, if you like.'

'You're very kind – very sympathetic.' He glanced down at his book again.

He was so damned obvious that Amanda almost groaned.

On the drive, she made sure that the slit in her skirt was parted to just above her stocking top. She exaggerated the movements of her legs, flexing the muscles in her thighs and calves far more than she needed to. Tom had to adjust himself in his grey flannel pants, twice. Oh yes! He had as many doubts about his sexuality as a mink in heat does!

When she parked in Sophie Sharpe's driveway, Tom asked her, 'Are you sure my mother is away and won't be back?'

'Not until quite late tomorrow, at the very earliest. Of course, if you don't want to ask me in ...'

'I do, I do!' He took a deep breath. 'Come on in, then.'

Tom dumped his backpack in the hallway.

Amanda unhooked her jacket's frogs and asked, 'Aren't you going to be a gentleman and take my wrap for me?'

'Oh – right.' His fingers trembled as he slid it off her shoulders.

Amanda turned, keeping very close to him. The tent of his erection brushed her high on her hip, almost at her waist. 'You're tall, aren't you,' she said. 'Big for your age?'

'Um ...'

'Take your jacket off, then, Tom. Let's get comfortable, shall we?'

'I – er – I've been travelling all day.'

And he wanted to be very clean, in case things went as he hoped?

Amanda played along. 'Why don't you go and take a nice hot shower, Tom. I'll be fine. I don't mind waiting.'

'Sure?'

'Sure.'

He took the stairs two at a time. Amanda considered. She could snoop around Sophie Sharpe's home, just a bit, while he showered, but he might not take very long. In any case, the thought of plucking the lad's cherry had her too horny to concentrate on spying. She kicked her shoes off and followed him upstairs. The sound of the shower led her through a chintzy pink bedroom that had to belong to his mother and to an ensuite bathroom's door. Amanda stripped quickly and went in. There was a roman tub and a separate shower stall with glass doors that were completely steamed over. All she could see through them were the movements of a vague pink shape. She took a deep breath, sucked her tummy in, opened the door and stepped inside.

'Oh! Ms Garland! I . . .'

He was slender and smooth, with pale-fawn nipples. His body was as hairless as his face, but the erection he clutched in his soapy fist was as big as any that Amanda had ever seen. It had a flared deep-crimson head.

'You weren't going to waste that, were you?' she asked, nodding at his erection.

'I . . .'

'I think I understand. You were nervous you'd come too quickly so you were going to jerk off first, before we got together, right?'

He nodded.

'But, at your age, you can come and come again and again, can't you?'

He nodded again.

'And who do you think about when you masturbate, boys or girls?'

That had him! He couldn't confess to it being either without revealing his lack of sexual confusion, and he wasn't sophisticated enough to say, 'Both.'

Amanda let him off the hook. 'By the time I'm done with you, it'll be me you fantasise about every single time you play with yourself. Now leave that lovely thing alone before it squirts. Lather me, all over. You'd like that, wouldn't you?' She turned her back to him to make his getting started easier.

His soapy hands smoothed over her shoulders, then down her back as far as her waist, where they hesitated, making nervous circles. Perhaps it was too soon to get him to caress the cheeks of her bum. At his age, it would be tits he dreamt of mostly. Amanda took hold of his wrists and drew his hands around her to place one on each of her breasts. Automatically, he began to compress and release them. She leant forwards to brace herself on the wall. Her hips pushed back at him, forcing him to lean over her.

There! That was nice. She could feel his balls loll against the base of her spine and his hot shaft rest up her back, all the way to her waist and beyond. He *was* a big boy.

'Nipples?' she suggested, and wriggled back at him.

Tom plucked and twisted. Amanda moaned to encourage him and squirmed back harder.

'Ms G-Garland!' he gasped.

Amanda quickly turned to face him. His face was strained and purple. She grabbed his waving manhood, low around its thick base, meaning to squeeze his climax back the way she'd often done for Roger, but it was too late. Tom jerked. A great squirt of man-cream hit her navel and drooled down the subtle curve of her tummy before the shower's jets rinsed it away.

'I'm sorry! I'm so sorry!' His face contorted in shame.

'Don't be, silly! I like the feel of a man's hot cream on my skin.' She demonstrated her pleasure by rubbing her belly, though by then all traces had washed away. 'Turn around and face the shower. I'll soon have you hard again.'

He turned.

'Spread your legs wide for me, Tom.'

He shuffled his feet apart. Amanda soaped her hands and reached around him with one and under him with the other. Toying with his balls, she slowly caressed the length of his shaft. In two strokes, it was erect. In four, it was throbbing with urgency.

'There! You see? Turn around and face me again, Tom.'

Warm water cascaded over Tom's head and shoulders. It sluiced down his young body. Amanda lapped at the cascade as it flowed over the smooth skin of his chest, then parted her lips to let the water flow into, and overflow, her mouth. She considered going lower to take him into her water-filled mouth and gargle but decided to save that idea for someone who would appreciate it more – and who would last longer.

Amanda opened the shower door and marched out, pulling Tom after her by his hard-on. He managed to grab a towel en route to his mother's bedroom but Amanda didn't give him time to dry himself. She turned his back to the bed and pushed on his chest. He fell flat on his back, plucking his shaft from Amanda's fingers. She flopped down and leant over him.

'You want to learn how to kiss properly, right?'

He nodded.

'Put one hand on the back of my head with your fingers tangled in my hair. Girls like to have their heads steered.'

'They do?'

'Most do. I do.' She quickly amended that to: 'Or I used to, when I was a lot younger.' It wouldn't do for her to reveal her submissive side, not while she was dominating the boy. 'Now, the other hand, on my breast. Play with it nicely. Good. Now tilt your head to the right and turn it towards me. Part your lips. No! Not like you're going to swallow me whole. Part them, that's all. Now ...'

She ran her hands down his bare belly and lower, taking him in hand again. Amanda leant in close, breathing in the smell and the sight of him. So fresh. So adorably young and unsullied. Tom's mouth really was quite feminine. She'd seen one quite like it, very recently. Now who ...? Right – Nola. Kissing Tom would be a lot like kissing her receptionist, except that the girl would have had more practice. A lot more. With Roger, for one.

She bit hard into Tom's sulky lower lip.

'Ouch!'

'Hurt? Here, I'll kiss it better for you.' Not feeling at all contrite – quite the opposite, she seemed to be turning into a real bitch – Amanda nibbled and suckled on Tom's bruised lip.

He relaxed. Her tongue slid into his mouth. He tasted of peppermint; either he'd popped a breath mint or he'd brushed his teeth before his shower. A very good beginning. Amanda's tongue delicately explored his, over and under, sampling the liquor of his mouth. His tongue responded, aggressively at first, but a sharp smack on the back of his head settled him right down. Once his tongue was tamed, she taught him the art of the tender kiss.

Her fingertips delicately stroked him. His hand moulded her breast with increasing boldness. Tom began to pant. Despite the care with which she caressed him, Amanda sensed that he'd climax again if they continued like that much longer.

She pulled free and fell on to her back, thighs wide apart. 'Finger me!'

'What?'

'You know – play with my pussy.'

It was Tom's turn to lean up on one elbow. His touch was diffident, as if he was awestruck by the intimate flesh he was being allowed to fondle. If he'd ever caressed a girl's pussy before, he was an excellent actor.

'I thought girls had hair there,' he said softly.

'We do. I wax. Do you like me without hair?'

'Oh yes! I didn't know. Doesn't it hurt – waxing?'

'Yes, but I think it's worth it. See all my delicate folds and creases?'

'Oh yes.' His tone was positively reverential.

Amanda was aroused enough that her inner lips emerged like new petals beyond the bloom of her outer ones. Tom's fingers had no problem finding their way into the centre of the rose.

'You're so ...' he gasped.

'Yes, I am,' she replied, having heard the 'hot' 'wet' 'soft' speech before, used it in fact, when egging on Ro – a lover.

'Complicated,' he finished.

Ah yes, that was what she loved about these boys. Their fresh ways of looking at things. She choked back a laugh. He'd think she was laughing at him, when really she was giddy with delight at his naive, yet entirely accurate, description of her womanly parts.

'Do you want to take a close look?'

'May I?'

'Go down there.' Amanda used both hands to press down on her outer lips and pull them up and apart, opening herself blatantly.

Tom knelt on the floor between her feet. 'Oh! You're so pink! And there's a – like – a little bump at the bottom, and ...'

'Look for the bump that's higher, here.' Amanda's index finger pulled back the tiny hood to expose her delicate clitoris. 'That's the love-button, Tom. That's what makes girls happy. Wet your fingertip and stroke it, very softly. It's sensitive at first, before it gets excited.'

She deliberately gasped and shuddered at his first tentative touch. If a man likes to believe that he drives a woman wild with his caresses, then certainly a boy would.

'Rotate on it,' she said. 'Round and round. That's good. Yes, that's *very* good.' She paused to enjoy the sensations for a while before saying, 'Now your tongue, Tom. Lick it. Show me what a man you are. Good. Nice and easy, like our kisses. Lick, lick. Lovely! Now finger me, inside, but keep licking. Feel up and behind, Tom. Yes. That's it. You can use two fingers, you know. Up there. A little higher. Higher. To your right. Good. Feel that? Like a spongy bump? That's my G-spot. If you know where a girl's clitoris is, and her G-spot, you can drive her crazy, Tom. I promise. Now massage me inside. Nice. Nice and tender. Now you're going to get a little more aggressive. Pump me a little, with your fingers. And lick faster. Over to the left a bit, that's it, right there. Good, Tom, that's the spot. Lick and rub, Tom. Don't stop. Little harder now. Lick and rub. I like a rhythm, baby, get a rhythm going, baby, work your hands in sync, that's it, yeah, yeah, that's it. Keep it going. Little faster. That's good. That's good. That's good. I'm close now, baby. Don't change a thing. You're gonna make me climax, baby. Ready? Are you ready? Oh yes! Fucking yes! Oh – fuck, fuck, fuck, fuck, fuck!'

Amanda curled her knees up to her chest as her orgasm erupted. Her fists clenched handfuls of sandy hair, keeping his head right there, right freakin' there! His fingers kept going, God bless the boy, pumping her through one paroxysm and into the next until there were no more and she could push him off her and shudder in peace.

Amanda was so lost in the flow of release she was barely aware of Tom gaping at her, and when she did notice it served to increase her pleasure. His mouth hung open in a big idiotic grin, and his caramel eyes were huge. Likely this was the first time he'd ever seen a woman's face *après* orgasm. The thought sent a final tremble through her gut. She lay utterly still, letting the afterglow light her from within. Boys were the best.

'You were the best, baby,' she cooed. She sat up, pushing her damp blond hair from her eyes. 'That was wonderful, Tom. Thank you.'

'I'm glad you liked it,' he said uncertainly.

Did he think it was over, now that she'd come? Poor darling, slumped on the floor like a puppy without a treat.

'It's my turn to make you see the stars,' she growled.

He cheered right up. 'You're very wet,' Tom said. His fingers twitched but, like the good boy he was, he waited for her to tell him what to do next.

'*Real* men like that,' she told him. 'They like to taste it. Lick me, Tom.'

Obediently, he lapped at her, timidly at first but with growing enthusiasm, until his cheeks were pressed between her pussy's lips and his tongue was squirming into her. She felt like laughing at his sloppy eagerness, but she felt something else, too, so she let him relish cunnilingus without comment, except once, when she said, 'No teeth.'

After a few minutes she said, 'Now you may fuck me.'

He jumped up and started to scramble on top of her.

'No, not like that.' She pushed him back with her foot. 'Stay standing up. Take hold of my ankles. That's it. Lift them up and spread them wide. Push them at me until my knees are in my armpits and my bum is tilted up off the bed. See how flexible I am? Girls will be even more so! Now come close. I'll put it in for you.' Amanda reached down with both hands. There was no need for her to use her hands to open herself for him this time. The slatternly lips were plastered apart by her spendings. With one hand under his balls and the other guiding his stiff rod, she worked its head inside her.

'First time?' she asked, just to be sure.

He nodded, wordless.

'You'll enjoy it, I promise. Go slow. Just ease into me, Tom. Relish every inch. In. In a bit further. Easy does it. Oh you're such a big boy, Tom! Deeper. Deeper. That's it – all the way. Wow! Now grind on me. See if you can get any deeper. Oh yeah. Twist your hips. Press hard. Put your weight into it. I promise you it won't hurt me.'

She squeezed hard with her internal muscles. Tom's eyes opened wide.

Amanda continued. 'Verrrry nice. Now pull back, there's a good boy. Take it just as slowly. Right, right … Now in again, just a tiny bit faster.'

The lad gritted his teeth in his effort to maintain control.

'On your toes, Tom. Lift up and lean right over me. That's good.' Amanda ran her fingertips up and down his sides and across his hairless adolescent chest. As the slow rhythmical pace of their coupling began to get to her, she raked her nails down his chest, making him wince and leaving livid lines. Amanda curled to get her arms around him and her lips to his chest. Her tongue traced the welts that her nails had left on his tender white skin.

Tom humped hard and slow. Either by instinct or luck, the head of his rod rubbed against Amanda's G-spot and she moaned.

Perhaps he took that as a signal, or maybe he simply couldn't hold back any longer. He cut loose and pounded into her. Amanda grabbed his hair and pulled him lower. Her other hand squirmed between their bodies to find her clit. Abandoning the idea that this was for Tom's benefit, she frigged herself furiously. She hissed her lust at him, spurring him on, and managed to bring herself to another goddam good climax just before he released inside her.

His face distorted. He yelled 'Yes' half a dozen times; he yelled 'Fuck' half a dozen times; and finally, he collapsed on his side beside her.

'Was that nice?' she asked. 'You looked like you liked it.'

'Fan-fucking-tastic!' He groaned. 'Was I too loud? Did I look stupid?'

'You looked beautiful, baby. Handsome, I mean. Happy. And you weren't one bit too loud. You come beautifully.' She sat up. 'Which reminds me, Tom, has a girl ever swallowed your come?'

He shook his head.

'But you've come in a girl's mouth, right?'

'N-no.'

'Been sucked off?'

'Never.'

'That's terrible! I'll have to take care of that. If you'd like me to?'

'Take care of ... ?'

'Suck your cock. Make you come. And swallow every last drop.'

Tom moaned, 'Oh, fucking hell, yes, please.'

'Remember,' Amanda told him, 'however many girls suck you off in the future, I was the first.'

'I'll remember. I'll always remember you, Ms Garland. You're wonderful. I – I love ...'

Amanda gave him a warning look. There was no need for him to make sugary declarations he didn't mean, not to her.

His face flushed. 'I love it,' he finished lamely.

Tom raised himself on one elbow to look down at his limp manhood. 'But it's gone ...'

'Soft? That's fine, Tom. You'll see.' Amanda spun round on the bed and lifted Tom's leg so that she could rest her cheek on the inside of his thigh. He was totally limp, in fact more than a little bit shrivelled. She lifted its head between her finger and thumb, parted her lips and took it into her mouth. Amanda let it just lie there, heavy on her tongue. After about half a minute, it twitched. Without her doing anything at all, it twitched again, and then a third time. Slowly, it thickened and lengthened, lifting and stiffening. Within a minute, it filled her mouth with its comforting bulk.

Involuntarily, Amanda swallowed. Tom reacted instantly. His hips moved a fraction, pushing the head deeper. Amanda squeezed his thigh as a signal that he should keep still. Her tongue rolled around the hard smoothness of his helmet. She turned her neck a little, working his knob into the pouch of her cheek, and then sucked air. Tom jerked. Amanda lined her throat up again. She relaxed her gag reflex. She nodded. Tom groaned.

Amanda found Tom's hand and laid it on the mound of her sex. Taking his cue, the boy curled a finger inside her while he found her button with his thumb. Incredible, how quickly he'd learnt the basic tricks to pleasing a woman! As he glossed her glistening pink seed, Amanda gurgled on his dome and slavered it with her tongue.

'Shall I . . . ?' he asked, licking his lips.

Amanda nodded and lifted her leg. It'd been years since she'd been in a sixty-nine. There had been lots of oral sex with Roger, but they'd fallen into the habit of him doing her and then her reciprocating. Of course, once Roger climaxed, he was done for the day. So much of their play, she'd come to understand, had been arranged around that one simple fact. Young men were gloriously different. They could do so many of the things Roger had lost the strength or ability to do, getting hard over and over again being just one of them.

But they couldn't dominate her.

Well, no problem. It wasn't as if she were restricted to one lover and had to choose between younger and older, submissive or dominant. Now that she was a dedicated libertine, she could enjoy the benefits of all ages of men – and boys.

And girls? Maybe. If girls were half as delightful as boys, she'd be a fool not to seek out the experience.

Sixty-nine can take a long time. A woman can't totally concentrate on either what's being done to her or what she's doing to her partner. Amanda decided to shorten it by giving all her attention to pleasuring the boy. With that decided, Amanda bobbed, fast and furious, until Tom squealed, stiffened and poured himself into Amanda's mouth.

She gave him a minute to recover before she jumped off the bed, stole a jar of expensive cream from Sophie's dressing table and returned. 'Next, how about a nice slow hand-job, Tom? Would you like that?'

'I – er . . .'

'Of course you would.'

An hour later, Tom fell fast asleep with his head on Amanda's breast, suckling at her nipple. She carefully worked her way out from under him. He looked so cute, lying there like a satiated little angel. It was a shame she didn't have a camera handy.

But she did! Roger had boasted that his cell phone did everything but make his coffee – and it had a camera function. Amanda ran, naked, downstairs to her bag. A door in the hallway was ajar. Through the crack, she could see a desk. Amanda strained her ears. Tom was still snoring softly upstairs. She gave her head a shake, appalled that she'd only thought of the camera in relation to pictures of Tom. There were other, much more important uses for it. Amanda tiptoed into the room and pulled the deepest drawer of the desk open. Bingo! It was filled with hanging files. The first one held bank statements.

That would be a good place for a spy to start. She spread them over the desk and started to study them.

Tom's plaintive voice called out, 'Ms Garland?'

Damn! No time to study, but she had the cell-phone camera. Quickly, she took snaps of as many of the documents as she could until the camera was full, then shoved them back into the drawer, dropped her phone back into her bag and hurried into the hallway.

Jesus! Tom was halfway down the flight, wrapped in a towel.

'I was looking for the kitchen,' Amanda told him. 'I'm thirsty. I'd like a glass of water.'

'Look,' he said, as he proudly pulled his towel away.

Her eyebrows rose. Obviously, the short nap had totally refreshed Tom. His manhood was once more fully erect. Amanda announced theatrically, 'Why drink plain old water when I can sip from the Fountain of Youth? Back up those stairs, boy!'

11

Amanda squirmed against the leather of her Lexus's seat. Her pelvis seemed heavy, like it was full of trapped energy, and she felt squishy inside, puffy and squishy and needy. Good God, what was happening to her? She must have stored up a hell of a lot of repressed lust during her long marriage to Roger. In the brief time since she'd entered the business world, she'd had sex with three callow boys and one virile man – one of the boys not more than an hour ago – and she was already starting to ache for more.

Should she be worried? What if she was turning into a nymphomaniac? That had always seemed, to her, to be a sentence worse than death. To need it all the time and never be wholly satisfied . . . Amanda shuddered. Then again, while she was with Roger, she'd masturbated daily as well as enjoying sex with him every couple of weeks. Since she'd become, well, 'sexually active', she hadn't masturbated once. Poor Mr Buzzy. Poor Rabbitty Rabbit and Rolphy the Dolphin. Her sex toys, once so important, lay abandoned in her bedside drawer. She simply didn't need them any more. She'd outgrown them, and that was a damn good thing! There was no downside, none at all, to her sexually charged life-style.

Amanda signalled, pulled out, passed the pokey driver ahead of her and smoothly slid back into her lane. She liked driving and she was good at it. Ever since the day she'd received her first driver's licence, which had been the very day she'd been eligible for one, she'd had a set of wheels, progressively more impressive wheels, until she'd finally landed the Lexus – her baby, her pride and joy.

The leather-covered steering wheel was smooth in her hands, though not as smooth as any of the three sets of boy-balls she'd recently fondled. If only the shoe stores weren't in such dire straits, she'd be able to immerse herself in a sybaritic lifestyle – though she wasn't doing too badly as it was. Amanda wondered what she'd find when she down-loaded the contents of her cell phone. Something useful, she hoped, though she hadn't managed to snap a photo of Tom, sleeping like a baby, no, sleeping like a man, sated by sex. And she'd been responsible for it. She'd taken command of the situation, of him, and made it happen exactly as she'd wanted. Heady stuff.

Amanda had done a lot of dominating, lately. Nothing but, in fact, with all three young men. What she fancied now was something different – submission, perhaps, like she'd enjoyed with Trevor, the security man. Perhaps he'd force her to bend over and then bugger her, no matter how much she begged him not to? She'd developed quite a 'to do' list, and being sodom-ised was right at the top! Amanda giggled. Second was girl-girl sex. The first was quite the opposite of the second, she mused, but both were very hot. She squirmed again, the leather seat pleasantly smooth against her bottom but providing no stim-ulation. She dropped one hand from the steering wheel into her lap. Should she?

No, she decided. She'd stick with her new lifestyle – mastur-bation with a partner, not instead of one.

Trevor. How easily he'd slipped from her thoughts, given what a big impression he'd made on her at the time. The man was a marvellous lay, although, now that she thought about it, she and Trevor hadn't actually had sex, yet. Not the 'tab A into slot B' kind, anyway. That was a serious omission. Next time they got together, she'd get him to do her both ways, if she could persuade him it was his idea, not hers. There'd be no bossing him around, she was sure of that.

At the next lights she made a left turn and headed back towards her office building. It was getting late. So Trevor would soon be on duty.

When she walked into Forsythe Footwear's darkened offices, there were vertical slits of light showing between the slats of her blinds. Had someone decided to do some snooping of their own? She crept over to the window and put her ear against the glass. There were some muffled sounds but she couldn't make them out. Squinting through a slit showed her a subtly moving shadow but no more. Amanda stepped out of her pumps and tip-toed along the window-wall to her office door. It was closed but half-glazed. She peeked in with one eye.

There was a couple tangled in an embrace by her desk. The man, in his immaculately pressed striped shirtsleeves, had his back to her so she couldn't tell who he was but the girl had hair like a pink dandelion. Nola! The cheeky little trollop! Just because she'd been in the habit of messing around with Amanda's husband in that office didn't give her the right to entertain her boyfriends there. That was disrespectful to both Roger *and* Amanda!

The couple disengaged long enough for Nola to peel her skinny-fit ribbed turquoise sweater up over her head and off. She was braless, of course. Nola needed no support, not with those childish little boobs, hardly more than bee-stings. Amanda had to admit they were pretty, though. The girl's puffy nipples were about the same shade of shocking pink as the inside of Amanda's pussy. The colour made them look vulnerable.

Nola pulled the man's head down to the nipple of her

diminutive right breast. Doing so half-turned him. He was Rupert, Amanda's new retail supervisor! The bastard! The bitch! Her hand closed around the doorknob. She'd fire them both!

Nola's head tipped back, a look of pure ecstasy on her face. Amanda hesitated. True, Rupert was her boy-toy, but it wasn't as if they'd promised to be faithful to each other. She'd only had him the once, that time in his shop. Amanda really had no business playing the betrayed damsel. She let go of the doorknob.

Rupert sucked and nibbled his way from Nola's breasts up her neck to take her mouth in a long lascivious kiss. His hand slid up under her short slit skirt. It looked as if they weren't just going to neck. The way they were going, before very long they'd be making out like minks right in Amanda's office. It might be fun to watch ...

Amanda's fingers popped her skirt's studs at her hip. Her hand stole into the slit. She found the crotch of her bikini panties and worked her fingertips inside.

No! Hadn't she just decided not to masturbate alone any more? Why should she lurk outside her own damned office and finger herself while her employees got all the action? Without another thought, Amanda threw the door open and marched in.

'What the hell do you two think you're doing?' she demanded.

The cliché 'They sprang guiltily apart' came to life. Amanda suppressed a laugh.

Rupert spluttered. Nola flushed and buried her face in her hands. The girl's shoulders quivered and she made sobbing noises but Amanda was sure the little slut was putting on an act.

Rupert said, 'Nola said you were gone for the day.'

'And that's your excuse?'

'No – I mean ...'

'And you aren't even doing it right, not for her.'

Rupert looked blank. Nola raised her head, wide-eyed and confused.

'You're being gentle. Nola likes it rough, don't you, Nola? She likes to be dominated, to be forced. This randy little whore likes a bit of pain to spice up her pleasure.'

'How do you ... ? What are you saying?' Rupert spluttered. 'I don't get it.'

'I think I've been abundantly clear, Rupert.' Amanda softened her tone. 'You've so much to learn about girls. I suppose I'd better teach you. Here, give me your tie.'

Bewildered, Rupert did as he was told.

Nola asked, 'Are you going to fire us, Ms Garland?'

Amanda considered using the threat of dismissing them to ensure their obedience but decided against it. That was the sort of dirty trick stuffy old men used to control their underlings. These two would do what she wanted, exactly what she wanted, because that was their natures. They *needed* to obey, just as she needed to command them – and just as she in turn sometimes craved to be dominated. She knew just how exciting it was to willingly submit and she wanted nothing less for Nola and Rupert.

'No,' she said. 'Your jobs are perfectly safe. You are both free to walk out of my office, right now, and I'll forget what I found going on in here.'

'But?' Nola said. Understanding dawned in her pale-green eyes.

Amanda grinned. 'You'd be opting out of my special "employee benefits programme." You wouldn't want to do that, would you?'

'Employee benefits programme?' Rupert asked.

'It's an educational one. You remember what I taught you – "just obey"?'

He nodded. Nola looked questioningly at him, then at Amanda.

'You'll see,' Amanda said to the girl. She took a deep breath. She'd had no doubts about her abilities to seduce and dominate her young men. Amanda was sexy and boys of their ages were horny by nature. They'd have sacrificed a testicle each for the chance to have her. Nola was different. Amanda had no idea how the girl would take to being fondled by another woman. What if she refused? Even worse, what if she went along with it because she felt she had to?

The other problem was that, for all her bluster, Amanda had never been with a woman, while it was very possible that Nola had, which meant the girl with the candyfloss hair might be more sexually experienced in this particular arena than she was! At any rate, Nola certainly couldn't have *less* experience.

Before she could chicken out, Amanda spun Nola round by her bare shoulder, pulled her arms behind her and bound her wrists with Rupert's silk tie. Nola didn't struggle or protest, which was a good sign.

Another deep breath.

Amanda turned Nola again. The girl's pale eyes had glazed over. Her pouty little mouth was lax, her pink lips wet and parted. Amanda swallowed. Her first lesbian kiss was waiting for her. How different could it be from kissing those boys, particularly the one she'd just had, Sophie Sharpe's androgynous son Tom?

She blanked her mind and put her lips to Nola's. They were plump and soft and tasted of cherry lip-gloss. Nola leant closer, her mouth, her entire body, yielding to Amanda's touch. The depth of Nola's surrender empowered Amanda. Suddenly confident, she parted Nola's lips with her tongue and invaded the sweet wetness of the young woman's mouth. Nola moaned and writhed, rubbing her mound against Amanda's. Amanda gripped her willing victim, one hand knotted in her hair, the other holding her chin, and ravished the girl's mouth.

Nola had a masochistic streak, as the pictures Amanda had found in Roger's desk had clearly indicated. Amanda nibbled on her lower lip, then bit, not hard enough to draw blood but hard enough to hurt and, maybe, to bruise. The more Amanda's teeth worried Nola's delicate flesh, the more eagerly Nola squirmed and whimpered.

Amanda drew back so she could see Rupert. The boy was dumbstruck, likely overwhelmed to see in the flesh what he'd feverishly imagined or gawped at on the internet.

She barked an order. 'Strip! Get stark naked.'

Returning to the girl, Amanda released her chin and reached down to the hem of her short skirt. Nola stiffened. Was that because she felt she was about to be invaded and didn't want to be, or in avid anticipation of pleasure? Amanda remembered what it had been like the first time a boy had put his hand up her skirt, back in her teenage years. She'd felt fearful but thrilled. Most of the fear had been about disappointing the boy, whatever his name had been, but some of it was about her intimate parts being touched by strong hands that might be cruel or, worse, clumsy.

Amanda's hand slid up over Nola's stocking-top. The girl was actually quivering. That made Amanda even bolder. The skin on the inside of Nola's thigh was warm satin stretched taut over firm young muscles. Higher, Amanda reached thin cotton that coated a plump mound. She palpitated. Nola's knees buckled. Amanda's fingertips felt the crotch of Nola's panties dampen.

This was fun! She might be faking that she was an experienced Sapphic dominatrix, but her act seemed to be working just fine. Perhaps she was a natural!

Rupert's polite cough reminded Amanda that he was there. She turned her head. The lad was standing naked with his hands hovering over his erection, almost hiding it.

'Here!' she said. Amanda grabbed Rupert's right hand and pushed it up under Nola's skirt. 'Finger her pussy. You remember how I taught you to do it. Get two fingers up behind her pubic bone and press on her G-spot. Squeeze her bone between your fingertips and the heel of your hand. Don't be gentle with her. Use your grip to lift her up on to the tips of her toes. I think she'll like that.'

With one hand in Nola's hair and the other gripping her chin, Amanda pulled the girl's sulky little mouth wide open and spat into it. Now where had that come from?

Amanda quickly continued. 'She's my toy. She'll accept anything I do to her, or anything I have you do to her.' She released the girl's chin. 'Isn't that right, Nola?'

Nola swallowed deliberately and licked her lips, relieving Amanda's concern that she'd pushed too far, too fast. 'Yes, Ms Garland, anything at all.'

Amanda felt a rush of affection for the pink-haired harlot she held fast in her hands. 'There's a good girl. We're going to have fun with this little slut, Rupert, you'll see. Lift her up by her pussy, like I told you.'

Amanda worked Nola's skirt up high so that she could watch the long muscles in the girl's slender thighs tense and quiver as Rupert's hand raised her. 'Bring her over to the sofa.' Amanda undid her own skirt and let it fall to the floor before following. 'Push her down to her knees.' Amanda stood in front of Nola's face. 'Take my panties off for me.'

With her hands bound behind her, Nola had no way to obey except by leaning forwards and taking the waistband of Amanda's panties between her teeth. She worked her head from side to side, dragging down, gradually peeling the sodden silk lower, down her thighs and to her ankles. Amanda kicked them off and spread her legs, her naked mound inches from Nola's mouth. She didn't have to look to know that the pink inner lips, slick and likely still a little puffy from her afternoon with Tom, were showing.

'You like to eat pussy?' she asked.

Nola nodded and licked her lips. Damn! Amanda had been right. The girl *was* more experienced than she was, when it came to lesbian loving. OK – she'd just have to keep faking it. She threw herself down on her back, on the sofa, flung one leg up on to the sofa's back and spread the other wide, her foot on the floor.

'Rupert,' she commanded, 'get rid of her skirt and panties. Bend her over the sofa's arm.'

The young man pulled Nola to her feet, stripped her of her skirt and panties and pushed her over the padded leather arm. Her cheek landed on the inside of Amanda's thigh. Amanda took control of the girl's head with one fist in her hair.

Amanda said, 'This nasty little slut has been a very bad girl, haven't you, Nola?'

She whispered, 'Yes, Ms Garland.'

'You are going to punish her for me, Rupert. You're going to spank her for me. We'll start with twenty slaps.' When that didn't seem to worry the girl, Amanda added, 'On each cheek of her bum. Cup your hand and bring it down hard. I want to hear it land. She can take it. She's taken a lot worse than that before, haven't you, Nola?'

'Yes, Ms Garland,' Nola admitted with a shy little smile.

Bitch! Sure, she'd been spanked before – by Roger. Amanda fought a sudden rush of anger. It only made sense to stop abusing the girl if she really felt anger towards her, and Amanda didn't want to stop. Her hand twisted in Nola's hair, raising her head. The look on the slut's doll-face somehow combined perfect innocence with eager depravity. Amanda's anger dissolved.

'Well, my sweet little fallen angel,' she cooed, 'are you going to be a big brave girl for me?'

'I'll try. I promise I'll try, Ms Garland.'

'And are you going to lick me nicely?'

'I'll do my best.'

'Then we shall begin.' Amanda pushed Nola's face down and guided her mouth into the soft wet folds of her pussy.

Unbidden, an inquisitive tongue teased Amanda's inner lips apart. God, the girl's mouth was so gentle, her tongue so slim, her face so smooth – it was like nothing Amanda had ever felt before. She wanted simply to surrender to the sensations, but if she did so it would likely plunge her two young sex slaves into complete confusion.

'Rupert, start the spanking. Take it slow. Count out loud.'

His hand rose and fell.

'Put some effort into it! That was a love-pat, not a spank.'

'Sorry, Ms Amanda. I'll start over.' His next slap whacked. 'One.'

Nola jerked. Her tongue circled, teasing the inner surfaces of Amanda's lips. Amanda pulled her in tighter and wriggled, spreading herself over Nola's cheeks. The girl's tongue flickered in a way that promised Amanda's clit pleasures to come.

By his tenth slap, Rupert seemed to be getting into it. Not only was his hand coming down with more force but his erection strained upwards at a 45-degree angle. Nola whimpered open-mouthed. The wet on her face wasn't just from Amanda's juices.

Amanda pulled Nola's head higher, directing that tantalising tongue to her aching bud. God damn, the girl was good! A sigh escaped Amanda's mouth before she could stop it, but it only served to encourage Nola. When Rupert reached 39, Amanda forced herself to pull the girl's mouth away and take a few deep breaths. She'd been balanced on the brink and didn't want to climax, not just yet.

Rupert exclaimed, 'Forty, twenty on each cheek!' He paused before adding, 'Ms Amanda, you should take a look at her bum. It's mainly a brilliant red but it's mottled with blue and purple in some places. I can't believe I did that.'

'Good.'

Amanda looked at Nola's face. Her eyes were glazed. Her lips were slack. She had a look of total surrender, but showed no sign of desperation. It seemed that forty hard slaps on her bottom were no more than hors d'oeuvres for the masochistic little sex-pot. Very well. It was time for the main course.

'Rupert,' Amanda said, 'there's a plastic ruler in the middle drawer of my desk. Fetch it.'

Nola's eyes widened. 'Not ...'

'You know what it feels like?' Amanda asked.

'Yes – no – I mean, I can imagine.'

'I'm sure that you can. Do you want out? You can leave right now, if you like, if you aren't brave enough.'

'I can take it.'

'Good girl.' Amanda pushed Nola's face back down into her lap. 'Rupert, just ten, five on each cheek. Aim low, where her bum meets her thighs.'

'But I might hit her –'

'Pussy lips? Yes, you might. That'll really make her squeal!'

Nola's tongue flickered harder and faster, as if the thought of having her tender nether lips clipped by the edge of a plastic ruler inspired her.

At the fifth hard crack of the ruler, Nola yelped.

Amanda lifted the girl's head. 'Do you want to beg for mercy?'

Nola shook her head.

'Very well. Carry on, Rupert.'

The ninth blow brought a long gurgling wail from Nola. From the sound of it, the little bitch had climaxed! The tenth and final whack elicited a deep grunt. Amazing! Amanda could understand, sort of, how a spanking could be pleasurable. She'd never imagined that one could actually give a girl an orgasm. She *had* to try it.

The 'to do' list she kept in her head never seemed to shrink. Now that she was trying Sapphic sex for the very first time, crossing one thing off, she was adding 'being spanked to see if it could make her climax'.

Nola, despite her orgasm, was still lapping avidly at Amanda's hard pink bud.

'Good girl,' Amanda purred. 'You were very brave. I'm proud of you.'

Nola's sincere 'Thank you' was muffled but understandable.

What next? Rupert's rigid cock reminded her. 'Rupert. Fuck this little tramp. Take it slow and easy, just like I taught you.'

That brought a questioning squeak from Nola. She obviously hadn't known that Amanda had had the boy first. Fair trade. Nola had fucked Amanda's husband and Amanda had fucked Nola's new boyfriend. Even Stevens, baby.

Amanda sat up and lifted Nola's head. Her mouth was very wet and kissable. Amanda's flavour was on the girl's tongue. As she sucked it off, Amanda peered past Nola. Rupert had to semi-squat to line his shaft up with the girl's sex. Nola tensed, no doubt because she felt Rupert's knob pushing at her pussy's bruised lips.

Both the girl and the lad grunted. He was in her! The young man was taking the young woman, and at Amanda's command! It was just too good! Beside herself with wicked glee, Amanda lifted her leg over Nola's head and rolled off the sofa. Much as she'd been enjoying the delightful things the girl's tongue had been doing, she just *had* to see what Rupert was up to.

What a sight! Rupert hadn't exaggerated when he said that Nola's svelte oval cheeks were bright red with blue and purple patches. And the livid stripes that had to be from the ruler were developing into pale ridges. It must have really hurt.

Rupert leant back to angle himself upwards. As he withdrew, Nola's pussy was exposed. Yes, he had clipped its lips. They were swollen and plum coloured. She had to be so tender that each time he ground into her it caused a fresh surge of serious pain.

He was holding her hip in one hand but the other still held the ruler. Amanda took it from him and set it aside. Whether or not Nola was up for it, she wasn't going to have her bum punished any more, not just then.

Rupert stretched up and angled his cock down. Amanda reached between the youngsters and groped around until she found the girl's clit. For the first time, she felt some sympathy for the fumblings of men. It wasn't as easy to locate a clitoris as it was to find a penis, that was for sure. Once she had a grip on it, she rolled it between her fingertips. Rupert's balls dragged across her hand. 'Good boy, Rupert,' she said. 'Make it last as long as you can.'

Amanda squatted for a closer view. She ran her other hand over the radiant heat of Nola's bruised skin. The girl clenched her ass-cheeks and quivered, as if Amanda's touch was electric. 'Please?' she sighed.

Please what? Amanda stroked again. Nola half-twisted her hips towards Amanda's fingers. She wanted to be touched – where? Oh! Amanda wet a finger and stroked its pad around the striated skin that ringed Nola's tight little bum-hole.

'Mm!'

'You like that?'

'Very much, thank you, Ms Garland.'

Amanda's fingertip spiralled in until it settled over the pinhole. To her amazement, she felt Nola's sphincter loosen without her applying an ounce of pressure. It was an invitation that Amanda couldn't resist even if she wanted to. Her finger pushed. Hot flesh clung. Amanda wriggled her finger and worked it deeper. What did that feel like for the girl?

Rupert gasped, 'Oh fuck!'

For a moment, Amanda thought the boy was about to climax but his exclamation had been a reaction to seeing his boss and mistress sticking her finger deep into the bottom of his young girlfriend. It must have been quite a shocking sight for him, considering how recently Amanda had first debauched him.

The boy pulled back. Amanda felt the bulky head pass beneath her finger in Nola's ass. The sensation was different; it was exquisitely delicate. He pushed in, dilating Nola again and pressing up at Amanda's finger. The two, the mature woman and the precociously depraved lad, exchanged knowing looks. The next time he pressed into Nola, it was for Amanda's pleasure more than for Nola's, she was sure.

Nola purred, 'Please, Ms Garland?'

'Please what?'

'Two fingers, or three?'

Some sadistic dominatrix she was: her victim had to ask for more intense abuse. Nola wanted more, did she? Very well!

'Stop fucking her, Rupert,' she ordered.

Rupert froze, his cock still halfway embedded.

'Pull out.'

He obeyed. Amanda twisted her finger out of the girl's bum and left off fingering Nola's clit. She took hold of Rupert's shaft and guided its slippery head to nudge at Nola's already relaxed sphincter. 'Ever done this before, Rupert?'

'No Ms Amanda.'

'You'll like it. Now push.'

Rupert took Nola's hips in his hands and pulled on them as he rammed unceremoniously into her bottom. Amanda gasped even louder than Nola. Rupert grunted and did it again. Nola squealed with obvious delight. OK then.

'As hard and as fast as you like, Rupert,' Amanda said.

He drove into the girl and swivelled his hips, grinding in as deeply as he could push. Amanda cupped a palm under and between them to toy with the girl's swollen lips and the boy's swaying balls. He pulled back, quickly, and slammed in again.

'Faster!' Amanda encouraged.

He pumped quickly and furiously. His face contorted. It looked as if he was about to climax and Amanda didn't want him to, not just yet. She snatched up the ruler and whacked it across his bottom.

'Wha –!'

She struck him again.

The sudden pain seemed to have pulled Rupert back from the edge he'd been balancing on but Amanda found that she was having far too much fun to let up. Each time his buttocks drew back, she swiped at him again, spurring him back in. They developed a rhythm that, almost as if by mutual consent, accelerated. Amanda wasn't counting but she was sure he'd endured far more than the ten blows he'd given Nola, yet he still hadn't so much as yelped. Amanda was astonished by the pain threshold of both Nola and Rupert. Clearly, she had a lot to learn. She drew her arm back and delivered yet another crack to Rupert's beet-red bum.

Rupert gasped, 'I can't hold back any more, sorry!' and skewered his shaft into the girl's bottom.

Nola, who'd been whimpering and moaning with pleasure,

suddenly screamed, 'Fill me up, you fucking bastard! Give me your hot load!'

The filthy words, delivered at top volume, electrified the boy. He ground into Nola, grunting and groaning with complete abandon. Nola thrust up to meet him, urging him on with her body and her unintelligible moans. It seemed as if a pulse ran through Rupert's entire body before he slumped, staggered back and sank to the floor. His cream trickled obscenely from Nola's bum-hole.

The frantic coupling had driven Amanda wild. She flipped Nola over on to her back so that she lay across the sofa's arm on her bottom, puffy pubes uppermost. Amanda hunched over Nola and thrust three fingers into the girl, found her swollen seed with the ball of her thumb and frigged her frantically. Nola reached out to Amanda's sex and fingered it the same way.

At last Amanda gave in to the sexual need that throbbed in her body with every beat of her heart. A few minutes of frenzied fingering later, they climaxed more or less simultaneously. Amanda threw back her head and let her voice express what her body was experiencing as she came for the umpteenth time that day. Nola's trills of delight joined Amanda's howls to create a Sapphic cacophony that rang in Amanda's head all through her drive home and right up to the moment she fell into her bed for a few hours of much deserved rest.

When she arrived at her office the next day, there were two gifts waiting for her. The first was obvious – a gigantic bouquet of white and pink roses in full bloom commanded her immediate attention, their scent as heady as the most concentrated rose-based perfume. 'Lovely!' she called to Nola, who was rather gingerly seated at her workstation. 'Who sent them? You? Rupert?' It was inconceivable that her two young playmates had either the funds or the sensibilities to arrange such an extravagant offering.

Nola shook her head, her full lips compressed into a thin straight line. 'No, *that's* not from me,' she grumbled.

Amanda closed the door to her office. She circled the bouquet. It was truly a superior arrangement. Unless she was mistaken, the vase was crystal. She began counting the blooms, putting off reading the attached card as long as possible, enjoying the suspense, but left off at 26. The flowers were from Buds, a shop so exclusive its name seemed self-effacing, rather than silly. The card read, 'A rose by any other name is not nearly as lovely as you. – Tom.'

Oh yes, young Tom Sharpe. She'd almost forgotten him in the excitement of her first ménage, her first time with a woman, her first time as a dom. He was a good lad, perhaps a bit – what was the word – 'vanilla', that was it; he was a bit vanilla for her taste. It took all Amanda's strength to move the great vase of roses from the centre of her desk to a low table under the corner window. They'd get plenty of light there, and she needed her desk. She'd have to call Tom and thank him, and she'd have to do so soon, as he was due back at college in a few days, if she remembered correctly.

Amanda sat down at her desk, aware that she was a tad disappointed by the name on the card. She turned it over in her hand. Exactly who had she hoped the flowers might be from? David Beckham? Leonardo DiCaprio? Jared Leto? Amanda giggled. Perhaps one of the British Princes, William or Harry? She flipped the card into her pencil drawer. Amanda could only hope that Tom had paid for the flowers himself and not charged them to his mother's credit card.

Now that the vase was off her desk, Amanda saw a thick manila envelope that hadn't been there the night before. It was marked: 'Ms Garland, Private'. When she opened it, she found a D&S magazine that featured a photo-story about a vicious-looking but gorgeous dominatrix wielding a leather paddle on the bottom of a worshipful little female submissive. The dominatrix had been labelled, in pen, 'Ms A.G.' The submissive's hair had been brightly coloured in with a pink felt-tip pen.

So, Nola had chosen Amanda Garland as a replacement for Roger Garland as her dominant, had she? In that case, Amanda decided she had better do some research. She left her office early; frankly, every muscle in her body ached from the debauchery of the day before. But, she noted with some satisfaction, sexually she was entirely sated.

After a long dreamless early-evening nap, Amanda surfed the web for material about domination and submission. The number of websites devoted to the subject was overwhelming so she concentrated on a few highly informative sites. Amanda was pleased to find that many of her instincts had been right on the money. She'd been correct in her assumption that it would be a mistake to inflict pain when angry and she'd used her voice well, by turns commanding and praising her two eager submissives. Amanda had good reason to be proud of her first attempt at domination, but she'd been lucky, too. What if Nola or Rupert had refused to do as she bid? She wouldn't have known how to deal with it at the time, but now she did.

This strange world of D/s was actually very well ordered, with strict rules that made perfect sense. Safe, sane, consensual. Next time – and she was sure there would be a next time – she'd assign the submissive a safe word, and she'd plan events in advance, but on the whole Amanda was content with the way she'd played things. It was simple, really, as long as the dominant stayed in control of the situation, which had been easy for Amanda, and in control of herself, which hadn't come quite so naturally to her. There'd been any number of times when she'd desperately wanted to abandon herself to the highly charged eroticism of 'scening'. But she'd been right not to do so. There were sacrifices to be made when one chose the dominant role but, as Amanda had discovered, the rewards were spectacular.

That night, when Amanda went to bed, she dreamt of an infinite daisy-chain that alternated dominant and submissive, command and obedience, absolute control and total surrender, everyone knowing their places and sublimely happy.

12

Mr Eggerdon was alternately ecstatic and despondent. With prices slashed at every Forsythe Footwear shop, the company's bank accounts were fatter than they'd been in years, and still gorging. On the other hand, the value of their inventory, in their assets account, was plummeting. The net balance was negative. They were, on paper, bleeding money.

On top of that, Ms Garland's juvenile team had reorganised the way inventory accounts were kept, so that no profit was shown until an item was actually sold. Ridiculous!

Mrs Carrey was frantic. In under a week, five shop managers had given notice, all panicked by rumours that Forsythe Footwear was going under. She'd never had to deal with that many severance packages at one time, not back in the days when *Mr* Garland had been in charge!

While trying on some of the sample shoes she'd had returned by all the shops that had some in stock, Amanda consulted with Rupert and Paul. Based on Rupert's knowledge of the managers' personalities and sales abilities and Paul's mathematical analyses of their ordering habits, they agreed that two of the managers who'd given notice should be allowed to go but two should be persuaded to stay, if at all possible. They disagreed about the fifth, Meg, the tall slender blonde who had been Rupert's assistant before being promoted to take his place. Rupert said she'd be an asset. Paul maintained that she was untried and too young, and female, come to that. By tradition, Forsythe's managers were always men. Paul suggested Rupert wanted to keep her on just because he was desperate to get into her panties.

Rupert and Amanda exchanged secret looks. Neither of them was about to explain that, what with Amanda and Nola, separately and together, Rupert was getting all the sex he could handle.

Poor Paul. Amanda suspected he was the brightest of her young stars and possibly the most dedicated – to her company and to her personally. She'd have to reward him for that in the future, but there'd be no future if she didn't get to keep Forsythe Footwear.

Amanda said, 'I'll go size the girl up for myself.'

Rupert smirked. Amanda shot him a look that should have fried his brains.

The intercom buzzed. Nola's voice announced, 'Trevor, the building's security man, would like a word, please, Ms Garland.'

Amanda ushered her handsome boy-toys out of her office and let hunky Trevor in.

He said, 'That woman, Ms Sophie Sharpe, was back again this morning, Ms Garland. I told her that you'd had her barred from the building and I escorted her out.'

'Thank you.' Amanda glanced guiltily at the now droopy roses in the window.

'Did she, um, say what she wanted?'

'You know what she wants. To take over your company.'

'Oh, right.'

'She told me that, when she's in charge of Forsythe Footwear, she'll have my job.'

'Does that worry you?'

He grinned. 'I don't work for the company, I work for the building. But there's something else.'

'Something else? What did she say?' Amanda's heart sank.

Damn that Tom Sharpe, he'd promised to keep their liaison a secret.

Trevor's face became stern. 'This has nothing to do with Ms Sharpe. There's something you and I have to talk about.'

Amanda said, 'Go ahead.'

'Not here. Not now.'

'When then? Where?'

'Somewhere more private.' He came closer, his bulk looming over her. His voice became more resonant. 'Tomorrow's Saturday. I think you should invite me to your home for dinner, don't you?'

Amanda's tummy fluttered. In her weakest, most 'little girl' voice, she said, 'Will seven-thirty be OK, Trevor?'

'Eight o'clock. Wear something pretty.'

'Yes, Trevor, I will – and thank you for keeping Sophie Sharpe out.'

He relaxed back into his employee self. 'No problem, Ms Garland. It's always a pleasure to take care of you.' He saluted her with two fingers to his forehead and left.

Amanda sat back in her chair, closed her eyes and allowed herself a long sweet moment of anticipation. It swept through her like a strong hot breeze. The intercom buzzed.

'Yes, Nola?' She tried to keep the irritation out of her voice.

'Tom Sharpe on line one, Ms Amanda. Shall I tell him you're out?'

Oh that boy! He'd been pestering her non-stop since their afternoon together. 'Yes – no, wait. I'll take the call.'

Enough was enough. She punched the button on the phone with such force her nail broke. Bloody hell! 'Tom?'

'When can I see you again? Please, please say you'll see me this weekend.' His voice was high, an annoying whine.

'Shouldn't you be back at school?'

'I told my mom I'm sick. I can't bear to be that far away from you.'

Dear God! 'Tom, don't be silly. You have to get back to your studies.'

'I can't concentrate. All I see is you. Listen, I wrote you a new poem. "The Goddess", by Tom Sharpe. Her face is heart-shaped like Athena's, her brow, like Hera's, is high and clear –'

'Stop!' Amanda's voice was stern. 'No more nonsense, young man. Get your ass back to class.'

'What about us?'

'There is no "us", Tom. We had a – a play-date. That's all.'

He groaned as if she'd stuck a knife in his belly. 'No!'

'I've tried to be patient but I've got work to do. Stop calling me, do you understand? No more flowers, chocolates, poems – no more contact. Is that clear?'

'But I'm in love with you.'

'It's a schoolboy crush. It'll pass. Find a girl your own age to play with, now that you know how. I have to hang up now, Tom. Goodbye.'

'No! Wait! I love . . .'

Amanda cradled the receiver. She jumped up, grabbed her purse and hurried out of her office. 'Get rid of those damn dead flowers,' she barked at Nola. 'And all those chocolates and stuffed animals and that ridiculous giant cookie.'

'Yes, Ms Amanda.'

'If Tom Sharpe calls –'

As if on cue, Nola's phone rang.

'– you tell him if he continues pestering me I'll take legal action. Understand?'

'Yes, Ms Amanda. Where are you going?'

'Out!'

Amanda took a taxi to the shop that had been Rupert's and that was now in Meg's hands. She'd learnt her lesson about trying to drive through that maze of one-way streets. Driving, like sex, she'd decided, should always be fun, never a chore.

She walked into chaos. The shop that had once been immaculate was now cluttered with stands and folding tables, all piled high with shoes, boots and slippers. There had to be a dozen customers poking through the displays and six more seated on the benches, being helped by Meg, who was wearing a rather smart tailored cream pant-suit but whose hair was dishevelled and flopped over her forehead. As Amanda watched, the young woman rose from the feet of one customer, exchanged a word with a second, dashed into the stacks, reappeared with a box and squatted next to a third woman's feet. A second later, she was back in the stacks, out, delivered a shoebox with a smile and a comment, and marched up to the front counter to ring up the purchases of a woman who seemed to have served herself.

As she made change, Meg threw Amanda a smile and a 'Hello, Ms Garland.'

'You're very busy.'

'I guess.'

'Why are you all on your own?'

'No payroll budget for help. Excuse me.' She tore to the back of the store, took a box from a customer and brought it back to the cash register.

'Can I help?' Amanda offered.

'Do you know the system for finding styles?'

'Not well enough.'

'Can you work a cash register?'

'I can try.'

'It's all yours, then.' She rushed off again.

Credit and debit cards were easy. Amanda fumbled with cash, at first, but thank goodness there wasn't much of that for her to deal with. Meg served four, five, six or sometimes eight customers at a time. Amanda was hard put to keep up with her, even just taking payments and bagging. Six o'clock came and went. As Meg hurried past her, Amanda asked, 'When's closing time?'

'Today's Friday. Nine o'clock.'

The next time Meg came near, Amanda asked, 'When do you get to take a break?'

'Good question.' She turned to a customer. 'It only comes in black, I'm afraid, madam, but black goes with everything, doesn't it, and, at that price, you can't go wrong, can you?'

A gaunt woman with a ragged unibrow brought a shoebox to the counter. As Amanda was ringing the sale in, Meg quick-stepped up through the maze of customers and rested her hand on the woman's box.

'Sorry,' Meg said, 'but I think I made a mistake.' She opened the box, took the shoes out and inspected them. 'Silly me! I've accidentally given you a size eight right and a size seven left. Which size was it that you wanted, madam?'

The woman muttered, 'I've changed my mind,' and headed for the door.

'What was that all about?' Amanda asked.

'Poor woman – her right foot is a size larger than her left. She asked to try both sizes on and deliberately mismatched them. We'd have been left with an unsaleable pair if she'd got away with it.'

'How did you know?'

'She asked me to bring her a pair in size seven and a pair in size eight. She didn't ask to try a seven and a half.'

'I see! That's very clever of you, Meg. Tell me, is it common for people to have bigger right feet than left?'

'Odd-sized feet aren't that rare. Nobody has two feet exactly the same size but, with most people, the difference is tiny. With some people it's the right that's bigger than the left and with others it's the left that's bigger than the right – then with some poor people it's both.'

'Both bigger?' Amanda blinked, then chuckled. 'Ah – shoe-shop humour?'

'Keeps us sane.' Meg hurried away to pluck the shoe a woman's sticky little boy was gnawing the heel of from his grubby little paws and wipe it clean with a wet-wipe.

As busy as she was, Amanda had plenty of opportunities to watch Meg as she swiftly but stylishly ran the busy shoe store. She had the grace of a ballerina and her svelte body suggested the same but her stance, in those rare moments she wasn't on the run, was not that of a dancer. Her shoulder-length chopped hairdo and long bangs framed a heart-shaped face, with those grey wide-set eyes and her lips, thin on a wide mouth, contributing to a gamine look that Amanda found irresistible. To think she might have let Meg go without even seeing her again made Amanda's tummy ache. This girl was a prize.

Half an hour later, Meg paused by the counter again. 'Want to hear a good one?' she asked Amanda. She leant on the counter, adopting the pose of storytellers the world over.

'I could do with a good one about now.' Amanda tried not to stare hungrily at Meg, but she felt as if she'd been starving for the company of this woman all her life.

'See that girl standing in front of the full-length mirror? The one in the very short skirt?'

'Redhead? Nice legs?'

'You noticed, huh? Well, she's trying on the highest heels we've got. Can you guess why?'

'Tell me.'

'She just bought that skirt from the shop next door. Now she's worried that it might be too short for her uptight boyfriend's approval.'

'So?'

'So she wants a pair of the highest heels we've got, to lift her legs up inside the skirt!' Meg burst into loud laughter, then covered her wide mouth with her hand in a vain effort to contain her mirth.

Amanda almost snorted. 'You're joking!'

'No I'm not.' Meg laughed again, even louder.

Amanda was amazed at what a big guffaw the skinny girl could make.

'And they say that us blondes are dumb!' Meg said, as she rushed away.

It was all Amanda could do not to call after her, 'Come back! Tell me another one! Let me hear you laugh again.'

Somehow, Amanda managed to make it to the end of the night. Though her feet hurt and even her back was starting to complain, it wasn't the physical discomfort that had her worried. It was her mental state that made her wonder if she'd actually lost her mind.

This was like nothing she'd ever felt before. She supposed some would call it a 'pash', a schoolgirl crush, but she knew it was much more. If 'pash' was short for passion, then, yes, there was that, but just for starters ...

At ten after nine, three more bargain-hunting women came in. Meg signalled to Amanda to lock the door behind them. Amanda was frazzled enough to run to the door to comply. By her count, they now had eleven customers still inside the shop. They seemed more like adversaries than customers to her. She wanted to scream, 'Take them, take the shoes and get out!' But that would never do. By some miracle, they ushered the last pair of shoppers out at nine fifty-five.

Amanda sank on to a bench seat with a sigh. 'How on earth do you keep this up?' She slid her shoes off her stockinged feet and rubbed her tingling toes.

Meg was counting cash at lightning speed. 'I won't have to for much longer. You can see why I'm quitting.'

'Yes, well, that's the reason I'm here.'

'I thought so.'

'Why don't you hire more help?'

'Ask Head Office.' As she totalled the receipts, Meg explained that each shop's payroll budget was based on the takings of the same month the previous year. At Christmas, that worked just fine. The shop could easily support two full-time people and four part-time. In February, the budget didn't even cover the manager's salary so Rupert had had to put in sixty-hour weeks and cut Meg's hours to the bone, and he'd still been in trouble for overspending on wages.

'That's not fair,' Amanda said.

'It's your company.'

'If I fixed that, would you stay?'

'Maybe as an assistant, not as a manager.'

'Why not?'

'Managers get salaries. Assistants get paid by the hour. Right now, I'm making less than I did before I got "promoted".'

'That's ridiculous! What if managers got bonuses or a percentage, or something?'

'Perhaps. I'm too tired to even think about it right now.' Meg handed Amanda a grey canvas bag full of cheques and money. 'Hang on to this for a moment, OK?' She disappeared into the stacks, before reappearing a moment later wheeling out a vacuum.

'You're going to vacuum, now?'

'And clean up. I hope to get out by midnight, if I'm lucky, then go to the bank with the deposit, then catch a late bus home, and then I'll be back here at ten to nine tomorrow morning, to open up. Thank God tomorrow's Saturday and we close at six, or as soon after it as the customers allow.'

Amanda said, 'That's preposterous!'

Meg shrugged. She flipped the switch on the vacuum, which burst into a roar.

Amanda rose, waving her arms to Meg. 'No, I mean it. It's slave labour. Meg, turn it off, turn it off.' When Meg had done so, Amanda continued her rant: 'No one should have to work like this. This is an outrage.'

Meg rested an elbow on the vacuum's handle, again adopting a timeless pose, this one of the cowpoke leaning on the rail of a fence. 'Like I said, ma'am, it's your company,' she drawled.

'I have to make this up to you. Forget the vacuuming, Meg, and get your coat.'

Amanda took her cell out and speed-dialled. 'Rupert? It's Amanda. You still have a key for your old shop?' She paused. 'Good. I want you to call Paul. Tomorrow, at eight, I want both of you here to tidy up and cover for Meg for the day. I'm giving her tomorrow off. Be prompt because you'll be clearing up and vacuuming before you open, and the place is a real mess.' Her head cocked. 'Well, if Paul doesn't know how to sell shoes as well as you do, you'll just have to teach him.' She grinned at Meg. 'I'm relying on you, Rupert. Don't let me down. Bye.' She hung up with a flourish. 'There,' she said, 'it's all fixed. No more slave labour for you!'

Meg commented, 'I bet Rupert wishes he could say that.' She handed Amanda her coat before she could reply. 'Come on. I can still make the ten-thirty bus if we hurry.'

Amanda followed Meg out the door. She couldn't let Meg leave her, not yet. 'When did you eat last?'

'I brought a couple of doughnuts in with me this morning. I had one for breakfast and the other –' Meg locked up as she spoke '– the other one was lunch, I guess, or else a series of snacks – I snatched a bite each time I passed it.'

'So you're hungry?'

'Ravenous.'

'You don't look like you eat anything.' Amanda was shocked to hear the words she'd just spoken. She didn't want to mother the girl but that wasn't how it sounded.

'I'm just naturally thin,' said Meg. She took the canvas bag from Amanda. 'I have to deposit this. But I promise I'll pick something up from my local Indian takeaway if I can get there before it closes.' She smiled politely.

Amanda realised Meg was poised for flight. She felt fluttery inside, as if this was an all-or-nothing moment, as if there were no tomorrows and Meg might disappear forever if she let her go now.

'I'm taking you out to dinner,' she blurted. Again her words resounded, loud and entirely inappropriate, in her ears.

'You've already been more than generous, Ms Garland. Um, do you mind if we walk?'

Amanda shook her head and Meg started walking, long strides that made Amanda hurry to keep up.

'I appreciate the offer but what I really need is a nice relaxing bath and to get to bed.'

'That sounds great! Where's the nearest four-star hotel?'

Meg laughed, that boisterous, full-throated laugh of hers. Amanda imagined she'd die happy if she could just die listening to Meg's laugh, and it was a good thing too, because she was embarrassed to death. Now she'd gone from motherly busybody to sexual predator, and neither was the image she wished to present.

'Listen, I don't mean to sound ungrateful but . . .' Meg stopped at the brick wall of a bank where there was a night deposit. She dumped the grey canvas bag, which disappeared with a resounding thud; the sound was not much louder than the noise of Amanda's heart beat pounding in her ears.

She was struck, again, with the feeling that Meg might

disappear forever, like an apparition, the product of a school-girl's horny dreams. But dammit she wasn't a school girl! 'Forsythe Footwear is undergoing massive restructuring,' she began. Much better. 'I have very little time at my disposal and there's a lot I want to talk to you about. And, frankly, I'm beat. My legs aren't what they used to be ...' Damn, she'd made reference to her age. But Meg was listening, her thin brows knotted in concentration. Amanda blundered on. 'Why not get a couple of rooms, or maybe a suite, and order in a good meal? We can relax, take our time, and I won't have to schedule another meeting with you. It makes perfect sense.'

'Well, now that you put it that way I suppose ...'

'We need a good hotel, no, a great one, with room service.'

'There's a real beauty just a few streets from here.'

'Perfect. But we're taking a taxi.' Amanda stepped to the kerb and raised her hand. 'What do you like to eat, Meg? When we get there I'll take care of room service while you take a nice long bath. Would you like a Jacuzzi tub?'

'I guess. Are you sure ... ?'

A taxi pulled up. Amanda opened the door. 'Very sure,' she said, ushering Meg inside.

As they rode, Amanda asked, 'What was Rupert like to work for?'

'He was pretty good to work for and great on the floor.'

'On the floor?' Amanda asked with a grin.

'You know what I mean – sales. I've seen him cover a dozen customers at once at Christmastime.'

'And personally?' Amanda underlined her question with a raised eyebrow.

'Him and me? No, nothing there. He fancied me, I think, but he's not my type.'

'No? A good-looking young man like Rupert?'

'Not my type,' Meg repeated, leaving Amanda to interpret it any way she liked.

The hotel's lobby had parchment-coloured moiré silk on the walls. The Muzak was by Mozart. The carpet dragged at their heels. Amanda booked them a luxury suite with two double beds and whisked Meg off to a boutique on the concourse level for toiletries before heading up to the twentieth floor.

Amanda collapsed on the bed nearest the door. 'That was a hard day's work.'

The tall blonde made straight for the bathroom.

'Put your clothes out and I'll have the valet service get them clean for the morning,' Amanda said.

Meg called out from inside the bathroom, 'So what'll I wear till then?'

'There should be two robes in there, one each. See them?'

'I do now. Nice!' Meg appeared in the doorway. 'Thank you for this, Ms Garland.'

'You're welcome. And please, call me Amanda.'

She used the onscreen system to order scrambled eggs with white truffles, wholewheat toast points with sweet Normandy butter, Royal grey-blue Caspian Beluga caviar, Turkish coffee with raw sugar and a dessert of mixed berries in Armagnac with Cornish clotted cream. To drink, she asked for a carafe of Buck's Fizz on ice. It was close to the meal that Roger had ordered for them on their very first weekend away together. The meal had complemented his seduction very nicely, she'd always thought. Not that she was trying to seduce Meg. Not exactly. She didn't know what she was trying to do, only that she wanted to be with Meg, to talk and laugh and yes, OK, she wanted to kiss Meg's ascetic mouth. She ached for a kiss from Meg. In fact, glad as she was that she'd played with Nola and so at least had some experience, a part of her wished it hadn't happened, so that her first girl-girl kiss would be with Meg. But after that ...?

This line of thinking only served to make her anxious so Amanda rapped on the bathroom door and walked in without waiting for an answer. 'I want a robe,' she explained. 'I'm putting my things out for cleaning as well. I hate to put anything on that's not really fresh, don't you?' She paused.

The Jacuzzi tub had whipped up a froth of bubbles that concealed Meg's breasts but her bare wet shoulders were pink and sculptured. The girl didn't seem at all embarrassed by Amanda's presence, so she continued, 'Room service will take about thirty-five minutes with our supper, so, if you don't mind, I'll quickly use the shower while we wait.'

'All girls together, right?' Meg observed dryly.

'Right.' Not wanting to push too far too soon, Amanda scooped up the girl's clothes and took a robe from the rack out into the other room. She stripped off quickly, bagged both of their clothes and hung them outside their door.

Amanda slipped into the fluffy white terry robe, took a deep breath and marched back into the bathroom. Meg's grey gaze was cool, impassive, as she watched Amanda shed her robe, hang it up and step into the shower stall.

Amanda washed as elegantly as possible, just in case Meg could see her shape through the translucent glass door. She knew she couldn't come close to the kind of natural grace that Meg displayed in every movement, but she could try. 'I wondered if you were a dancer,' she called over the sound of the running water.

'Not me!' replied Meg. 'Clown school!'

The Jacuzzi motor hummed into action, putting an end to any chance for conversation.

When Amanda was done she left the shower gracefully and took her time slipping into her terry robe, giving Meg a chance to look her body over if she wanted to.

Did the girl like girls? Amanda guessed the answer was yes,

reading between the lines of what Meg had said about Rupert not being her type. Though really, that could mean anything. And, even if the girl did like girls, did she like women? Amanda thought she'd die if Meg didn't want her, so better she give Meg a good look at the goods she had to offer and then, if Meg wasn't interested, Amanda might be able to figure it out without having to offer and so, perhaps, having to suffer the humiliation of being rejected. Then, at least, she could crawl away and die alone.

The wall-to-wall vanity was opposite the bath. Amanda loosened the tie of her robe and turned the hair dryer on. With both of her elbows up, one hand brushing her hair and the other directing the dryer, her robe naturally fell wide open, displaying her breasts in the mirror in a most complimentary way. Amanda kept a surreptitious eye on Meg. Was it a coincidence that Meg chose that moment to wash her own hair and so sat up higher in the water, arms raised? Like Nola, she had small breasts but, whereas Nola's were gentle swellings tipped with puffy pink nipples, Meg's breasts were more prominent, like pale soft cones, with turret-shaped light-brown peaks. Like her eyes, her breasts were widely spaced, her clavicle prominent above them and her ribs equally prominent, below. Amanda caught herself staring in the mirror at Meg, something she'd vowed not to do, and now Meg was looking her way and had caught her gawking. God, what does a woman say to a girl who's caught her leering at her naked body, and who is now salaciously eyeing her in turn, if she'd not got her signals crossed?

A rap on the suite's outer door saved Amanda. She tightened her robe's belt as she hurried to answer it. The meal came on a little wheeled silver cart. Amanda signed for it, aware that she was flushed and breathing quickly. She steered the cart into the bathroom.

'Supper in the bath, Meg?' she asked. 'Or would that be too decadent?'

Meg turned off the Jacuzzi. 'Decadent seems to be the order of the day, and I haven't had the opportunity to be decadent in ages.'

Amanda sat on the toilet seat. She laughed. 'I'd say you're too young for anything to be "ages ago".'

'I suppose.' Meg's grey eyes clouded. 'Although I'm older than I look. I'll be twenty-eight on my next birthday, you know.'

Amanda laughed. 'You're a baby.'

'If you say so.' Meg stretched her long limbs and sighed. 'Sometimes I feel ancient.' She leant against the curved back of the tub and closed her eyes.

'You really do work too hard.'

'That wasn't what I meant, but you're right. I do work too hard. My boss is a killer.'

She laughed her boisterous laugh then, and the sombreness of the moment passed. 'So what's to eat?' She sat up again.

'Scrambled eggs.'

'Since when are scrambled eggs decadent, anyway?'

'When they're served with truffles.' Amanda scooped fluffy eggs on to a triangle of toast and presented it to Meg.

Meg took the toast and popped it in her mouth. 'Yum.' She gestured at the tray. 'Is that caviar?'

'Yes,' said Amanda.

'I've never tried caviar.'

'Want to?'

'Absolutely. I'll try anything once, or twice, even three times. If I don't like it the first time, I might acquire a taste if I give it a chance. I think all the best experiences are acquired tastes. Like, every kid likes sugars right off, but the grown-up pleasures, like espresso or martinis, those take time to appreciate. They require a mature palate, don't you agree?'

'I think so. Although there are some adult pleasures that I've taken to as a fish takes to water.' Amanda spooned up a few of the glistening grey globes and presented them to Meg's lips. 'Just hold them on your tongue for a moment to appreciate the texture, then pop them between your teeth to release the flavour.'

Meg's face was thoughtful as she absorbed the feel of them, then surprised as she burst the salty little morsels. 'Different,' she mused. 'More, please. And more plain old scrambled eggs too, please.'

Amanda fed her several tiny spoonfuls of caviar and then some eggs on toast.

'I could get used to this,' said Meg.

'Me too,' said Amanda. The extreme nervousness she'd suffered all evening had mercifully passed and now she was calm. She'd be content to sit by the tub and serve Meg treats all night long, if that's the way it turned out. Amanda raised a flute to the girl's mouth. 'Buck's Fizz?'

'What is it?' Meg asked.

'Just orange juice and champagne. I like it because it reminds me of Regency times.'

'Regency times? Men in tight buckskin pants and girls in flowing empire-line dresses? Yummy!' She put her lips to the flute and drank.

'What's yummy? The men in tight pants or the girls in their flowing dresses?'

'The orange juice and champagne.' Meg laughed so boisterously that her breasts bounced on the surface of the water. She opened her mouth, like a greedy baby bird, and Amanda obligingly held the glass to her lips and tipped it. Meg slurped noisily. When she was done, Amanda tipped the glass to her own lips.

'What about you?' Meg asked. 'Not about the drink, about

the men in tight pants and the girls in flowing dresses. Which would you prefer?'

This was it, the pivot point. 'Both,' she answered honestly.

Meg reached for Amanda's hand, dipped two of her fingertips into the dish of caviar and lifted them to her own mouth to daintily lap the morsels off. Her cool grey eyes met Amanda's. 'Want to fuck?'

'I do,' replied Amanda. 'Very much.'

'Me too,' said Meg.

The meal went rather quickly, after that. When they were done, Amanda wheeled the cart into the hallway, keeping the Buck's Fizz and two glasses, and hung the 'Do Not Disturb' sign on the door handle. She sat down on her bed and waited for Meg. Perhaps she should arrange the lighting? Get under the covers? Find some music on the clock radio by the bed or on the TV? She found she wasn't thinking clearly enough to do anything and anyway Meg was with her, now, naked and rosy from the bath, gracefully crossing the room to sit beside her, and it seemed the only thing to do was kiss Meg and, when Meg kissed her back, to kiss her longer, more deeply, until both of them were panting and Meg was helping her out of her robe and they were falling back on the bed, twining their limbs and pressing up close, still kissing as if there was no such thing as tomorrow.

The first time was rougher all around than Amanda might have imagined, had she had the capacity to think. Since she'd only known Meg a matter of hours and had been in one peculiar state or another for all of that time, she hadn't actually imagined anything beyond the feel of Meg's skin against hers, lips to lips and breasts to breasts. Amanda didn't have anything planned and her usually precise mind and persistent manner utterly deserted her. Hence the 'rough' part – where she would turn one way and Meg the other so that they bumped heads or poked ribs. As Meg was so thin her bones seemed able to dig especially deep into Amanda's flesh but at least she had natural grace. Amanda felt bigger than normal, like she was taking up twice her usual space, so she was uncoordinated and once discovered she was suffocating Meg with her thigh only moments before it might have become dangerous.

None of it mattered. Each woman was intent on having the other. Each used her hands, her mouth, her feet, her hair, her breasts, her sex to entice and entrap the other. Breast to breast, they sucked tongues and pinched nipples and licked and bit earlobes and shamelessly thrust out their mounds. Side by side they used their fingers, first, to find every crease of the other's sex, marvelling at each other's hooded bead, small, then not so small, emerging from the safety of shelter to come out and play.

They tasted each other and in that way and in many others made each other wet. And, when both were glassy-eyed and loose lipped and dripping and panting, they tried to ride each other's hard places and clumsily knocked bone against tender flesh. Neither cared. A murmured gasp, a quick apology, 'Never mind,' whispered in response and on they went, always forwards until Amanda found the perfect curve of Meg's hipbone and rode it without pride or grace but like a wild thing that has caught its prey and will not give it up. Meg urged her on, her language that of the gutter but her voice as lilting and soft as an angel. Amanda's passion rose so high she was almost afraid to let go but Meg was unrelenting; she ground her hip against, almost into, Amanda's wetslippery centre, caressed her breasts with slender fingers and half-sang, 'Show me how you come, sweet Amanda. Splash your come all over me, that's a good girl, such a good, pretty, wet, lezzy, slut-whore.'

When she came, it was like tumbling from the peak of the highest mountain into free fall through a blazing white sky with no ground in sight. She whimpered as each spasm clenched and released, like a parachute deployed and almost instantly cut away so she jerked once, twice and then kept falling. The breathless descent continued until she landed, mewling and safe, in Meg's arms.

They were close, so close Amanda breathed in the air that Meg breathed out. She nuzzled her way through Meg's hair to find her ear and taste the rim with her tongue, suck the lobe with her lips and whisper, whisper sweetly. She'd have liked to stay curled up in the warmth and softness of Meg, but the other woman was on the move. 'Fold your hand like this,' she said, pushing Amanda's thumb and little finger under the other three fingers of her right hand. 'Fuck me with your hand, Amanda. Please?'

Amanda found energy where she'd have sworn there was none. She worked her fingers into the other woman, keeping them stiff. Meg was soft inside, a small warm cave with walls of wet satin that Amanda penetrated as deeply as she could. In truth, she hoped her fingertips would touch Meg's cervix, though she guessed that might not be pleasant for her lover. But to touch it, just once, the mouth of the womb?

'Put your hand inside and curl it into a fist. Your whole hand.'

'Silly,' said Amanda, before she realised Meg was serious. 'Is it possible?'

'Yes. Please, Amanda. I like it.'

This must be the way Rupert had felt, or Paul, when she'd told them to do something they'd never imagined, though in this case it was a request, whereas with her young men she gave orders. 'OK.'

She kept her hand in the position that Meg had shown her and pushed, giving no notice to how tightly her hand was squeezed or how wide Meg was opening. When her fingers were as far past Meg's pelvic bone as they could get, she started to curl them. Her knuckles scraped satin-draped bone. Meg groaned, as deep and loud as her laugh. Amanda made a fist. It fit.

Meg was blissed. Her eyes were open, pupils dilated, unseeing. Her cheekbones seemed softer, as if all her bones had slackened to let Amanda in.

An utterly peaceful moment came and went.

'What's this then?' began Amanda, her tone very gentle. 'There's a cunt stretched around my fist. My whole hand is inside Meg's cunt, and what a sweet sweet cunt it is. What happens, I wonder, if I pump it?' She flexed her fist.

Meg groaned. She nodded, or maybe she was nodding, like a junkie on a high; either way, Amanda took it as a cue to continue.

'What if I turn it?' Amanda turned her fist. Her hands were small and she kept the fist tight but still, knuckles rippled silky flesh and made Meg whimper. Amanda turned it the other way, just a little, and Meg shivered. The girl was like a hand puppet, with Amanda's hand inside, clear to the wrist, easily manipulating it. 'I never even thought of this,' she admitted.

Incredibly, Meg laughed. Not her usual guffaw but a half-embarrassed, half-proud tiny sound. 'Does my clit look like it's been squashed by a steamroller?' She giggled, then groaned as the slight movement of it reached her pussy.

'It does,' remarked Amanda. 'It looks like I could stamp my thumbprint on it. I think I'll give it a try.' She swiped her thumb with some of the copious cream on her other wrist and pressed it in the centre of Meg's flattened clit.

'Thank you. Don't come out, please ...' Meg trailed off. She was nodding again.

Amanda pressed with her thumb as she gently turned and clenched and unclenched her fist, each movement causing Meg to shudder and moan until she was shaking and groaning and coming. The first spasm squeezed Amanda's hand like a too-small glove and for the first time she feared for Meg's safety. She became totally still, her thumb pressed hard on Meg's clit and her fist curled tight inside her, until Meg stopped moaning and all the spasms ceased.

Amanda opened her hand as she carefully slid free of Meg. She could breathe again. Her hand was covered with white cream.

Meg was limp and quiet.

Amanda lay down beside her and placed her cream-slathered hand on Meg's breast. She slipped her other arm under Meg's shoulders and pulled her close. As much as she'd wanted, only a little while ago, to rest in Meg's arms, now she wanted to hold this ethereal creature in hers and keep her there, safe and blissed, forever.

13

Amanda was up and showered and still Meg slept. Though she yearned to wake the girl, Amanda moved about the room as quietly as a mouse. There were dark circles under Meg's eyes and, in repose, she looked like an angel who'd lost her way as well as her wings. Amanda had promised Meg a long lie-in and she intended to keep that promise.

The valet service had returned their clothes, laundered and ironed. On a whim, Amanda took Meg's white cotton bikini panties and left her own black satin thong behind. She hoped that Meg would consider it a romantic gesture. At any rate she'd get a kick out of the joke – each 'getting into the other's panties'. She recalled Meg's guffaw, so at odds with the delicate being now murmuring softly in her sleep.

Meg was overworked, underpaid and dead tired. And whose fault was that? Truthfully, Amanda rarely considered the plight of the working poor. She'd done nothing but scheme, either for sex or business, since her husband died. Had last night been an exception? Or more of the same? Silently, she left.

Amanda took a cab from the hotel to the office parking lot to collect her car. She took a route that passed a few shops, where she absently collected the things she'd need for dinner tonight, with Trevor. She was of half a mind to cancel and spend the rest of the day alternately resting and attending to some rather important matters concerning the upcoming business meeting. She'd be wise to be ready for that. But Trevor didn't strike her as the type who'd suffer a postponement gladly. They'd agreed on a time and a place and she suspected she'd better stick to it.

As she manoeuvred her way through the morning traffic, Amanda tried to organise her thoughts. She had a lot to accomplish before the fateful meeting, but there was still time to accomplish a few tasks before she started preparations for Trevor, if she could only concentrate. But she kept returning to the last few hours, from the moment – and she could narrow it down to exactly the moment – when she'd fallen head over heels for Meg. It was hard to believe so little time had passed, especially when you consider the hours they'd spent sleeping. Even then, they'd fit perfectly, 'like' moulded to 'like', curled up as contentedly as two kittens on a couch. Last night she'd have sworn she was in love, and, if the fact that the one she loved was a woman made her a lesbian, so be it. This morning she was rushing to get ready for her next assignation: to submit herself to the rule of the mighty cock.

It had all been so much easier when Roger had been alive. Damn him! Damn him for cheating and double damn him for dying from it! Her eyes filled with tears and she eased up on the accelerator. 'Fuck you, Roger.' Amanda tilted her head, as if Roger was beside her in the passenger seat and she was giving him a piece of her mind. Oh, it had happened, from time to time; after all they'd been married eight years. 'You had your fun. If I had me waiting at home for me I'd be organised too, like you were. But I'm all alone. You didn't even fucking provide for me properly, you bastard.'

Amanda wiped her eyes with the back of her hand. 'Fuck you, pal. I'm going to fuck whoever I want when I want and I'm not going to feel one bit bad about it, either.' She punched the radio on. Rock and roll filled the car. 'That's right, Roger. I rock!'

The house was already close to perfect. Now that there was no messy man living in it, there was very little housework to take care of. All Amanda had to do was tidy up a bit. After that she spent an hour or so at her desk. She looked up Meg's address on the Forsythe's employee list and called Buds to order an exotic bouquet to be delivered the next day. She and the florist settled on a brilliant combination of Bird of Paradise and Calla lilies.

That taken care of, she summarily dismissed memories of Meg from her mind. Saturday night was fast approaching.

Dinner was going to be simple. She'd bought steaks to save defrosting any. There was beer to put in the fridge, just in case Trevor was a beer man, and wine to decant. The sideboard had plenty of spirits. That left Amanda with just herself to prepare. It was a time-honoured tradition with her. But now she was doing it for Trevor, not for Roger!

Trevor. She imagined the bulk of the man, his dark brooding craggy looks and his remarkable body. In a way, sex with him would be relatively relaxing. Now that she was responsible for Forsythe Footwear, about a hundred and fifty people relied on her for their jobs. The company's future depended on how well she performed as its president. In her sex life, she was still in control, totally responsible for the pleasures and performances of Rupert, Paul and Nola. No wonder last night had been so fantastic, at least with Meg they'd been mutually responsible for the success of their love-making, so the pressure had been halved.

But, with Trevor, she could give up all responsibility. She could stop scheming and it was unlikely she'd feel the same tug at her heart-strings that she'd felt as she'd watched Meg sleep. All she had to do was to prepare herself for his arrival. Once he walked in her door, he'd take over. Success or failure was in his hands, not hers. She simply had to obey him. And, if anyone gazed tenderly at a sweet sleeping form tomorrow, it would be him, admiring her fragility; it would be his heart-strings that felt the tug, not hers.

Amanda took a two-hour scented and oiled soak. Since she had it in mind to be buggered, she paid special attention to her back passage. This was followed by a long slow full-body lotion treatment. Ever since she'd transformed herself into a sexual predator, she'd kept her pubes perfectly bald, so she had no need to wax again. Inspecting her privates gave her a minor thrill. What she saw, the smoothness, the plumpness, the crinkled pouty pink lips, Trevor would soon be gazing at.

And he would sodomise her, she was sure. He'd already explored her there, with his fingers, so it had to be something he liked. She was sure she could send him a signal, wiggling her rear as she served him dinner or maybe wriggling into his lap, blushing and stammering a request. 'Please would you take my ass?' No, not sweet or hot enough. 'Please, Trevor, would you kindly fuck my virgin bum?' Much better.

Amanda knelt on her bed. She sucked on her fingers to wet them and reached behind herself. One fingertip rimmed her sphincter. It felt nice! She pressed gently and willed her tight little hole to relax. There! One fingertip slid in quite easily.

It was tight inside, though, and that was just a finger. Trevor's cock had to be at least as thick as four of her fingers together, and thicker again at its bulbous head. A lot longer, too. Her finger pumped experimentally. Hm! The sleeve of her rectum dragged, which a man would likely enjoy feeling on his cock. Still squirming that finger in her bottom, Amanda toppled forwards on to the bed. She felt between her thighs for her clit. Um, yes. The two caresses worked together beautifully. No wonder Nola had got off so hard on being taken in two different places at the same time.

That was another 'to do', to replace the sodomising she was certain she'd experience that night – two men or boys at once, one taking her from behind while the other buried himself to the hilt in her pussy. She imagined Trevor ploughing her rear while Rupert, or perhaps Paul, fucked her. Oops! There was another thing for her growing 'to do' list, *three* men at once! After all, she had three holes. What would it be like to have her bum, pussy and mouth all stretched over hot thrusting . . .

Stop!

She'd been close, very close. Of course, Amanda, unlike some old man whose name she seemed to have forgotten, was able to come many times in an evening. She could have climaxed and still been horny when Trevor arrived, but that would have spoilt her ritual. When she was preparing for a man, she allowed herself to play with herself but never to reach orgasm. That way, she was especially eager when he arrived, and it showed.

Amanda already knew what she was going to wear. That night in her office, Trevor had obviously taken great joy in her acting like a total slut. If 'slut' was what he liked, 'slut' was exactly what he was going to get, in spades, vulnerable and doubled. She had an outfit that had inspired Roger to call her a 'super-slut' when she wore it. The sooner another man got the benefit of what had been one of Roger's favourites, the better!

Amanda's fishnet stockings had seams, which meant ten minutes of pinching and tugging to get them perfectly straight, but she had lots of time, and the more painstaking her preparations, the better she felt she was serving her man. By the time she was satisfied with the straight lines that ran up the backs of her elegant legs, she'd started to sink into a submissive frame of mind. Amanda the dominatrix had disappeared. She had been replaced by an Amanda who not only was an abject sex slave, but was also immensely proud to be one.

Her thong was made of fine black mesh. She moulded it to her pouting pubes and then drew a fingernail up between her pussy's lips, tucking the fabric between them. The transparent wisp blurred the details of the plump treat it covered without concealing a thing.

Her long-sleeved, high-necked top had come as part of the same outfit as the thong. When off her, it was just a handful of shimmery black cloth. When she'd stretched and struggled and tugged and smoothed it into place, it compressed her flesh and obscured it about as much as a deep shadow would have done. Amanda didn't need support but the tightly clinging garment lifted and projected her lush breasts quite deliciously.

She looked absolutely stunning. Amanda wondered what her young men would think of her in this outfit. Or Meg? At the thought of her willowy playmate from the previous night, Amanda's deliciously simple state of mind disappeared, replaced with a dozen persistent confused questions.

Damn!

Amanda had no choice. If she wanted to enjoy an evening of submitting to Trevor, and she did want to, she'd have to banish Meg from her thoughts, just as she'd banished Roger. Well, not exactly as she'd banished Roger. He was relegated to a dusty corner, slouched among the cobwebs, with a dunce cap on his head. In her imagination, Meg, on the other hand, would simply stay as she'd been when Amanda had last seen her, sleeping peacefully in a comfy bed in a deluxe hotel suite. She giggled. Paul and Rupert and Nola were no threat to her peace of mind, but she was happy to give them a room in the same fantasy hotel, with one bigger-than-king-size bed, ample room for all three of her toys, and always room for one more.

She imagined that she tucked the covers neatly up under Meg's chin, sent the youngsters off to bed and gave the finger to a pouting Roger. Done. She had just enough time to finish getting ready before Trevor arrived. At the thought of him, excitement surged through her body, making her arms and legs tingle and igniting an ache in her groin. God, he was so big and powerful, sort of dangerous but at the same time a source of absolute security. This was going to be great!

Her skirt was very short, in glossy black satin, with slits to the tops of her thighs. Amanda chose simple black patent pumps with slender four-inch heels. She considered wearing higher ones but she was trembling all over now. Amanda couldn't trust herself to serve a meal. Falling flat on her face while carrying plates of food wouldn't be sexy.

Amanda loved the anticipation of a planned night of sex. She'd touched herself occasionally during her preparations, and the one time when she'd fingered her own bum she could've come. But she was saving it all for Trevor. Every glance, every smile of hers would be her most alluring; she'd pour admiration on him until he felt like a king bathing in a waterfall of adulation – powerful and exhilarated.

And, in return, he would approve of her. He might not say so but it would show in his gaze and his tone of voice. He'd be as overwhelmed by her regal sluttishness as Caesar had been by Cleopatra's when she'd emerged from that rolled-up carpet – especially once Amanda had finished doing her over-the-top black kohl eyes. Using a lipstick that was so expensive it smelt good, Amanda gave her lips the colour and shine of molten maraschino cherries.

She admired the finished product in the mirror. 'Trevor,' she purred. In that one word, she promised her expected guest absolute and eager obedience – in all things sexual.

Seven forty. She put the steaks on and set the microwave's timer for Trevor's jacket-baked potato. A foil-wrapped baguette was already warming in the oven. The salad was a simple one, just iceberg lettuce, green onions, julienne orange bell peppers and paper-thin slices of cucumber, with an assortment of dressings on the side. She'd be serving fried onions, fried pea-meal-coated slices of yellow tomatoes and lightly sautéed sinfully black Portobello mushrooms with the steaks.

Seven fifty-eight. Time for one last preen and primp in front of the full-length hall mirror. She gave in to vanity and rejoiced in her curvy shape, perfect legs and adorable face. What a looker!

Would he be on time? She'd enjoyed every moment of her preparation but anticipation could so easily slip into anxiety if tested. Amanda took her position at the door with her hand on the knob of the lock. A car crunched gravel in her driveway. Yes! Amanda tweaked her nipples. The door's chimes sounded.

Another deep breath and she opened it.

Trevor's bulk blocked the light. His cologne might have been Lapidus but she wasn't sure. He was in his uniform, which she'd hoped he'd be. One thing was different. Now there were handcuffs dangling from his belt. The sight of the cold bright metal made her shiver.

She said, 'Welcome to my home!'

He looked her up and down, very slowly. Amanda kept her eyes downcast while meekly submitting to his inspection.

Trevor said, 'Good. I approve.'

Glowing, Amanda looked up. 'Dinner will be about five minutes, Trevor. Oh! May I call you "Trevor", or would you prefer something else?'

'Such as?'

'Well – "sir", perhaps? "Master"?'

'Good girl for offering. "Trevor" will be fine.'

'Thank you, Trevor. The dining room is this way.' She was extremely aware of his bulk behind her as he followed her through the living room.

He paused at the piano. 'You play?' He pressed a few random keys.

'I love to play,' she replied, and was thrilled to bits when he laughed at her little witticism. God, this get-together was already making her giddy.

He took the chair at the head of the table.

'May I get you something to drink?'

Trevor picked up the decanter of wine, poured an ounce into a glass, swirled it and sniffed. 'Plum, oak, mushroom, caramel, a little earthy? A Merlot? Um.' He sniffed again, took a sip and decided, 'Chateaux Petrus.' It was a statement, not a question. 'This'll be fine.' He poured his glass half full.

'Thank you.' Amanda repaired to the kitchen. He had depths, this brawny security guard. Not only did he bear himself with the certainty of a natural dominant, he obviously knew his wines. Amanda resolved to never condescend towards him, even when they were in their public roles.

Out of deference to his size and build, she'd broiled him a 24-ounce, three-inch-thick Porterhouse. Her steak was a six-ounce Filet Mignon. She served them and went back into the kitchen for his potato, the onions, tomatoes and mushrooms.

When she returned to the table there was wine in her glass and her steak had been cut into bite-sized pieces. She put the potato on Trevor's plate and poised with a knife above it. 'May I?'

He nodded. Amanda halved his potato, scored it, salt and peppered it, spooned on a healthy portion of sour cream and sprinkled it with freshly chopped chives. While she did so, he helped himself to the other vegetables.

Amanda sat down kitty-corner from Trevor on his right and picked up her cutlery.

He said, 'No.'

Amanda set them down again and looked questioningly at him. Trevor speared a morsel of steak from her plate, added a piece of mushroom and held it to her lips.

'Thank you!' Amanda was delighted. What fun!

Trevor ate some of his steak and potato before feeding Amanda another forkful of her own meal and lifting her glass to her lips to wash it down. His arrogant mastery was working its mojo on Amanda. She felt she should be on all fours, grovelling and wagging her tail.

As he ate and fed Amanda, Trevor talked knowledgeably about the latest films and the top TV shows. It seemed that he was a movie stuntman by choice but that was a precarious living. Working nights in security guaranteed him some income and left his days free for film gigs and the karate classes he taught. He was a black belt. 'Never sneak up on me,' he said to Amanda. 'I mean it.'

Amanda nodded. Add karate skills to his size and Trevor was potentially very dangerous. To submit to such a threat was as brave a thing as she'd ever done. She was sure he wouldn't damage her, so long as she didn't jump on to his back out of nowhere.

Amanda cocked her head. 'But you've been in the building by day, as well. You've been keeping that ghastly Sharpe woman off the premises.'

'That was for you. I was off duty, officially.'

'You worked extra unpaid shifts, for my sake?'

'Yes.' His eyes narrowed. 'Look at me.'

Amanda lifted her eyes to meet his intense gaze.

'Ours might just be a casual *affaire* and nothing more than sexual, Amanda, but we *do* have a relationship. We've had one ever since that night I caught you playing burglar, remember?'

'Yes, Trevor, of course I do.'

'If I have a sexual relationship with a woman, I am responsible for her safety. Accept that. It doesn't mean anything more than that but, for as long as we continue to fuck, no matter how casually, I will protect you to the best of my ability. Is that clear?'

Amanda lowered her eyes. 'Yes, Trevor, thank you.'

He set his knife and fork down. 'Clear the table and return to me.'

Amanda's tummy did flip-flops. The time was here. When he'd done her at the office, it had all happened in a rush, totally unexpectedly. She'd had no time for doubts or anticipation. Now, however, she'd gone through her preparation ritual, gradually building up her ... What was it she'd built up? It wasn't fear, exactly. It wasn't just desire, either. It was both of those, and more. Amanda knew that once his hands were on her she'd feel more comfortable but, until he touched her, she was like a girl on the highest platform at an Olympic pool. Eager to disappear into deep blissful oblivion but scared to make the leap.

When she returned to Trevor, he'd taken off his uniform jacket and turned his chair away from the table. He pointed to the floor in front of his feet. She moved to that spot. He signalled for her to turn her back to him. Amanda glanced at the silently threatening handcuffs that lay on her table and obeyed. Her wrists crossed behind her without his instruction. She felt the cold steel click, the grating of a ratchet on her right wrist, then on her left.

She was helpless. What did she know about this big powerful man, whose broad hands she'd put herself into? He might be a . . . Her mind skittered away from that line of thought. If she'd delivered herself into the hands of a maniac, it was too late to worry about it now.

His finger turned her to face him. The back of his hand smoothed down the satin of her tiny skirt from her navel almost to the swell of her mound.

'You've been a very bad girl, Amanda.'

'Yes, Trevor.'

'Do you know what I'm talking about, specifically?'

Amanda shook her head.

Trevor meandered a fingertip up from her pubes to her navel and down again. 'You know what I do for a living, don't you?'

Amanda nodded.

'You know that I patrol the offices at night.'

'Yes, Trevor.'

His tantalising fingertip made circles on the satin of her skirt. 'Four nights ago, you were in your office, late.'

Four nights . . . ? Yikes. Nola, Rupert, the spanking and the plastic ruler, and . . .

'It didn't occur to you that I'd be making my rounds?'

'Um. No.' She dimly recalled that her original intention in returning to the office was to bump into him, but then she'd caught Rupert and Nola in her office and . . . She grimaced. Had he seen her playing. 'You . . . ?' she gurgled.

'Yes, I saw you. I watched every nasty perverted thing you did to those two young innocents, and what you forced them to do to each other. You humiliated and debauched them. You're a corrupter, Amanda.'

'Is that bad?' Amanda dared to look up at him, to gauge his seriousness.

'What do you think?' His face was unreadable.

'I – I guess I am a corrupter.' She paused. 'But I didn't make them do anything they didn't want to do.'

'Noted.' His fingertip drifted down again, over the swell of her mound, almost stroking her pink pearl. 'Still – you should be punished. Do you agree?'

Amanda tried to think. Her quandary was clear. She could either agree with him and be punished, or disagree with him and be punished for disagreeing. She was in such a state of submission she was honestly confused until she remembered that she *wanted* to be punished. Then her answer came easily to her. 'Yes,' she pronounced.

A chuckle escaped Trevor. He continued, 'What punishment do you think is appropriate for your sin?'

Darn, more thinking. 'A spanking?' she asked.

'Agreed. A spanking for starters and more, much more. You debauched them, so, as a punishment, you will be debauched in turn, by me. As you assure me that they were willing, or eager even, so shall it be with you. I'm going to test your limits, madam. I am going to subject you to the deepest humiliation and most extreme depravity a man can inflict on a woman, but in no way more than you secretly crave. Do you understand?'

'Yes, Trevor. Thank you, Trevor. Will it hurt?'

'You want it to, don't you?' he stated.

'I'm not sure.'

'Well, we'll just have to find out. He spread his knees and patted his left thigh. 'Lie across here, Amanda.'

She obeyed, trembling. His leg was solid and bulky under her tummy. As best she could, Amanda tried to relax and just hang over his leg with her hair brushing the carpet and her toes touching the floor. His big hand smoothed up the backs of her thighs, pushing her flimsy little skirt up on to her back. Feeling suddenly very vulnerable, Amanda jerked on her manacles. It did nothing but hurt her wrists.

She felt thick fingers hook into the waistband of her thong

and drag it down to dangle around her knees. The night he'd caught her searching desks, he'd put his hand up under her skirt to touch her, but he hadn't actually inspected her bottom the way it seemed he was doing now.

'Are you ready to be spanked?' he asked.

Amanda nodded. Time to close her eyes and plunge off the platform.

Trevor raised his hand.

'Oh! I wanted to ask a question!' She wasn't ready – she needed more time; she was too scared. 'How many am I to have?'

'Forty, for a start.'

Jesus ... She shivered. 'On each cheek, or total?'

His hand came to gently rest on her bottom. 'You've got such a dainty little bum, my hand pretty well covers it all, so the forty will be on both cheeks at once.' His voice was low, a soothing rumble. He caressed her supple curves as if testing her flesh for resilience. Are you ready to be spanked?'

Once again Amanda nodded.

'Remember what you told that lad, about smacks clipping Nola's pussy lips?'

Amanda groaned. What had seemed quite tolerable when she was handing it out seemed absolutely cruel now that she was to be on the receiving end.

From the feel of it, he swung horizontally, clipping the undersides of her bottom cheeks and rocking her across his thigh. 'One,' he said.

It stung! How could she have thought there could be pleasure in it? She remembered Nola's joy. Maybe it got better?

Trevor's second slap landed a bit higher, where her bottom was at its fullest and roundest. The third struck her again where the first had. Amanda's bottom burnt.

Against her own will, her legs bent up protectively. Trevor

hooked his right calf over them and forced them back down without losing his slow steady rhythm. Helplessly she writhed to try to escape the relentless rain of pain. It seemed as if her bottom had blossomed so that the smacks now landed sooner than before, and that it glowed from the heat of the beating. The glow began to spread, down and then between her thighs, from the surface in, until not only her skin but her insides were on fire and her blood simmered.

Amanda began to drift. Each stinging slap sent her deeper into a rosy fugue-state.

She lost count. She didn't care. It didn't hurt any more, quite the opposite. It was delicious. God, Trevor was wonderful! She'd never had a lover like him. Submitting to him was rapture.

Amanda climaxed, a short hard convulsion that came and went almost before she realised it. It was effortless. She burst into tears at the ease of it.

Her sobs did nothing to slow him down. If anything, they spurred him on. The spanking continued. Lust, reignited, seared through her veins. Darling Trevor! Whatever he wanted from her, no matter how depraved, she would do for him. Anything, Christ, anything, just so long as he promised to always make her feel like this.

Another orgasm was building, like a tornado it whirled faster, almost ready to touch ground. Amanda squirmed, trying to rub herself on the hard muscle of his thigh. The climax eluded her. Sudden desperation. The smacks to her ass started to hurt again. She'd never been so tender in all her life. It was cruel – he was cruel and once she'd come she'd say so. She managed to position herself so that her red-hot clit was squashed with each blow. So close ... Amanda was making little wet sounds with her mouth and what was the wet on her cheeks? Tears? Never mind. So close ... so close ...

The spanking stopped. Her precious orgasm retreated. She babbled, 'More, please, Trevor. Just a few more?'

He gathered her up in his arms and cuddled her head to his massive chest. His body felt like a thinly padded, leather-covered brick wall. 'Greedy girl. Perhaps I'll spank you again later, but for your first I promised you exactly forty smacks and I always keep my word. That *was* your first proper spanking, as an adult, wasn't it?'

She nodded.

'You were very brave, Amanda. I'm proud of you. It's a shame that you had to wait so long to find out.'

'Find out?' Her head was thick, as if she'd just woken up. 'Find out what?'

'That you're a pain-slut.'

'Really?' She frowned. 'What's that?'

Trevor laughed. 'It's just what it sounds like, silly. You get off on pain.'

She tried to hide her face in his shirt, suddenly embarrassed.

'Hey, be happy. It's a special gift. There are pleasures available to you that a lot of women are denied.'

'OK.' Amanda's voice was muffled. She pressed as close to him as she could get. Trevor rocked her in his arms and smoothed her hair. Amanda felt like a girl who'd done something really clever and now was being properly appreciated for it by some big important man.

He was hard under her bare and tender bottom. She wriggled until she'd trapped his length between the cheeks of her burning bottom. Amanda wanted one thing only, to please him in some way that would make him keep appreciating her, just like this, for endless days to come. 'Would you like me to suck you, Trevor? I'd like to, if you'd let me.'

'You're a good girl for asking and, later, you will, but I have other things in mind for now.'

She'd never offered her mouth to a man before and had it refused. Still, Amanda didn't feel rejected. Trevor had planned things for them to do. That was as it should be. He'd command and she'd obey. With her young toys, Rupert, Paul and Nola, it was the other way around. Exerting command is just that – exertion. Surrendering could be physically strenuous but in all other ways, mentally and emotionally, it was incredibly relaxing.

Hm? What if she gave Nola to Trevor play with, sometime? It was within her power to do that. Nola would get a kick out of being humiliated by being 'loaned out'. Would that be a good way for Amanda to express how she felt about the big man? Come to that, how *did* she feel about him? Was it love? But yesterday and that very morning she'd sworn she was in love with Meg. Did she even want to be in love? She'd 'loved' Roger and look where that had got her!

Damn! She was thinking! Being cuddled and stroked was lovely but, if Trevor didn't do something sexy to her soon, she'd lose her beautiful blurriness. Amanda snuggled her face into the hollow of his muscular neck and lapped at his skin.

'Fully recovered from your first spanking, are you? Ready for something else new?'

She whispered, 'Yes please, Trevor.'

'Very well.' He stood up and deposited her on her feet. He slithered her thong down her calves to the floor. In a few deft movements, he'd stripped naked.

His body was gorgeous! Perhaps it was because of his work as a stuntman that he'd shaved or waxed his sculptured chest. His pecs were hard plates with tiny dark nipples like raisins. His abdomen was ridged, like a sandy beach after the tide has retreated. His thighs would have filled jodhpurs. She knew that he was hung – she'd had it in her mouth, after all – but even half-erect and drooping it was much longer now than she remembered it being. Of course, last time he'd still had his pants on. It seemed that he'd only showed her half the package that night.

Amanda fought the urge to drop to her knees and worship it. Her tongue ached to lick and her lips to surround and her mouth to adore it. First she was eager to trace the prominent veins that made fascinating ridges up its entire thick length.

Jesus. Unless she was very mistaken, she was going to be forced to take that powerful monster up her bum! Maybe she should have had Rupert or Paul take her bottom's cherry first. Oh well! It was too late now. She'd never refuse Trevor.

He took her by her hair to the edge of the table. She stood where he left her while he grabbed a cushion and set it in front of her. Then he pushed her forwards until the fronts of her thighs pressed against the now cushioned edge. Lifting her wrists and pressing down on her head, Trevor bent her over to squish her breasts flat on the hard wood.

'Brace yourself.'

That was a pretty unceremonious way for him to announce that he was about to bugger her! Amanda stiffened her legs and gritted her teeth. His belly brushed against her back. It was coming!

The sensation of his hard wet knob pushing against the lips of her pussy seemed anticlimactic. Then it wasn't. He was entering her slowly but the thickness of him distended her pussy further than it had ever been stretched, and deeper, much deeper. Amanda felt as if she'd been impaled by a warm smooth log.

'You're very tight,' he said.

'Mm. You're so big,' she said.

His hand pulled her hair back, arching her. His other arm wrapped around her hips, its hand spread wide over her tummy, bracing her and locking her in position. One finger found her hot spot.

He rocked. Amanda moaned. The fingertip rotated, then flicked from side to side. The way Trevor was moving, so slowly and so controlled, he'd never reach a climax. Amanda tried to squeeze him but she was so dilated her internal muscles had no strength.

The only part of either of them that was moving with any speed was that flickering fingertip, driving her higher and higher and higher again . . .

Until it stilled.

Trevor crooned into her ear, 'Poor baby.'

She tried to push back at him but, with his strength and weight, she doubted he noticed her efforts.

The finger began to rotate again. Perhaps . . . But no. He was pulling back. She tried to wriggle, to no avail. His muscles held her as securely as his handcuffs held her wrists. Goddam it, was he ever going to let her come.

He reached past her to the dish of butter. Amanda knew what that meant, but denied it. It was something she'd thought she wanted to try but, now that it was imminent, it didn't seem like a very good idea. She retreated into a place where she could feel but where she couldn't form a single coherent thought.

Something parted the cheeks of her bottom. Cold slipperiness was slathered over her tight knot. Something thick prodded the greasy stuff up into her and then pushed deeper and deeper, oiling her hot dry inner tunnel. The invader pulled out, leaving a vacuum of need behind.

Something really big pressed against her sphincter. Her knot tightened by reflex but Amanda knew that was wrong. It had to relax. Relax. The big intruder was inexorable. It forced her weak female flesh to part, to yield to its superior male strength.

Her back passage was pierced by the invader. It hurt. He pulled back a fraction, then pressed forwards, deeper. She was being stretched wide to accommodate him. It didn't hurt as much. Again he pulled back a fraction, then thrust all the way in. God. She was being violated and it was absolutely delicious.

Something slippery was tantalising her joy-button. A kind voice murmured in her ear, though she had no idea what it said. The thing that had claimed her back passage reached its greatest depth and paused. Gradually, as her body accommodated itself to the obscenity of its desecration, Amanda drifted back to full consciousness.

'Are you all right?' Trevor asked.

She nodded.

His hips moved forwards an inch and then drew back again. 'Do you want me to?'

Amanda summoned the ability to speak. 'Yes. Do it, please. I want to fuck like this. I can do it if you make me, so make me do it.'

'Good girl.'

His thrusts started slowly and gently but rapidly became faster and fiercer. Despite the lubricating butter, her tunnel clung to his shaft, so that each deep impalement and partial withdrawal seemed to move her entire insides. His fingertip punished her button until pleasure bordered on pain in not one but two places. With each stroke, his swaying balls slapped against the swollen lips of her sex.

'Fuck, fuck, fuck.' It was her voice, muttering, rising with each expletive, growing louder with the climax that rose like the tide from the place where his finger touched her, and the place where he plundered her bum. It raged like a stormy sea, each wave crashing closer to the surface, pounding in her ears so she had to shout to be heard over the noise, 'Fuck, fuck, fuck!' until she drowned.

Amanda was sated, floating in a warm dream state, without a care in the world. She was boneless, completely limp.

Trevor lifted her into his arms. 'Are you OK, Amanda?'

She could feel his erection's hard wet crown tap against the base of her spine. Somehow, she managed to croak, 'Blissed. Totally blissed.'

He chuckled. 'I'll take that as a compliment. Up to bed with you.'

'But what about you? You haven't ...'

'For a nap, that's all. We've lots of time, and I want you to be fully alert.'

14

Amanda woke up in her bed feeling a pang of guilt. As far as she knew, Trevor hadn't climaxed yet. How long had she neglected him for? The bedside clock told her it was a few minutes after midnight. She couldn't have been asleep for more than an hour. Amanda was naked now, no stretchy top, no handcuffs and no hose. He'd undressed her and put her to bed.

Amanda rolled on to her side and reached back to palm her own bottom. It was not much warmer than usual, despite the severe spanking it had endured. She worked a finger between her bum-cheeks. Her knot felt no different than when it had been innocent. She contracted the muscles in her rectum experimentally. As far as she could tell, it was still as tight as it had been when she'd been a virgin back there. She tried relaxing her opening. Ah! There was a difference. The next time Trevor, or someone, pushed into her back there, he'd encounter less resistance.

Unless she wanted there to be.

Water started running in her ensuite bathroom. Amanda relaxed. That was OK then. Trevor was just taking a shower and would be back with her soon. She hadn't failed him – and there would be more pleasure yet to come!

She leapt from bed and dashed to her dressing-table for half a dozen miniature breath mints, a spritz of Joy in her hair and a quick repair job on her makeup. The water stopped. Amanda threw herself back into bed, pulled the covers up to just below her navel and posed prettily for him.

Trevor came in damp and naked, towelling his hair. His magnificent purple-crowned stem wagged at her. That oversized shaft had been all the way up her back passage. She'd taken the whole damned thing, to the very hilt, and she hadn't cried out or begged for mercy. That was pretty impressive!

'You're quite the little switch, you know,' he said.

'What does that mean?' She was pretty sure he meant it as a compliment, whatever it was.

'When I saw you with Rupert and Nola, you were so dominant I wondered what had happened to the sweetest little submissive I'd ever met!'

Trevor strode to the bed and threw her bedclothes aside. His hand wrapped around the back of her neck and pulled her face up to his. Amanda realised that Trevor had fucked her face, pussy and bum, but he hadn't kissed her, not once.

Her mouth started to water even before his lips met hers, even before his thick tongue pushed its demanding way into her mouth. His hand cupped her left breast firmly but gently. It was a delicate fluttering thing that wasn't being crushed, despite the power of its captor. It was safe simply because the hand that held it cherished it. If he hadn't been so careful, his strength could easily have ruined her tender flesh.

Amanda groped with both hands and found his shaft and his huge swaying balls. One hand stroked, the other jiggled. Her subtle caresses seemed to spur on the tongue that mastered her mouth. It lifted her tongue and sought out the nectar that was pooling beneath it. She began to pant. At the same time, she was filled with pride. Her weak little hands were exciting a man who could have broken her with a careless gesture. It was like making love to a lion. The peril compounded the pleasure.

Trevor broke the kiss, grabbed her left leg just above her knee in his left hand and lifted it until only her shoulders and neck were still resting on the bed. Her right leg flailed in the air. His right hand pushed it down, and wide. In his grip, Amanda was no more than an anatomically correct rag doll, and he was inspecting her most anatomically correct parts. She relaxed as best she could in that awkward half-suspended position.

His hand turned, casually flipping her over on to her face. 'There's hardly a mark on your bum now, just a trace of blush,' he observed. 'You heal quickly.' He turned her back. 'Keep those lovely thighs spread wide apart.'

Amanda stiffened. Trevor's hand rose and fell. Three powerful fingers smacked her, right on her sex. That blow was followed by a staccato tattoo of short sharp slaps. Sometimes Amanda masturbated that way, with a carefully controlled two-finger spanking on her sex, usually aimed directly at her clit. His blows were twice as hard and twice as fast and covered the entire delicate area. Within moments, her outer lips pouted and she was so wet his fingers splattered each time they landed.

Once more, it was the indignity and her helplessness as much as the sensations that excited Amanda. It seemed he'd only just started when her climax convulsed her dangling body. Without pausing, while the after-shocks still wracked her, he spun her round, dropped her leg, took her throat in one hand, her hair in the other, and directed her gaping mouth on to his rigid manhood. He pulled her face in so close that her nose was buried in his pubic hair and his shaft's crown was buried in the back of her throat. She was good at this but, still, she was scared. Amanda tried to cough but she couldn't. Her mouth was too full of his hard flesh. She could breathe, but only just. Each time she inhaled, her breath rattled. Her mouth flooded with saliva. Amanda felt her face redden. A pulse began to throb in her temples.

He wouldn't hurt her. He wouldn't. He wouldn't.

Her eyes turned up to his, begging. No sooner had their eyes met than he pulled his hips back, unplugging her throat. Amanda took a long wet bubbling breath and wiped her drooling mouth.

'Thank you,' she gasped.

'You're safe,' he assured her. 'I might scare the hell out of you once in a while, but I'll never harm you. Do you understand that?'

'Yes I do. Thank you.'

'Now I'm going to teach you some special ways to please me.'

'Thank you, Trevor. I'd like that.' An errant traitorous thought reminded her that whatever erotic tricks he taught her would likely work just as well on other men, and boys.

He continued, 'While I'm teaching you, you may touch yourself whenever you like. I'll enjoy watching you. Climax at will, but this is going to be about you pleasing me, nothing more.'

'I understand, Trevor. I'll do my best to make you happy with me.'

'I know you will.' His grin promised, or threatened, a surprise. 'You'll have no choice but to please me. You're only a doll, after all. You're my beautiful, incredibly sexy, very light and very flexible, doll, but no more than a doll. You'll see what I mean.'

One big hand took her right shoulder, the other her left thigh. Without so much as a grunt, he heaved her up off the bed and high into the air above his head. It felt as if her bottom was almost touching the ceiling. Trevor looked up at her. His arms flexed, lowering Amanda's left breast down to his lips as if it was a dangling bunch of grapes. He flicked her nipple with the tip of his tongue and then sucked it into his mouth. His teeth gripped her tender nub. Trevor pushed her up, away from him. Amanda's breast was elongated into an obscene pear shape and further, until jagged streaks of pleasure/pain lanced her.

Amanda revised her previous thought. *This* wasn't a trick Paul or Rupert, or most men, could duplicate. She was as buoyant and weightless as a balloon, tethered to earth only by the tip of her nipple in his mouth.

'Trevor?' she asked, unsure what her own question was.

He tossed her on to her back, on her bed. 'My bendy doll!'

Before she could take a deep breath, his hands took her ankles, spread them wide and doubled her knees up into her armpits. 'I'll strain you but I won't break you,' he promised.

Trevor knelt beside the bed. His extended tongue stiffened. With a nod, he stabbed into the core of her sex. He nodded some more, making love to her with his tongue. When he looked along her body to her face, his cheeks were glistening with her fluids. 'Do you like the taste of your own juices?'

'I . . .'

'Of course you do.' He released her left leg but kept her doubled up by her right. Three fingers of his right hand united into a stubby dagger that he plunged deep into her delicate folds. He stabbed and stabbed again with force that was just short of bruising.

Rough sex. Amanda could tell that Trevor must have had a lot of practice at it. Although he seemed careless of her, each move he made was carefully calculated to send thrills of fear and waves of helplessness through her without ever doing her any actual harm.

Trevor rotated his hand, scooping out her essences, and stretched his fingers up to her mouth.

'Suck!'

She obeyed.

'Nice?' he asked.

Amanda nodded. 'But you taste better.'

'Later.' He buried his face between her nether lips.

The crude snuffling noises that he made inside her tickled and made her want to giggle but she wasn't sure that it wouldn't break the mood. Anyway, bendy dolls don't laugh, do they?

His mouth moved lower. His tongue was tantalising the sensitive patch of skin between where her pussy's lips joined and her bottom: her perineum, or – what was that word – her 'taint'. That felt so good. Any impulse to laugh left her. Amanda's fists grasped handfuls of bedclothes and twisted them.

Trevor took hold of her free ankle again and pushed it up to join its mate, and forced both further back. Amanda grunted. Her knees were pressed into the bed next to her ears. Her breasts were squished beneath her thighs. Her body was bent in two. Her sex and her bum were pointing straight upwards. Trevor's tongue was slavering from her clit to the fleshy cup where her pussy's lips joined at the bottom of her slit, and back, and down again, and then lower.

Amanda sucked a deep breath. The tip of Trevor's tongue was dancing around her bum-hole. That was obscene, but the sensations were so delicious that she felt herself opening to him.

Trevor nodded again, but now it was her back passage that his stiff wet tongue was stabbing into. Oh damn! She pulled her arms in and worked them down her doubled-up torso to her sex. Her left hand's fingers squirreled into her pussy. The fingers of her right spread into a fan and flickered across her joy-button as best they could in the cramped space.

His tongue was actually inside her bottom and squirming deeper! Hell, she'd climaxed just a few minutes before but already she felt hornier than she'd ever felt in her entire goddam life.

She started to come. The orgasm reared like a winged beast but it was as if her contorted body trapped its escape. The captive climax seemed about to claw its way to freedom when Trevor reared up over her, took both of her ankles in one massive fist and used his other hand to steer his cock to her bum-hole. He drove down into her and her orgasm took flight.

'Fill my bum with your cream, Trevor, flood my insides,' she begged. God, she wanted him to come with her.

His thrusts paused. 'Little sex dollies don't get to make requests,' he told her, and withdrew.

'I'm sorry! I'm so sorry!'

'They don't get to apologise, either. Don't you remember, this is when I use you as my toy?'

Amanda nodded but dared not speak. The sternness of his words was just a part of his game, she was almost certain, but she wasn't absolutely sure. Silence seemed the best policy.

But she yelped when he suddenly pulled her legs down straight and tugged her right off the bed by her ankles, to sit with her back to it and with her mouth agape just inches in front of the purple head of his rigid wagging shaft.

His hips swung from side to side, slapping his stem across Amanda's face, smearing her cheeks with his juices. She wanted to try to catch his glistening dome in her mouth, but she was learning that, in this particular game, any initiative on her part was absolutely forbidden. If he wanted her to suck on him, he'd simply put himself into her mouth and order her to.

Trevor grabbed Amanda under both armpits and tossed her back up on to the bed. Her head was in a whirl. What next?

He stepped up on to the bed and loomed over her, legs

astride. Amanda gazed up between the impressive columns of his muscular thighs, at the underside of his jutting rod and at his dangling balls, and licked her lips lasciviously. She might not be allowed to ask for anything but there was no rule against body language, was there?

Trevor squatted. Facing away from her, he lowered himself slowly towards her face. Her lips parted in invitation but it wasn't his erection that he presented to them. The crinkled hairs on his left testicle brushed her lips. His balls were huge. Even though Amanda strained to open her mouth to its fullest, his one ball nestled halfway into it, much like an egg sits in an eggcup.

'Lick,' he said. 'And remember that you can play with yourself if you like.'

She took that reminder as a command. Her tongue flickered as well as it could in the confined space of her flesh-filled mouth. Amanda drew her knees up high and wide, parted her nether lips with the fingers of her left hand and started to make slow circles around her pink pearl with the index finger of her right. It was her guess that she was supposed to diddle herself as an erotic exhibition, just to amuse him, rather than for her own pleasure. Strangely, her showing off her self-love made it far more exciting than doing it just for herself. She humped her hips to show him that she was getting off on the play.

Trevor lifted a little, moved sideways a fraction and lowered himself again. Amanda had a new ball to please with her tongue. Fingers took hold of both of her nipples and rolled them into tight spirals. She moaned her appreciation.

Trevor said, 'Hmm! That's nice. Good little doll!'

She moaned some more, with more vibration. It must have got to him, because he stopped toying with her left nipple and, from the feel of his movements, started stroking himself.

It would have been nice if she could have watched that. She'd always had a thing for watching men masturbate. Maybe another time, or perhaps he'd do it for her later, as he seemed tireless. How could Trevor hold his position like that? Impressive, that was the word for him, all around.

Trevor hitched up and came down again. This time it was his perineum that pressed against her lips. Well, she'd enjoyed that caress when he'd done it to her, so that was fair, not that fairness was relevant. She licked from side to side and then up and down.

'Use your teeth,' he said. 'Nibble gently and scratch my skin with your teeth.'

Amanda did her best to comply, though she was finding it hard to breathe with her nose nestled between the cheeks of Trevor's hard-muscled rear. Her attentions to his perineum seemed to be having an effect on him. She could feel that he was rubbing himself much harder now. She stopped toying with her joy-button and began diddling it in earnest. If she timed it just right, perhaps they really could climax together.

Trevor hitched up again. Amanda sucked a deep breath while she could. When he lowered himself once more, his firm buttocks spread across her mouth.

OK. He expected her to lick him there. He'd done that to her and it'd been incredible, but licking a man's bum-hole? Could she? Could anything be more degrading?

But her being degraded was part of this game between them; she knew that. Amanda extended her tongue, as stiff as she could make it, and slavered it in tight little circles around his ring.

Trevor sighed and jerked harder on himself.

Amanda managed to pull her head back into her mattress a fraction and spat up. A feeling of power flooded her. Straining up,

Amanda squirmed her slippery tongue into the forbidden pinhole above her.

Trevor grunted. Amanda's fingers flickered on her clit. Her other hand wriggled two fingers deep inside her and spread them wide to stretch herself open. She was giving him an obscene eyeful while she orally serviced his perfect bum. It would be enough to make a stone statue give up its cream, she was sure of it.

Trevor babbled, 'You fucking wonderful beautiful depraved superb little sweet-cunt witchy-fucking-slut-bitch, I'm going to ...' His words became a strained bellow.

Trevor, losing control? It should have frightened her, especially the way he was howling, but Amanda found it tremendously exciting. Hot, wet man-come flopped across Amanda's body in a splatter from the nipple of her left breast to the crease of her right groin. That triggered her. Another orgasm ripped through her, so fast and deep she felt as if she'd been torn in two.

Trevor toppled sideways. At last, he'd climaxed. It hadn't quite been simultaneous, but so what. It'd been absolutely glorious.

15

Amanda woke with her back pressed against Trevor's solid chest. His hard and hairy thighs were curled up beneath her soft and smooth ones. His massive arm pinned her. She tried a subtle wriggle and felt his shaft, trapped between his belly and her bottom, thicken and rise.

He whispered, 'A quickie, before breakfast?'

Amanda groaned. 'No more! I ache all over.'

He chuckled into her hair. 'That's what I like to hear.'

'What about you?'

Trevor stretched. 'Me? I feel like a well-oiled machine. A hungry well-oiled machine.'

While Trevor took a long shower, Amanda laid out a big breakfast of free-range eggs, back bacon, wholemeal toast and a crunchy oat cereal. There was a bowl of fruit, milk and orange juice on the table and a fresh pot of coffee brewing. Amanda, not one for a big breakfast, nibbled a piece of toast and sipped a cup of tea. She wasn't ready to indulge herself by recalling the events of last night yet; she needed to be alone for that. Oh God. Oh God Oh God Oh God. The man was a freakin' sex machine. His plan was obvious in retrospect. Satisfy her every desire until she's limp in your arms, let her have a little nap and then use her like a toy. 'My little bendy doll,' he'd said, plainly delighted. She smiled. It hurt her lips. Her hips were on fire and her groin ached. Her nipples were swollen and so, she suspected, were her insides. Her spanked bum was tender, though, interestingly, her back passage was perfectly fine. God. She needed him to leave so she could collapse.

But she needed him to come back, too.

'Good morning,' he said. He was dressed but this time there were no handcuffs dangling from his belt. He sat at the spot she'd set for him at the head of the table.

'Coffee?' She raised the pot.

'You bet.'

Amanda served, though not the same way she had the night before. Here in her kitchen they were in a sort of neutral zone; neither their work personas nor their dom/sub roles were relevant. The lack of structure made her nervous.

She sipped her tea, while he ate.

'Trevor, I have a couple of questions.'

'Shoot.'

'Did you ever see Roger with another woman?'

'Hmm. I don't like to tattle on the staff but ... let's just say he liked the circus.'

'The girl with the candyfloss hair? I already know about Nola. Anyone else?'

Trevor shook his head. 'But I wasn't paying as much attention back then as I started to once you came on board.' He grinned. 'Next question?'

'Last night you said I needed to be punished for corrupting young people. Was there any truth in that?'

'Nope. Just playin'. And may I say you play very nicely.' His eyes twinkled. He helped himself to another serving of eggs.

'So you don't think I'm corrupting kids?'

'They're young adults. Like me. I'm much younger than you are.'

'Not *much*.' She laughed. 'You're a *little* younger than I am.'

'The bigger question is the fact that they work for you. You need to be very clear with them about that – that they are free to refuse you without losing their jobs. If they are, that is.'

'Yes, of course. I've tried to be clear.'

'And they should have safe words. Oops. Something I guess I forgot to offer you.' He mocked chagrin. 'I suppose it's too late now.' He grinned.

'Hey, that's right. I never even thought to insist. I even had one picked out, my first safe word ever.'

'What is it?'

'I thought about it a lot. It's "potato".'

'Oh is that so? I'll try doubly hard not to make you use it, now that I know what it is.'

'Hey!' She mocked indignation. They both laughed.

'I've been a player for a long time,' he said. 'You're safe with me.'

'I know. And I knew that, last night. I always feel safe with you. Which is why I'd like you to come work for me.'

He stared at her, clearly surprised. From the look on his face, Trevor would need a moment to consider her offer.

The telephone rang, and Amanda reached for the receiver. 'Hello.'

'I don't think you're the one who should be threatening me with legal action,' whined the tremulous voice of Tom Sharpe.

'This can't go on. You have to go back to school.'

'My school buddies are coming here to collect me.'

'Good. Go back to class and forget about me.'

'I'll never forget you. I'll love you as long as I live.'

'OK. That's fine. But we're – we're finished. Over.'

'We'll never be over.'

For the first time, Tom hung up on her. Amanda cradled the phone. She met Trevor's concerned look. 'That's why I need you to work for me. I want to be able to call on you any time, Trevor.'

'Who is it?' His voice was grim.

'Oh just a – a man. A young man. He's leaving town now so . . .'

'Are you sure? If he bothers you again, you call me. Understand?'

Amanda nodded.

'As for me working directly for you, you do see how the dynamic between us would be affected by that, don't you?'

'I don't see why it has to make any difference at all. Anyway, I think it would be worth it, for me to know you're always there.'

'Amanda, I'm already always there.'

A few moments later Trevor was gone. He didn't kiss Amanda goodbye but that didn't surprise her. She was beginning to understand him. Kissing equals intimacy and, for him, intimacy only occurred after the nap a woman needed to take after he'd fully satisfied her with his tremendous sexual prowess. Intimacy was when he could hold her above his head and call her his 'bendy doll'. The rest, for Trevor, was play.

16

Amanda paused outside the door to Purchasing.

Paul's raised voice came through the door: '... consider each season as an entity in itself. As it nears closing, we clear everything out.'

Rupert, his voice taut, said, 'But only the seasonal styles. There'd be no reason to dump classic black pumps, for example, just because of a date on the calendar.'

'You don't understand at all, do you? No matter how "classic" a shoe is, next year's version will be slightly different, somehow. You know, when you talk about "classic" styles, you sound just like Humpty-Dumpty Dumphries or Slimy Sophie Sharpe.'

'Fuck you!' Rupert sounded livid. 'Just you wait. When Ms Amanda makes me a VP, you'll see how we'll run things around here. There's always the bottom line to think of, remember!'

'Fuck you! Ms Amanda make *you* a VP? That'll be the day.' Paul's voice rose even louder. 'I'll be your boss any time now. Ms Amanda and me, we have a special understanding. She recognises real talent when she sees it.'

'You think *you* have a special "in" with Ms Amanda? *I'm* the one she's relying on to help her save Forsythe Footwear. Her and me – we're like this.'

Amanda imagined Rupert holding two parallel fingers up. Damn! She'd never considered that her young stars might squabble. The way their row was going, one of them was likely to blurt something like: 'And I'm fucking our lady boss. What do you think of that?'

She rapped on the door and marched in. Both of her young lovers were red-faced and tight-fisted with anger. 'Paul,' she barked, 'aren't you supposed to be checking on Shop Number Nine today?'

Paul mumbled something and made for the door. Rupert smirked.

Amanda continued, 'And you, Rupert, our shops' shelves are almost empty. Shouldn't you be doing something about your plans to refill them once the big sale is over?'

Paul glanced back, grinning, before he closed the door. Rupert scowled, picked his phone up and dialled a Milanese number.

Damn! She had to do something quickly, before their petty rivalry ruined everything.

Back in her office, she wracked her brains. She had to come up with something before her carefully established team started slithering sideways out of control. Amanda came to a decision. It was risky, but anything was better than nothing and, anyway, she'd become somewhat of a risk-taker recently so why stop now? She made a list before buzzing for Nola to come in to her.

'Look at this list,' she ordered the girl.

Nola stood beside Amanda and read. Amanda took advantage of the girl's position by running her fingers up between her legs, under her short skirt.

'Most of what's on the list you can likely find, some around the offices, the rest somewhere else, right?'

Nola swallowed and blushed. It wasn't because of what her boss's fingers were doing, Amanda thought. It was the contents of the list and Amanda's assumption that she knew where to find them that likely embarrassed her, or perhaps excited her.

'I – um – think I can lay my hands on most of this stuff, somewhere or another,' Nola admitted.

'What you can't find, buy out of petty cash. This is confidential, right?' Amanda's fingertip scratched at the cotton gusset of Nola's bikini.

'Of course, Ms Amanda.'

Amanda moved the crotch of Nola's panties aside. 'How are things going with you and Rupert?' she asked in a conversational tone of voice.

Nola squirmed. 'Good, but it's not the same as ... Not as good as ...'

'As when it was the three of us?' Amanda's fingertip wormed its way into the folds of Nola's sweet young sex.

'Yes, Ms Amanda.'

'You liked that, didn't you?'

'Yes, Ms Amanda. It was very – very special.'

'Do you think you love Rupert?' Amanda began to pump gently.

'Me? Love him? I don't think so. It's ...'

'The submission and the sex that you love?'

'I think so. With Rupert, the sex is good, but ...'

'He's not very dominant, right?'

Nola nodded.

'And you're bisexual, like me, aren't you?'

'Yes, Ms Amanda.'

'What if I told you that I was thinking about lending you out to a very dominant, very demanding male friend of mine to be his sex-toy for a night. Would you like that?'

'Would you be there, Ms Amanda?'

'I could be. If I were, you'd have a master and a mistress doing you, both at once, wouldn't you?'

Nola bore down on Amanda's invading finger and wriggled. 'Oh – both at once?'

'We'll see – if you're good.' Amanda took her hand from beneath Nola's skirt and held her finger up to the girl's lips.

Nola sucked automatically.

'Now go see about that list,' Amanda ordered.

'Are these things for a party?' Nola asked.

'Sort of.'

'Will I – will I be invited?'

'Not to this one but you will be to the next one, I promise.'

The girl looked disappointed but she said, 'Thank you, Ms Amanda.'

The next day, just before five thirty, Nola wheeled a dolly with a carton on it into Amanda's office. 'It's not that heavy or full,' she explained. 'I thought this looked better than me carrying it. Like a disguise.'

'Good thinking. Did you get everything?'

Nola came to stand beside Amanda at her desk. 'Everything, Ms Amanda. Ms Amanda?'

'Yes.'

'I'm not wearing any undies.'

Amanda suppressed a smile. 'And why's that?'

'Well, yesterday? I thought, just in case? Like, if you wanted to feel me up again, I should be prepared.'

'I'll remember that my little Girl Guide. Tell me, does Rupert "feel you up" at work?'

'Only at lunchtime, Ms Amanda. Never during working hours.'

'But I get to touch you whenever I like.'

'Well, you're the boss, Ms Amanda.'

'Hold on. Just because ...'

'I don't mean because you pay me. I mean because of your nature, and mine. I couldn't dream of refusing you anything, unless I really didn't like it.'

'But then you could?'

'Yes.'

'But you can refuse Rupert any time?'

'He's just a boy, Ms Amanda. He's sweet, and cute, but ...'

'I understand.' Amanda glanced at her watch. 'It's after hours now. Did you close your switchboard down?'

'Yes, Ms Amanda.'

'Then perch that pretty little bum of yours right here.' She patted the edge of her desk.

Nola sat herself on Amanda's desk, close to her boss.

'Pull your skirt up, Nola, all the way. Prove to me that you aren't wearing anything under it.'

The girl put her fingers to the hem of her skirt and hesitated. She peered back over her shoulder at the office's window-wall. 'People might see.'

'Everyone will be leaving now, but the blinds are almost closed. Someone would have to stand right up close to see in, and then you've got your back to them so all they'd see would be us having a nice little chat.' Amanda's voice became demanding. 'Do it, Nola.'

The girl pulled her skirt to the tops of her legs, did a little hitch and tugged it past her bottom. Proudly, she inched forwards a little and spread her thighs to show herself to Amanda. As Amanda remembered it, and she wasn't likely to forget, Nola had had a small neatly trimmed patch of sandy fuzz decorating her mound. Now it was as bald as Amanda's. Another tribute?

The girl's outer lips were plump, divided by a tight slit, with no sign of the sweet pink treasures within.

Amanda said, 'Play with yourself, Nola. Show me how you get off when you're all alone.'

Nola nodded. 'Yes, Ms Amanda.' She bit her lower lip and hooked a finger into herself, vertically, and worked it up and down for a dozen curved strokes. As she played, her nether lips became swollen and parted, exposing pink inner lips that were tinted with crimson at their edges. Nola curled over to peer down at herself.

'Do you ever use a mirror to watch yourself?' Amanda asked.

Nola nodded.

Amanda was tempted to part her own skirt and join in but that would have been a different game – a 'girls playing together' game. For now, she wanted it to be 'submissive debasing herself for her mistress's amusement'. If Amanda wanted sex with an equal, she liked to think she could call on Meg, though there'd been no communication between them since Meg had called to thank her for the bouquet. Truth be told, Amanda wasn't sure how to handle the way she'd felt with Meg.

Nola used the fingers of her other hand to part herself and lifted the finger that had been rubbing her pleasure bud. That little pink nub had swollen to the size of a large pea and had extruded from its sheath. That seemed to have been the objective of the first part of Nola's game. She took the sensitive polyp's sleeve in a delicate finger-and-thumb grip and began to work it backwards and forwards, like a little boy jerking off.

That was interesting. When not using a vibrator, Amanda rubbed hers, and flicked it, and patted or slapped it, but she'd never pulled on it. She'd have to try that someday, but not now.

The girl's fingers moved faster. Her head fell back. She was panting.

'Close?' Amanda asked.

Nola nodded. Amanda reached out and pushed the girl's hand aside.

'What?' The girl shuddered with need.

Amanda's fingers took over from Nola's and jerked at a furious pace, deliberately driving her over the edge. As she reached her climax, Nola flopped back flat on to Amanda's desk and humped up at her boss's hand before letting loose with something between a scream and a sigh.

Her aromatic honey oozed from her pussy. Nola gasped, 'Thank you, Ms Amanda. That was absolutely fucking wonderful.'

Amanda said, 'I've changed my mind about inviting you to my "party", except it won't really be a party. You are going to have to follow my instructions exactly. You can do that, I know. Now that I've decided to include you, we'll have to add to the things you brought me. It'll all happen tomorrow evening, starting at eight, and this is what we are going to do ...'

17

At seven forty, Amanda and Nola shoved Amanda's desk across her office until it was just about three feet from a side wall. Amanda sorted some of the carton's contents out and gave them to her pink-haired receptionist. 'Take these to Mr Eggerdon's office. You needn't hide them. Just leave them on his desk.'

When the girl returned, Amanda told her, 'You might as well get stripped off now. Rupert is due in about ten minutes. He might be early.'

It only took a second for Nola to lift her floaty little organza shift up over her head and off. Amanda had told her to be ready to get naked quickly, so the flimsy dress, her pink Dim stay-up hose and her pink mock-croc kitten-heels were all she'd worn. Amanda was also ready for instant nudity, in a short navy coat-dress with white polka dots that had just three over-sized white buttons, also worn over nothing but her creamy skin, blue suede high heels and dark-blue figured Leg Avenue stockings.

Nola squeaked across Amanda's desk on her bare bum, dropped over the other side and crawled out of sight underneath, just before Rupert tapped diffidently at Amanda's office door.

'Come in!' Amanda dropped Nola's dress into the girl's lap.

He was wearing sneakers, faded blue jeans and a creased brown leather bomber jacket over a black turtleneck. Perhaps he was making a statement. Usually, he was quite the dandy.

It could be that he thought the way he habitually dressed, taken with his boyish features, feminine lips and pale complexion, plus his having submitted to Amanda's dominance so quickly, brought his masculinity into doubt. Poor Rupert! Perhaps what Amanda planned would be therapeutic for the lad.

'You wanted to see me?' he asked nervously.

'Exactly. Strip.'

'What?'

'I said, "Strip." Rupert, we're going to play a game that's by way of being a test. To pass, you have to obey me absolutely, which is something I've already taught you, I trust, and you have to keep silent, not a word, not a grunt, not a sigh. Don't even hiccup. Can you do that?'

He frowned. 'I don't understand.'

'You don't have to. Rupert, when I first met you, in your shop, you obeyed me. Think about where that has got you. Your obedience so far has got you some spectacular sex, right?'

He nodded. 'Right, but ...'

'Obey me always, but especially now, and the erotic rewards will blow your mind. If you have any reservations, any at all, you may leave me right now. It won't affect our working relationship, I promise.'

'Oh, I'll do as you say, Ms Amanda – exactly as you say. I trust you completely.'

'Good boy. So, go ahead – strip off.'

She'd fucked and sucked him. She'd had him go down on her. They knew each other's body well, but he still undressed like a shy little boy, turning his back to her mostly and trying to shield himself with his hands when he had to face her.

When he was naked, Amanda pointed to her office chair and told him, 'Sit!'

He obeyed nervously but with his erection fully engorged. Amanda took a long leather strap from the carton. His eyes widened. When she passed it behind the leather chair and around his waist, he opened his mouth but managed to swallow his words before they spilt out.

Amanda pulled the strap tight behind the chair and buckled it. Rupert's arms and legs were free to move but he was trapped, strapped down. There was no possible way for him to reach the buckle.

The next thing out of the carton was a blindfold that was something like a sleeping mask, except that most of those aren't made of stiff black patent leather and lined with thick soft lambskin. Amanda had tried it on herself. Anyone wearing it was unable to see a thing, not even a glimmer of light.

Strangely, once Rupert was blindfolded, he seemed to relax more. Perhaps he'd decided to resign himself to whatever fate Amanda planned for him. Surrender can be comforting, as she well knew.

'Hands linked at the back of your neck, and keep them there. Now, Rupert, I'm going to ask you some questions. You may answer by nodding or shaking your head, nothing else. Do you understand?'

The lad nodded.

'You must be absolutely truthful. If I catch you lying, or even shading the truth, I will be *very* disappointed with you, and you don't want that, do you?'

He shook his head vigorously.

'Good. Rupert, do you ever look at porn sites on the net?'

He hesitated before nodding.

'Good boy.' She drew her nails down his chest and made him shiver. 'Do you watch girls making out with girls on those sites?'

Nod.

'How about sites with boys doing boys?'

Amanda beckoned Nola out of hiding.

Rupert contorted his upper body, half-nodding, half-shaking his head and shrugging, all at once.

'Is the answer to my question too complicated for a yes or a no?'

Nola, suppressing giggles, clambered over Amanda's desk.

Rupert nodded his answer to Amanda's question.

'Is it threesomes that you've seen, two men with one girl or two girls doing one man?' she asked.

Nod.

'But when it's been two men, sometimes the men touched each other by accident, even their sexual parts, right? After all, if one man is screwing a girl while another one is buggering her, some sort of contact is inevitable, isn't it?'

Nod.

'You've seen three-way kisses, either two men's tongues and one woman's or the other way around?'

Nod.

'Did it turn you on to watch that?'

A hesitant nod.

'When people have sex for fun, it's nice to share, just like having a party. Two men can share one woman, or two women one man, or any combination of people can all share. The important thing is, they all have to like each other, or at least not dislike each other. Does that make sense to you? It has to, doesn't it? After all, you enjoyed it when it was you, me and Nola, didn't you?'

Another nod.

'What if it was you and me and a very good male friend of yours? Could you handle that?'

Rupert shrugged.

'You like to watch sex. You've told me so. What if you watched while I was giving head to a good friend of yours, who you trusted? That'd be you watching, and at the same time, instead of jerking off, you could be making love to me. Wouldn't that be fun?'

His nod was decisive.

'Have you seen pictures of girls wearing strap-ons? Dildos in harnesses?'

His nod was confident.

'Doing each other?'

Nod.

'And you've seen men sucking on girls' strap-on cocks?'

Rupert's head cocked in thought before he nodded.

'Would you do that?'

His head wagged vigorously, as if the idea was very appealing.

'How about ... No, there'll be more questions in the test later, but, for now, I'm going to test your self-control. You have to keep perfectly still and absolutely quiet while your cock is played with. I warn you, you'll be teased dreadfully, but, whatever is done to you, you mustn't react. If you can't stand it any more and you want the game to stop, just say, "No more," and it will stop. OK?'

He grinned widely and nodded at the same time.

As Amanda had planned, Nola reached out and ran a fingertip up the underside of Rupert's straining shaft. Amanda tiptoed out of her office, leaving the door wide open behind her.

In Eggerdon's office, Amanda found Paul waiting for her. She gave him much the same speech she'd given Rupert, including, 'Strip naked for me.' When he was bare, blindfolded and strapped securely into Eggerdon's swivel-rocker, she told him, 'Remember, this game is to be a test. A lot depends on how well you do – not in your career but in your personal life, your sex life. Now, you must be silent, not a word or any sound, unless you really want me to stop, and then you may say, "No more." Otherwise, you must be silently obedient. You must be . . .'

Eighteen minutes after she'd left it, she wheeled Paul into her office, and paused. Nola was playing a game where her hooked finger pulled Rupert's straining cock down to where her cheek lay on his thighs. She held his cock there between her mumbling lips for a moment and suddenly released it to smack up against his belly before she tugged it down again. Clever girl! He'd never get off from that slow torment, but it would certainly hold his interest.

Amanda lined Paul's chair up next to Rupert's. As planned, Nola stood and took a position between the two lads and stroked both of their cocks at once. Amanda popped her three buttons and shrugged out of her dress.

Amanda said, 'We were talking about girls wearing strapons. I'd like you to picture that. Let's imagine it's me, or perhaps our little Nola. She's pretty, isn't she?'

Both young men nodded, each unaware of the other.

As Amanda talked, she fitted a harness around her hips and pulled the straps tight. A lifelike eight-inch purple jelly dildo was already fitted into the harness's socket.

Both young men nodded.

'I agree with you. Imagine her lovely slender body, her cute little tits, curvy little bum, stark naked except for the straps around her hips and a very realistic plastic cock sticking up. Got the picture?'

More nods. Amanda's fingers took over from Nola's, freeing the girl to strap her own plastic cock into place, this one black as night.

Amanda continued, 'Now think of me, in the same sort of

harness, and Nola goes down on her knees to gobble on the cock I'm wearing. Is that an exciting image?'

Enthusiastic nods.

'How about it's *you* who's sucking on my mock-cock? Or you and Nola taking turns at it? What if I was to bugger Nola with my strap-on? Would you like to watch me ream her tight little bottom?'

Their nods went into overdrive. Nola took over the stroking.

Amanda purred, 'You know what – I bet Nola would enjoy watching you suck on my dildo. Better, if she was here, I'm sure she'd love to watch me work my stiff plastic penis up into your bottom and give you a thorough bum-fuck.'

Nola grinned and joined in with the young men's nodding. Her fingers tightened on their cocks a little.

Pushing ahead, Amanda suggested, 'How about we imagine something really kinky now – your cock pumping up Nola's bum while you wrap your arms around her and stroke her imitation cock, just like she was a boy and you were jerking her off as you buggered her, and, at the same time, I'm buggering your bum with my plastic prick.'

The expressions on their faces said more than their violent nods. It seemed that the more perverse the scenes that Amanda described, the more excited the young men became.

Amanda continued. 'What if I told you that Nola was right here with me, now, and that we are both wearing strap-on cocks?'

Rupert's mouth opened but quick-thinking Nola covered it with hers before he blurted anything out.

'Remember the "keep quiet" rule!' Amanda snapped as soon as Nola's lips had left Rupert's.

Paul frowned, obviously not understanding why Amanda had said that. Nola's fingers, by stroking his cock a little more forcefully, smoothed the creases in his young forehead.

As one, the women went behind the chairs and unbuckled the straps that held their prisoners in place.

Amanda said, 'Now I'm going to move you. This is a test of your sensitivity and obedience. Let yourself be guided by my touch. No matter what is done to you, just let it happen. Not a sound, not unless you want the game to stop and then you say, "No more," otherwise not a sound, no matter what!'

Nola led Rupert from his chair and, with a push here and a prod there, made him kneel on all fours.

Amanda took one of Paul's hands and guided it to the dildo she wore. He stroked it tentatively at first but with more vigour once she imitated his action with her fingers on his cock.

It was Amanda's turn to lead Paul by his shaft and make him kneel, just a yard away from Rupert and Nola and at right angles to them. As one, the woman and the girl spread their victim's bum-cheeks. Each applied lube to their mock-cocks and guided their heads to nestle against the young men's clenched sphincters.

Amanda said, 'I said this game is by way of a test. It is. It's a test of depravity and of trust – and of masculinity. A man has to be very sure of himself to let a woman bugger him, just as a woman had to be very feminine to let a man do her that way.'

She signalled to Nola. As one, they applied gentle pressure.

Amanda continued. 'I like my man to be sure of himself, and to be depraved. Are you? Depraved and sure of yourself?'

Both young men nodded.

'Depraved and sure of yourself enough to be OK with a foursome, provided the other man was into it as much as you were?'

Both Rupert and Paul paused but eventually nodded.

'Very well . . .' Amanda hunched over Paul.

Nola arched over Rupert's back. Both the woman and the girl reached down to grip her willing victim's shaft.

'Now!' Amanda thrust deeply into Paul's rectum, as Nola did into Rupert's. They looked across at each other and grinned. It was strange, and exciting, to do what they'd only had done to them before.

Rupert grunted but Paul took no notice. He likely assumed it was Amanda grunting, from the exertion of skewering his bum with her plastic cock. The woman and the girl watched each other, and the men they were buggering, intently. When the tendons of Rupert's neck stood out and his face turned red, Nola's pumping fist slowed down and Amanda's accelerated. Timing was everything.

Somehow, likely more by luck than judgement, both men rumbled from deep inside their chests at the same time and both straining shafts spat their foam on to the floor. As quickly as they could, Amanda and Nola toppled the men on to their sides and swooped to take their knobs into their mouths to suck out their second ejaculations. Even as they finished sucking, they whipped the blindfolds away.

Each young man, while at his most vulnerable, looked into the eyes of the other.

Amanda wiped her mouth. 'There, see what fun four people can have together, if they're all good friends and don't let silly emotions, like possessiveness, get in the way?'

The men looked sheepish, but grinned, first at Amanda, then at each other.

Amanda unbuckled her straps. 'That's enough of girls doing boys, for today. Nola, swap with me. Let's show these two lads how quickly our mouths can get them stiff again, given a new girl to do and with two eager little bottoms waiting for their cocks.'

It went very well, Amanda considered, but there was one

small disappointment. By the time she and Nola had both been taken fore and aft by both men, with the men growing comfortable enough to do one girl while kissing and caressing the other girl, they were drained. Amanda had hoped to try her first double penetration, but men, it seemed, have their limits, even virile young ones.

18

Amanda and Nola took two large brown paper bags of Chinese takeaway each down to Purchasing. The desks in that department had been pushed together to make one large working surface so she'd been able to have a table and chairs brought in. As often as possible, Amanda and her sexy little submissive receptionist joined Rupert and Paul for lunch. It was all part of Amanda's plan to strengthen the bonds that united them all into a dynamic team. Her theory was that working, playing and eating together made for – well – togetherness.

Nola set out the paper plates, the plastic utensils and the little cardboard cartons.

At the desk, Rupert hung up the phone and told Paul, who was pinning a chart on to a cork-covered wall, 'They've only got four cases of a broken range of sizes left, but none of their size forties – that's our size seven.'

'Damn! It's sevens we need the most. I'd take what they've got, anyway. It's a nice-looking little number.'

Nola spread out plastic packs of soy sauce. She said, 'I always thought that a case of shoes had some of every size in it? Have I got it wrong?'

Amanda opened a steaming container of Moo Goo Gai Pan and inhaled the aromatic steam. 'Explain what we're doing to Nola, Rupert.'

He sat down and picked up his chopsticks. 'You're basically right, Nola. Now remember that we're talking about high-fashion shoes here, not Dumphries's so-called "standard classics". So, let's say a manufacturer makes five thousand pairs of a new style. Half or more of those are divided into cases that contain, usually, every size from a three or a four to a ten, or sometimes an eleven these days. Those cases are for orders that were placed much earlier, often a full year ahead.' Rupert speared a crisply battered shrimp and dipped it into warm plum sauce.

'The rest of the manufacturing run of the shoes is for back-up,' he explained around his mouthful. 'If a shop initially ordered two cases of a style, that would mean it only got two pairs of size four, for example. If both fours sell early in the season, the shop, if it isn't too far away, can order individual pairs from the supplier or wholesaler, to replace them.'

Paul interrupted. 'But if the shoe is from China, India or Manila, there are no replacement shoes available.'

Rupert continued, 'By the end of a season, the manufacturer or the wholesaler is left with odds and ends, covering maybe a quarter, a half or perhaps three-quarters of the original range of sizes. All he wants to do then is liquidate them, get rid of them for whatever he can get.' He tucked into his fried rice.

Nola asked, 'But don't shoe shops always want a full range of sizes in every style?'

Paul took over the explanation. 'Of course they do, in theory, but, in practice, they never have, not for long. A case comes in, someone buys the only size five in it and someone else buys the only ten, bingo – a broken range. Then, if a customer wants a shoe in a size that isn't in stock any more, it's up to the salesperson to offer the closest other styles that they do have in the customer's size.'

Nola clapped her hands as she realised what the young men were doing. 'So – you're buying odds and sods of hot styles from abroad, ones that haven't reached us yet, and you're relying on the salespeople to switch customers from the style they asked for to a slightly different one, when necessary.'

'And we're buying them at fifteen or twenty per cent of their original prices,' Amanda added. 'That's how we'll tide our shops over from the time our giant clearance sale ends until we get a proper purchasing system rolling. That'll take another two full seasons, at the very least.'

'We can do it,' said Paul.

Rupert nodded his agreement. Both boys shot Amanda questioning glances.

Rupert added, 'We can with Ms Amanda in charge.'

Nola grinned adoringly at Amanda. 'Oh, Ms Amanda, I sure hope you get to stay President of Forsythe Footwear!' The girl's exclamation was so ingenuous the three businesspeople in the room laughed. It was the question on everybody's lips, though neither Paul nor Rupert would have said it out loud.

Affection surged through Amanda. They were all three as devoted as they were adorable. Two of them had exceptional business skills and the third was as sweet as candyfloss. 'I expect the meeting to go very well,' she said. 'But I can't guarantee it.'

'We're behind you all the way,' said Paul.

Rupert nodded.

Nola giggled. 'Behind you,' she repeated. 'That's funny!'

Amanda intended to spend the rest of the day calling the other shareholders. There had been no time to woo them as Sophie Sharpe had likely done, and anyway numbers don't lie, but it would be a good PR move on her part. She sent Nola off to the warehouse with a list of questions she needed answered, and set to work in her office, starting alphabetically on her list of shareholders.

By the time she'd reached 'J', Amanda's face was frozen into a fake smile. She hadn't seen any of the shareholders since the funeral and so every single one had seen fit to express his or her condolences over Roger, so she'd had to feign a bit of sadness at her husband's untimely demise. When the conversation turned to the upcoming meeting, most of the shareholders assured her they'd be there, while quite a few, when pressed, admitted they'd already promised their proxies to Sophie Sharpe.

Just as she reached for the phone to dial Jim Jacobek, the next number on the list, it rang. She picked up immediately, glad of the distraction.

'I've got news for you, Ms Garland.'

Damn. Tom Sharpe.

She put on her most commanding voice. 'Haven't your friends come to collect you yet?'

'Forget that. Something's come up. I've heard my Mom talking. She says she has a way to ruin you, *and* Forsythe Footwear.'

'Yes, well, she's obviously been busy wooing the shareholders.'

'It's much more than that. Meet me and I'll show you. She's gone until Thursday morning.'

Amanda was sorely tempted. Getting more information about her opponent was tempting but, if it meant meeting up with Tom, she had to refuse. 'We're over, Tom. I'm not meeting you.'

'Then I'll call the police. How do you think the shareholders' meeting will go with you in jail?'

'What – what are you . . . ?' Amanda sputtered. The cheek of the boy!

'I'm talking "rape", Ms Garland. Statutory rape.'

'You're of age! Right?'

No answer.

'You're in college, Tom, you must be of age.'

'I skipped two years because I'm so bloody brilliant.'

'Oh my God.'

'That's right, lady. Jail time. Major scandal.'

'Oh my God. Tom, does your mother know about us?'

'No. This has nothing to do with her. I'll never tell her about us, Ms Garland, if you'll just come see me this one last time.'

She knew when she was beaten. 'When, and where?'

'My mom's house. Tonight at seven. Come alone.' His attempt at a threatening tone might have made her laugh had she not been so thoroughly shocked.

Her next call was not, after all, to Mr Jacobek, but to Trevor. 'I need your help. Are you free tonight? Around – um – seven?'

'I can arrange it. Why?'

'I might have got myself in over my head.'

'Does this have to do with that phone call you received the other day?'

'Yes. Trevor it's Tom Sharpe. Sophie Sharpe's son.'

Trevor chuckled. 'You'll do anything for Forsythe Footwear, or anyone.'

'It wasn't like that, honestly. There was an attraction between us, and I – maybe I let it go further than it should have but I – I thought he'd appreciate having his cherry popped by someone with experience. Instead he's gone crazy. One minute he says he loves me and the next he's threatening to have me put in jail.'

'Charged with ... ?'

'Statutory rape,' she whispered. It was horrible, horrible! 'He says he's not of age.'

'Could he be lying?'

'Yes.' She breathed a sigh of relief. 'That's probably it. He's probably lying. Still, I think I'd better meet him tonight. Will you come?'

'I'll lurk, close by, and listen in, just in case.'
'Thank you, Trevor.'
'Bring your super-dooper spy machine.'
'Huh?'
Trevor laughed. 'Bring your cell phone.'

19

They took Trevor's van. Amanda sat in the passenger seat and watched his biceps flex as he turned the steering wheel. He was wearing black pants that were tight over the bulging muscles of his thighs and a matching muscle-shirt, so that his enormous arms were bare. He looked so dangerous that it made her groin ache.

'I emptied Roger's cell-phone camera like you told me,' she said. She was about to say more, but she thought better of it. Instead, she asked why he'd told her to wear a pant-suit for the occasion.

'The little toad doesn't deserve to look at your lovely legs, Amanda.'

'But you do,' she teased.

'And when I want to see them, I'll have you take your pants off.'

Not 'ask'. Not 'tell'. Just 'have'. When they were in dom/sub mode, he was that confident of his control of her.

He parked a few houses down the street from Sophie Sharpe's home. Trevor checked that Amanda's cell, concealed in her over-sized Carriage bag but with its antenna slightly sticking out, could pick up her quiet voice and transmit it to his cell. He'd given her a small flat square of metal that had sticky stuff on one side. As he helped her from his van, he told her, 'I'll be listening closely. Just call my name and I'll be there.'

'What if my gimmick –' she opened her palm to show the metal square '– doesn't work?'

'Then I'll just have to damage Sophie's door, won't I?'

'Oh!' She had a quick and thrilling mental image of Trevor battering Sophie's door down.

Tom answered the door quickly. His eyes were bleary. He had booze on his breath. Those weren't good signs.

Amanda walked in 'at him' to make him back up, which gave her the chance to slap her gimmick over the slot the door lock's tongue went into before she pulled the door closed behind her. Did she hear the tongue click into place? She wasn't sure. If she'd screwed up, that would delay Trevor's charge to the rescue, if one was needed.

'Thish way,' Tom said and led her into the living room.

The room stank like a rundown slum pub, with traces of smelly old socks and stale teenage testosterone as grace notes. There was a stained towel on the sideboard, put there to protect the French-polished finish, no doubt, and it certainly needed protection. A dozen empty beer bottles lay on their sides and half a dozen bottles of cheap liqueurs stood on the towel, all opened and all streaked with sticky spills. The virulently coloured drinks seemed to be based on banana, chocolate, something green, two kinds of orange and one clear, anise, perhaps. All of them looked and smelt like synthetic treacle. Amanda couldn't imagine a more nauseating selection of drinks.

Tom waved his arm in a broad gesture that almost unbalanced him. 'These are my mates,' he announced, as if he was inordinately proud of having the uncouth duo that lounged across the room as friends.

One youth was large, with a bulbous nose that was pitted with blackheads. The other was a bit shorter than Tom but twice as wide, built like a fireplug. Whereas Tom had reminded Amanda of cricket, this one made her think of rugby and wrestling and gymnasium showers. Under other circumstances, Amanda might have found him reasonably attractive, in a crude sort of way. But not now.

'Nice to make your acquaintance,' he said with a smirk.

The other contented himself with a snort.

A slimy coldness invaded Amanda's tummy. Somewhere near the top of her extensive repertoire of masturbation fantasies, she'd imagined being kidnapped and forced to perform obscenities for a gang of crude toughs. Being subjected to a gang-bang was a common female fantasy, or so she'd read.

But this was real, and nasty. It didn't excite her one little bit.

'I want to see your ID,' she said to Tom, trying to take control. 'Something with your birth date on it.'

'Zat so? Like my driver's licence?' Tom leered in close. 'I want to see something of yours, too.'

Amanda struggled to keep fear from her voice. 'You had something to tell me about your mother,' she reminded Tom.

'Only one thing you need to know about my mother. She's not here! And she won't be back for a couple of days. Me and my pals are having us a bit of a bash before I head back to college. And you are invited to be the guest of honour, and to provide the entertainment.'

'Guest of honour?'

'I told my mates about all the really dirty things you and me got up to that day. They want you to do the same things for them, right?' He turned to his friends.

They agreed. 'Right! Right!'

Amanda wanted to breathe deeply but the smell in the room was revolting. Everything about this scenario was disgusting beyond belief. She tried to keep a level voice. 'And what if I don't want to do those things for your stupid friends?'

Trying to sound menacing but failing because his voice cracked, Tom snarled, 'It can be real nice for you if you play along, or we can make it real nasty if you don't, but you're going to do us, all three of us, and do us every way there is, whether you like it or not.'

'I don't believe you'd do that to me, Tom. Not after what we had together.'

That was precisely the wrong thing to say. Anger flushed Tom's face bright red and tears shone in the corners of his eyes. 'I loved you. You used me. I don't love you any more.'

Amanda shrank back. 'I need help,' she whispered.

The fat boy lumbered up out of an armchair clutching his groin. The leering wrestler elbowed himself off the wall he'd been leaning against.

'Might as well enjoy it, lady,' the fat one suggested.

'No!' Amanda lifted her bag closer to her face, abandoning all attempts at secrecy. 'Trevor! I need you. I *really* need you!'

'What the fuck?' Tom asked.

'Who's this "Trevor"?' the fat one wanted to know.

There was a crash in the hall and then the door behind Amanda burst open. The three would-be rapists each took a quick step backwards.

'Party's over, lads,' Trevor announced.

The wrestler told him, 'Take off, you, before you get hurt, bad.'

Tom squeaked, 'This is a private house. I'll call the police on you.'

'That's a stupid threat,' Trevor observed. 'Here.' He scooped an ornate antique phone off a side table and tossed it at Tom, who fumbled his catch. The phone jangled to the floor. Its dial rolled away under the sideboard.

'Go ahead, call them,' Trevor challenged.

The wrestler said, 'You've got a count of three to get out, or else!'

'One-two-three,' Trevor counted. 'Now what?'

The wrestler rushed Trevor, fists swinging. The heel of Trevor's right hand met the boy's forehead, whipping his head back and sending him crashing against the wall. He bounced off it as if he was made of rubber and charged again. Trevor stepped inside his swinging fists and bitch-slapped him half a dozen times, driving him backwards until he fell over his own feet.

Tom hadn't made a move but Trevor reached a long arm out sideways and took his lower lip in a pinch-grip between his finger and thumb. As Trevor twisted, Tom sank, gurgling and streaming tears, to his knees. Trevor patted him down, located his wallet in his rear jeans' pocket, extracted it and tossed it to Amanda.

It was the fat one's turn to charge – and to be met by a thrust from the heel of Trevor's free hand into his flabby chest. He back-pedalled, gasping for air, and tripped over a stool.

'Next?' Trevor asked calmly.

The three teens looked questioningly at each other but none of them volunteered to attack Trevor again.

'Damn,' Trevor complained, 'I didn't even get to use my karate.' He took the open bottle of chocolate liqueur and poured it over Tom's head. 'Lap that up while I decide what to do with you,' he ordered.

Tom meekly obeyed.

'What's his ID say, Amanda?' he asked, as he poured a bottle of thick red liqueur over the big boy's head and a vile yellow liquid over the head of the other. Like Tom, they lapped up the liqueur that had reached the floor.

'He's more than legal, the little bugger,' said Amanda.

'You scared Ms Amanda, Tom. Apologise.'

'I'm sorry, Ms Amanda,' whispered Tom.

Trevor said, 'I don't think that's good enough, sonny. Amanda, go see if you can find a pair of scissors somewhere for me. The kitchen, perhaps?'

When Amanda got back, she found Tom still squatting, awkwardly shuffling his pants off his feet. The other two boys were in the process of dropping theirs. All three had sticky chins and shirts. They stared, bug-eyed, at the scissors in Amanda's hand.

'Trevor,' she whispered, 'I did hurt Tom's feelings. Maybe ...'

'He and his buddies were going to rape you, Amanda. Give me those scissors.'

'What are you going to do with them?'

'Don't worry, I'm not going to snip their cocks off, though I wouldn't mind doing that, actually. Here –' Trevor kicked Tom's pants over to Amanda '– you do it instead.'

He jerked his head to the other two. 'Give 'em to the lady, boys.'

To Amanda, he said, 'Cut their pants up, please. Nice small pieces if you don't mind.'

Amanda laughed out loud with relief. She commenced cutting up the boys' pants.

Trevor turned back to the teens. 'Underpants off as well, if you please. You, the one who thinks he's got muscles, I want you to sit in the armchair. Come on – move it. We're gonna make a movie, kids! Get your cell-phone camera ready, madam director. We're gonna make a porno movie starring Tom and Dick and over here – Harry.' He dragged Tom to his feet and released his bruised lip. 'OK, Tom, you promised blow-jobs and sodomy to your friends, I'm sure. It's not nice to renege on a promise, so on your knees, there's a good lad, and get sucking.'

Tom went white. 'Suck ... ?'

'That's right, suck your mate's cock. Let's get on with it.'

'I won't do it!'

'No?' Trevor's hand shot out. He took Tom's cock and balls into his massive fist. 'Want to change your mind? Ever heard the sound of a man's balls bursting from being slowly crushed?'

'N-no.'

'Me neither. It was a trick question. You can't hear it, you see, on account of all the screaming.'

'Ms Amanda,' implored Tom. 'Help me?'

Amanda looked up from the cell phone, which she was setting to 'movie mode'.

'How about if the boys pretend they're doing each other? It'll look the same on "Yoo-hoo tube" or whatever it's called.'

'I don't know,' said Trevor. 'I think they're dying to fuck and suck each other off.'

'No,' shouted Tom. 'I swear I'm not.'

'Me neither!' chimed in the stocky one.

Interestingly, the fat one remained silent.

'All right,' conceded Trevor. 'But I think all three of you owe a big thank you to Ms Amanda.'

A chorus of heartfelt thank-yous were offered to Amanda. To think only moments earlier these grovelling cowards had actually frightened her. She cast a grateful look at Trevor. 'Quiet on the set!' Let him have his fun. He deserved it.

Trevor directed Tom to kneel in front of the boxy boy, who sat on the couch with his legs splayed. He beckoned the obese one over. 'On your knees, you, down behind Tom. I want you to make it look like you're buggering him.'

When all three red-faced boys were in place, he said to Amanda, 'Be sure to get their faces, and their bare bums and their silly little cocks, of course. I want hard-ons! And I want to hear you boys make some noise.'

The boys pumped up their pricks and practised moaning.

'Action!' Amanda took close-ups and wide panning shots, while the boys groaned and humped like pros. After a while, she pressed the 'stop' button. 'New positions, please,' she said sweetly.

Trevor repositioned the boys so that the one on the couch was now apparently being rogered by Tom, while he took the large boy's member in his mouth.

Amanda shot for a few more minutes, then said, 'I think we've got enough.'

The boys collapsed.

Trevor moved among them, nudging them with his toe. 'You know how quickly I could get these clips to your parents or your college? Or just on to the net? Still, no rush. I think I'll just keep them for now. Maybe I'll upload them tomorrow, or next month, or even next year. I might just wait until one of you achieves something, not that that's likely. Won't it be nice, your name and picture in the local paper because you won first prize in an ugly contest, or got a half-decent job, or something? Or maybe because you managed to get married? And that jogs my memory so I go online, press "Send", and ruin you? Think about it.'

From their snivelling, it seemed the boys were doing just that.

Trevor asked, 'Done, Amanda?'

'All done.' She knelt by Tom to stare straight into his miserable eyes. 'I'm sorry it came to this,' she whispered. 'I'll keep the movie, Tom, not him.' She jerked her head at Trevor. 'I won't use it as long as you stay away from me. OK?'

Tom nodded. His puppy-dog eyes were grateful.

The fat boy blurted, 'I think I'm going to throw up.'

The wrestler said, 'Me too!'

'That's fine,' Trevor allowed. 'Just so you don't follow us. If you do, I'll thump you hard. Come on, Amanda.'

The room's door closed behind them a full second before the sounds of retching started.

As Trevor drove them away, Amanda cuddled up to his massively muscular arm. 'I don't know how to thank you,' she said.

'No need. I told you, remember? I protect you. It's part of the package.'

She ran her fingertips up the ridge of his cock, through his pants. 'It's a great package, Trevor.'

He covered her hand. 'No, Amanda, not now.'

'Why not?'

'That was pretty disgusting, back there. You can't feel like sex, not after what you just went through.'

'But I really want to thank you, and ...'

'Not that way, Amanda. Our physical relationship isn't all there is to us. At least, I hope not. I'm happy I was able to help you. And just think, now you have Sophie Sharpe over a barrel. Once she sees that movie ...'

Amanda sat up straight. 'No, Trevor. Sophie Sharpe will *never* see that movie.'

'But –'

'For all his bluster, Tom never told his mother about us. Even though he's of age, I'm sure his mother would still have had plenty to say to me, and to the other shareholders, about the morality of the President of Forsythe Footwear. No, what went on between me and Tom is still private, and it'll stay that way, as long as he behaves himself from here on in.'

'Even if it costs you the company.'

'I don't think it'll come to that. I learnt a few things from that boy.'

'That's for sure. For instance, always check their ID.'

'Yes, that.' Amanda had to laugh. 'Although I think, if I simply made it a rule not to have sex with people who still live with their parents, I should be OK.'

20

Dark as midnight, her naked body bathed in warmth. Safe inside a steel cocoon. Brilliant calm in the middle of chaos ... Amanda wondered what it would be like to masturbate inside the tanning bed. Her hand skittered down her belly towards its target. Her pink pearl, the one that so delighted in a good polishing, roused itself at once.

Damn! Amanda stilled her hand. She'd come to the tanning salon for a few moments' respite from either running a company or screwing her brains out with one or more of her five new lovers. She needed to quiet her thoughts, centre her being and get a base tan started so she'd be glowing for the shareholders' meeting. The absolute last part of her body that needed attention was her so-called 'love' button.

There was the rub. Was any of it love?

If not, was that mostly her choice? Or was it because deep down she wasn't loveable? After all, even Roger had had to seek ... something in another woman's arms.

Much as she was enjoying her current sybaritic state, she would not have entered into it had Roger not widowed her in such a publicly humiliating way. She was sure of it. But when she'd been exposed as a bad wife – or, no, as a lousy lover! – and left a widow at the same time, she'd truly lost all interest in monogamy.

There were two ways to avoid it. One was to be celibate. The other was to take multiple lovers. Amanda chuckled. The first option wasn't worth considering. It was glorious to be so sexually alive. She could have more lovers, too. Somehow she'd become a walking siren, a present-day goddess, Cleopatra in a business suit. If she wanted, she could already have had the parking attendant and at least one sales rep. Just wait till the shareholders' meeting. Her sexual charisma would probably win the day all by itself!

Especially with a little glow on.

Silence. Darkness from the goggles over her eyes and heat all around.

Again, Amanda wondered what it would be like to masturbate inside the tanning bed.

Forget it. A woman with five lovers needs to rest when she's alone. Amanda grinned as she counted them. A hunk o' burning love, Trevor. Rupert and Paul. And then there were the girls. Nola. Meg.

She hadn't thought of Meg much since the girl had called to thank her for the flowers. That conversation had been very short. Well, Amanda hadn't known exactly what to say and it wasn't up to Meg to say any more than she had, which was thank you.

What had it been about that girl that had so turned her head? It was lucky, really, that Trevor had come along that very night to screw the lezzy right out of her. God, what a man.

And what was she? A 'switch', Trevor had said. Maybe it was the extreme femininity of Meg that had so called to her, as heady an invitation as the extreme masculinity of Trevor, so attractive to one who is presently neither or both.

God, it was fun to combine the allure of woman with the power of man. No wonder she had five lovers. Amanda's forehead wrinkled. Not five lovers. Six. Tom counted. She had to be more careful in the future, and not just with checking ID. The first time for anyone is important. Certainly hers had been. Just because so far her virgin lovers had all been male didn't mean that losing their virginity wasn't momentous for them. She should have seen the Heartbreak Kid coming and been more careful with him or even have avoided the whole thing entirely. She'd been lucky, really, that Paul and Rupert had genuinely welcomed her advances. And welcomed her they had. Both boys had fallen into her clutches with grateful eagerness. Or would it be eager gratefulness? Either way, those initial shoe-store encounters had been divine.

Once again, Amanda wondered what it would be like to masturbate inside the tanning bed.

Damn!

21

Amanda's fingernails dug under the edge of the hard shell of wax that coated Nola's pubes. 'Ready?'

The girl nodded. Amanda ripped. Nola yelped. Most of the wax came away in one piece, leaving Amanda to pick the last few fragments off. 'Stand up and turn around.'

Nola lifted her bum off the tiled surround of Amanda's bathtub and turned to face it.

'Bend over.'

The easiest place to miss short fine hairs is on the 'taint' but Amanda's close inspection, with her eyes and with the tips of her fingers, failed to find any strays. 'There,' she said, 'that's better than shaving, right? It'll last longer, as well.'

'Thank you, Ms Amanda.'

'Turn around again.' Amanda poured soothing lotion on to her palm and smoothed it over Nola's freshly bald, newly sensitised, bright-pink skin. 'I want you to be absolutely perfect for my guest.'

'Me too. Is he ... ? I don't know what to ask. What sort of man is he, Ms Amanda?'

'You've met him – he's Trevor, our office building's security man.'

'Oh? He's a big one. I didn't know that you knew him, not socially.'

'More than "socially",' Amanda corrected with a smile. 'He's been very helpful to me, Nola, in all sorts of ways. You are to be my "thank you present" to him, because you are the very best toy in the whole world.'

'Thank you!' Nola smiled so wide her adorable dimples made her cheeks even more apple-like than usual. 'I've never been a "thank you present" before.' She giggled. 'I like it!'

'I thought you would.' Amanda sprinkled pink-tinted talcum over Nola's mound and brushed it off. 'I can't believe you and Trevor were never . . . introduced,' she commented.

'Oh. I dunno. I wasn't there after five much, except when . . . Roger . . .' Her voice trailed off and her face, just a moment earlier the picture of sunniness, clouded over.

'I'm sorry, Nola. I wasn't thinking.'

'No, I'm sorry, Ms Amanda. I never would've hurt you if I'd known what you were like.'

'It doesn't matter now,' said Amanda. 'I know it wasn't you in the hotel room.'

'No way! I always said to him to go home. I *never* went to a hotel with him. Honest.'

'I believe you. I do. But, tell me, did you ever see him with anyone else? Another woman?'

'No. And that's the thing I don't get. With you *and* me, what more could he want?'

Amanda chuckled. 'A good question, Nola. There, now your pussy is purr-fect. Do your face and don't spare the paint.'

Pink-haired Nola did her eyelids in silver, with glossy white highlights. She coated her lips with the same shade, and with the same wet look, as the delicate skin that lined her pussy.

When Nola was done primping, Amanda produced several rolls of pink ribbon. She'd decided not to put hose on the girl but to embellish her slender young legs with ribbons, tied around her thighs about where the tops of stockings would have come. A much wider ribbon went low around Nola's hips and tied in a big floppy bow, right over her mound. Narrower pink ribbons decorated her wrists. Finally, Amanda tied a pink ribbon as a choker, with its bow at the nape of Nola's neck.

'And now you're a pretty pink kitten for Trevor to pet,' Amanda announced.

She took Nola into her bedroom, where Roger had had several full-length mirrors installed. He'd so loved to watch himself and Amanda making love, the rotten cheating bastard.

'I'm gift-wrapped!' Nola squealed, delighted. 'Thank-you-thank-you-thank-you!' She looked Amanda, who was still in a plain terry bathrobe, up and down. 'What are you going to wear, Ms Amanda? And, may I ask, who is supposed to do what to whom? Is it to be all three of us tangled together, or mainly you and him with me assisting, or me and you with him watching, or me and him, doing whatever you tell us to do?'

'You and he at first, obviously, as you're the gift, and then we'll just see what happens.' Amanda realised she hadn't considered how she'd manage to 'switch' with a dominant man and a submissive woman as playmates. Oh well. She rushed on. 'He has amazing staying power. Don't be fooled by his manner at work, outside work he's dominant, *very* dominant, and extremely fond of spanking pretty little girls' bare bottoms.'

Nola smiled. '*My* sort of man, Ms Amanda.'

'I wouldn't be giving you to him if he wasn't.'

It was Amanda's turn to do her face. She used gold and green on her eyes and wet cherry on her lips for an effect that was a little bit over the top, even for evening wear, but nowhere near as theatrical as Nola's.

Amanda still hadn't decided what she'd wear. If she dressed dominant, that would be in conflict with her submissive relationship with Trevor. If she dressed sub, it wouldn't fit her relationship with Nola. She certainly couldn't seem to be trying to compete with the girl. Then again, she just as certainly didn't want to fade into the background. Not dom, not sub, not total slut and yet not blandly vanilla. Hmm!

Hadn't she recently read an article somewhere, *Cosmo,* most likely, about how to dress to go straight from the office to a hot date? The writer had recommended layers, worn in such a way that removing them one at a time could take a girl from daytime demure to 'let's go dancing' and all the way to downright daring, if she so desired. Amanda had those high-slit skirts that did something similar for her, but both Trevor and Nola were familiar with those by now.

Well, begin at the beginning. In this case, that would be with what went next to her skin. Amanda started searching the oversized chest of drawers that she used exclusively for her sexiest underwear.

One good thing about being rid of Roger, all the erotic play-wear that she'd accumulated over years of trying to keep her marriage exciting was as good as brand new again. None of her new lovers, young or mature, male or female, had seen her in any of it, apart from that one fishnet outfit she'd worn for Trevor.

The middle drawer yielded a waspie that she hadn't worn in ages. Seeing it again, she realised why Roger had bought it for her. It was very restrictive even though it only covered her from immediately below her breasts to just above her navel. She hadn't taken it as a subtle hint that he'd like to explore bondage. His loss! He should have been more explicit.

The waspie had wide vertical stripes that alternated golden satin and green velvet, which went very well with her makeup. Amanda's waist was still trim. Her hips and bust were both bountiful, so that, when that waspie was cinched tightly enough to restrict her breathing, it gave her a dramatic hourglass figure that was emphasised by the way the stripes narrowed and widened. That would be a good start.

'Nola,' Amanda said, 'come help me get into this.'

Nola oohed and aahed. She tugged at the laces with so much enthusiasm that Amanda's waist was whittled down to narrower than it was when she was twenty. The constricting whalebone stays made it impossible for her to bend, from her waist up, but left her hips free to sway and wiggle.

'Ms Amanda,' Nola declared, 'any man who sees you in that is likely to cream in his jeans before he even touches you.'

'Thank you. We'll have to see to it that Trevor doesn't see me like this until his pants are off, then, won't we?'

Nola giggled. 'Leave that to me, Ms Amanda. I'll have his pants off him in –'

'When he wants them off,' Amanda interrupted, reminding Nola of her submissive role.

'Sorry, Ms Amanda. I got carried away.'

'That's OK. Now come and help me decide what to cover this up with.'

'Seems a shame to cover it at all, Ms Amanda. Can't you find a way to let it show?'

Amanda thought for a moment. 'You know, Nola, that's a very good idea. I might just be able to do that.' She led Nola into her walk-in closet.

'Way cool!' the girl exclaimed. 'Sorry. It's just that you've got so many nice things.'

'One day I'll have you over for a "girl's day" and you can try some of my outfits on,' Amanda promised, 'but for now . . .' She pulled out a padded hanger with a green velvet military-style jacket. It wasn't a perfect match for the green in her waspie, but close enough. Amanda chose it because the jacket was very short, just long enough to overlap the top of her waspie by a couple of inches. It had a high stiff collar and long fitted sleeves and was fastened with a series of six green plaited silk frogs. Doing it up compressed her breasts some, but not uncomfortably so.

'Now for the matching velvet skirt that came with this jacket.' It was fully circular and meant to be mid-calf length. It came with a matching suede belt. In a few minutes, Amanda had punched extra holes and eased a couple of seams, so that she was able to buckle the belt very low around her waist, just a fraction of an inch above the lower edge of her waspie, and let the skirt hang almost to her ankles. The finishing touches were golden mesh stay-up stockings and a pair of strappy gold sandals with four-inch pencil heels.

'You're so beautiful,' Nola said with a sigh. 'So elegant. So classy. I really envy you your lovely figure, Ms Amanda.'

'Thanks, but you don't have to be jealous. You have a delightful shape.'

'It's OK, but ...' She sketched an hourglass in the air with her hands. 'That's what real men like best.'

'Well, I think you have a delicious little body,' Amanda said. 'And a lovely face to go with it.'

The women swayed closer. Amanda's fingertips rested on Nola's bare hips. Their lips parted as the doorbell downstairs rang.

'That'll be the caterers,' Amanda explained. 'There are pink pom-pom mules beside my bed. They should fit you. Put them on and come on down once the delivery men have gone.'

She went down and supervised, as men in chef's whites brought in a bowl of crushed ice with two dozen oysters on the half shell and then a dish of Beluga caviar and half a dozen platters of shrimp and scampi that were prepared in as many ways. There was a salver of cracked crab claws and another of split lobster tails and four kinds of bread plus three ready-dressed salads, a selection of dipping sauces, a platter of citrus slices on a bed of parsley and a pyramid of *escargots en brioche*. Trevor had once mentioned that the best thing about going to the coast was the shellfish. That was the sort of thing that Amanda prided herself on remembering.

Damn! What if he'd meant plain old cockles and whelks? Well, it was too late to do anything about it if he had. The escargots, which weren't strictly speaking shellfish, would have to substitute for whelks. A snail is a snail is a snail, right?

When Amanda had tipped the caterers and let them out, Nola came downstairs. The girl gaped and gushed as Amanda set up the drinks on a trolley, drew a couple of corks and stripped the foil and wire from the neck of a bottle of champagne. Knowing that Trevor was a wine enthusiast, she'd taken special care in her selections.

'When do I come in?' Nola asked. 'Am I to be here when he arrives, or jump out at some point, or what?'

'I didn't think to get a cake for you to jump out of,' Amanda teased.

'That's OK,' said Nola, taking her mistress seriously. 'I'd get all mucky with the icing.'

'Good thinking,' said Amanda. She suppressed an urge to laugh. Nola was already fading into that oh-so-literal state that made submission a delight to experience or to observe. 'I think we'll do it like this. We'll put this trolley in the kitchen and you can wheel it out when I call for it. You can serve us and then ...' Amanda looked around the room. 'Right!' She took an oversized decorative crimson and gold satin cushion from the couch and dropped it on the floor beside the chair that Trevor would be sitting on.

'Once you've served us our drinks, you can sit here. He'll be able to feed you titbits if he wants to, and touch you, which he's bound to want to. When we call for refills for our glasses, you can show off how graceful you can be as you get up and down, right?'

'Lovely! You think of everything, Ms Amanda. This is going to be such fun!'

'I wouldn't eat too much,' Amanda advised. 'He has hard thighs. You are likely going to be laid across them on your tummy at some point.'

'Yeah!' Nola stuck her bare bottom out sideways and gave it slap. 'I'll like that!'

Amanda lit the butter warmers. The doorbell sounded.

'That's him. Scat – kitchen!'

Amanda had asked Trevor to come casually dressed. He was in neatly pressed jeans and a white dress shirt with the sleeves folded back. He hugged her and then held her away from himself to admire her outfit. 'I'm impressed, but is this what you meant when you said casual?'

'I meant *you* casual, not me. This is to pay you back for your gallantry.'

'I'm paid in full by just one look at you, Amanda.'

'Flatterer! Well, you might think so, but I beg to differ. There are more treats to come.' She turned to lead him into the dining room.

'You've recovered, emotionally, from what you went through at Sophie's house?' he asked.

In answer, she gave her hips an exaggerated swing for him.

'It looks like you have,' he muttered.

When he saw the spread that had been prepared for him, he looked stunned. 'Just how many people are coming to this party?'

'I'm not expecting any more guests tonight. You don't have to eat it all you know, and I'll be eating, too. Take a seat and help yourself, Trevor.'

He sat and reached for a wineglass before scanning the table and seeing no bottles. His raised eyebrow asked Amanda a question.

'Oh – right!' she said. 'Drinks.' In the direction of the kitchen, she called, 'Pinkie! Drinkies!'

Simpering, Nola wheeled the cart out.

Trevor whistled. 'What wonderful service, and so nicely presented.'

Amanda feigned taking his reaction for granted and said, 'I thought Mumm's Carte Classique with the oysters, and a simple white Burgundy, a Cote de Beaune, to follow.' She held her breath for his reaction.

'Excellent choices!'

'I have a bottle of Chopin potato vodka in the freezer, if you'd prefer it?'

'Nice thought, but much later, perhaps – after . . .'

'Yes, "after" would be better,' Amanda agreed. Neither had to specify after *what*.

Trevor took the magnum of champagne from its ice bucket and eased the cork out with a steady twist of his wrist so that its pop was soft and no wine was lost. Nola held out two flutes for him to pour into. He topped them up but, when she turned to take Amanda's glass to her, his finger on her bare hip stopped her.

'Head back,' he told her.

When she'd tilted her head, he put the magnum to her lips. 'Don't swallow.' He poured, filling her mouth until the sparkling wine overflowed her lips. 'Hold it.' His tongue lapped the spillage from between her virginal little breasts. 'Now take what's in your mouth, and what's in the glass, to Ms Amanda.'

Nola walked around the table with her head up, to Amanda, who turned her face towards the ceiling. Nola bent over, carefully and slowly, and let champagne trickle from between her lips into Amanda's waiting mouth.

'Nice,' Amanda commented, when she'd swallowed.

Nola returned to Trevor's side and sank on to her cushion with her back to him and her nape resting on his upper leg. She arched and stretched to rest the back of her head on top of his thigh and gazed big-eyed straight upwards at him. Crafty slut! What man could resist?

Amanda shifted her chair so that she could see better.

Trevor's big thumb rubbed behind Nola's ear. His powerful fingers curled over her throat. Amanda imagined what that subtle threat felt like. She became aware of the feel of the fabric of her skirt, where she sat on it, and wriggled. Trevor's index finger tapped on Nola's lips. They parted and closed on its tip. Her cheeks hollowed as she sucked. Amanda imagined that the tip of Nola's tongue was doing its best to tease Trevor's finger.

Amanda tilted an oyster and let its slippery meat slide over her tongue to her throat. Trevor tipped an oyster between Nola's parted lips. The girl made an erotic exhibition out of savouring it. She rubbed the back of her neck on his leg, likely feeling for where his cock lay.

Amanda grinned. Trevor, she'd noted, 'dressed left'. The leg that Nola's neck was pressing against was his right.

Trevor ate, and fed Nola. He put morsels of scampi and shrimp between her lips and once bent over her to drop an oyster from his mouth into hers. His big hand split a lobster tail's shell. Trevor held the meat that he'd extracted all in one piece over a plate while he poured melted butter over it. When he touched the slippery six-inch length of white lobster flesh to Nola's lips, she sucked it in, whole, slowly, until it disappeared, and pushed it up and out again, still in one piece. Trevor grinned. Nola sucked in, and pushed out, fellating the treat as if it was a cock.

Trevor snuffed the candle under a container of melted butter. He waited a few seconds before testing its temperature with one thick finger. Seeming satisfied, he dripped melted butter on to first one of Nola's nipples, then on to the other. She squealed as if it hurt but her act fooled neither of her spectators.

Trevor rolled an oily nub between finger and thumb. Nola writhed, overdoing it, Amanda thought.

Had Trevor forgotten she was even there?

But he looked across the table at her and suggested, 'Isn't that jacket just a little too warm?'

Amanda was about to tell him it wasn't when she caught the glint in his eye. Of course! He wasn't dominating her overtly, because of Nola, but that question had really been a command. 'I could undo it,' she offered.

He nodded.

With deliberate slowness, Amanda unhooked one frog, then the next, all the time being watched intently by Trevor. As each plait of silk was released, her confined and compressed breasts expanded. Her jacket gradually parted. Each frog she unhooked exposed deeper and wider cleavage until her jacket finally fell completely open. Her nipples weren't quite exposed, so Amanda reached for a bottle of Burgundy, revealing her left breast in all its plump pouty-tipped beauty for a few seconds.

Trevor grinned his approval. 'Very nice. OK, Amanda, come over here . . .' He paused for a significant length of time before adding, '. . . please.'

Amanda followed his pointing finger around to stand with her toes touching Nola's cushion and her skirt brushing the girl's slender backward-arched midriff. Trevor's right hand pulled Amanda's head down to his. His tongue, his very strong, very male tongue, parted her willing lips and invaded her mouth. Amanda was aware that his other hand was moving

Nola's head and then felt the girl's lips and teeth on her pendant left breast's nipple.

Unbalanced, constricted by her tightly laced waspie, Amanda spread one palm on the table and gripped the back of Trevor's chair with the other hand.

Nola suckled, drawing shards of pleasure through Amanda's breast. Trevor's fingers were busy at Amanda's tummy, working on the buckle of her skirt's belt. Velvet slithered down over her hips and thighs, to the floor. Her sex was bared. The flat of Trevor's hand urged her thighs apart. He worked her pussy's lips between his thumb and fingers, engorging them. He tickled, teasing them apart, but, when they were ready, more than ready, for him to force his thick strong fingers up into her, his hand deserted her.

Amanda couldn't protest, not with his tongue commanding her mouth. Through slitted eyes, she watched him fumble for and find another naked lobster tail. Once more, he poured melted butter over it. And then ... Trust Trevor to make her gasp with shock. God but it was obscene! She felt firm but slippery lobster meat push at the parted lips of her pussy, and enter her. In it went, filling her, prodded by his degrading fingers. He drew it back, his fingers gentle on the delicate morsel, and pushed it in again, and again. Oh hell! He was fucking her with a lobster's thick tail, and Nola was watching the perverse act from just inches away.

As Trevor pistoned her, the ball of his thumb found her Trevor-ready bud and worked it insistently. Amanda fought against it but the sensations and the humiliation of it were irresistible.

She climaxed. It was a hard deep contraction, one only, but the violence of it extruded two dripping inches of lobster meat. She shuddered from head to toe.

Trevor pushed Amanda upright and gave her bottom a pat,

thrusting her hips forwards. Nola was as stunned as Amanda, judging from the look on Nola's face. Sure enough, Trevor guided Nola's head to Amanda's sex by his grip on the back of her head. 'Eat,' he commanded.

The girl obeyed, devouring a lobster tail that was now slick with both melted butter and Amanda's equally tasty juices.

When she was done, Trevor said to Nola, 'You liked that, didn't you?'

Nola nodded up at him.

Amanda could see that she was telling the truth. She relaxed a little, even managing a smile when Trevor looked her way.

He shook his head slowly. 'This is one depraved little whore you've brought to my attention.'

Amanda shrugged, playing along and, at any rate, at a loss for words.

He continued, 'I think she needs to be punished. Do you agree?'

Amanda nodded, grateful to Trevor for continuing to behave as if her opinion mattered, for the benefit of Nola, while making it crystal clear to Amanda that she was powerless in his hands.

Her face greasy, with mischief dancing in her eyes, Nola's eager voice asked, 'Are you going to spank me now?'

Amanda gasped for the second time that day. The cheek of the girl!

22

Amanda just *felt*.

It was a state she went into sometimes, if the sex was especially intense. The rational part of her mind, the part that thought in words, just drifted away. She was left at a nexus between sensation and desire. Perhaps not 'desire', exactly. Desire needs. In this state, she felt no urgency. She accepted each sensation and enjoyed it for itself, not as a stage in her journey towards her climax. Urgency would come; she was aware of that and would enjoy the greediness, in due course. Meanwhile, she was in a state she'd reached in other ways, from time to time: in the tanning bed, for example, and when she'd stood on the top of a mountain for the first time, breathing in thin air and with it the vista before her, and more than once, for a split second, while driving, but mostly during transcendent, mind-blowing sex, the state of 'Be Here Now', content to do nothing but *feel*.

Amanda just *felt*.

Her heels were elevated by her shoes, so that there was extra pressure on the balls of her feet. Her insteps felt a slight but delicious strain. The small subtle muscles in her ankles were flexed to hold her steady. Her calves were taut, as were the long muscles in her thighs. Now that Trevor had bared her from the lower edge of her waspie down, she was aware of her sex being fully exposed. It felt the coolness of the air, especially between fevered lips that were fat and scarlet-stained. Her pink pearl was tingling and tight.

Nothing was touching the skin of her mound but Amanda was intensely aware of its smoothness. It was almost as if 'nothing' was a tangible thing that caressed her. The cheeks of her bottom felt fuller, riper, more vulnerable than usual. That had to be because of the tightly laced waspie that compressed her midriff like erotic armour. Her waist couldn't bend freely. She was held in her waspie's close embrace. Strangely, what bound her also freed and protected her, so she was safe to just feel.

Amanda just *felt*.

Her brief velvet jacket hung loose, the soft fabric covering only her arms, really. With each breath she took, the lining of the velvet jacket caressed her nipples. The things that Trevor had done to her earlier must have made her perspire. She could feel a slight dampness in the crook of her neck and in the hollows of her collarbones.

Lips parted, Amanda breathed in.

Her nose filled with the aroma of seafood, fleshy and salty, evocative of the flavours of sex. Her mouth watered. Oysters tasted like Trevor's semen. Lobster meat reminded her of how sweet a girl tasted when she was at her wettest.

Amanda listened and watched.

Her ears sucked in the rhythmic sound of Trevor's big hand, clipping obliquely across the glowing skin of Nola's trembling bottom. They savoured the obscene slobbering noises that poured from Nola's mouth as she babbled pleas for mercy even as she begged the man who was tormenting her to force her to endure more.

Amanda's eyes gloated on the myriad colours that infused the cheeks of Nola's bum and the ripples that each slap sent through the girl's flesh and at the glistening of Nola's spending that coated the inner thighs of her thrashing legs. The girl had somehow lost the ribbon that had wrapped her hips, and the one that had bound her left thigh. The one that circled her right was stained dark now with her own lust's liquor.

Trevor paused. He held his hand out to Amanda. For a moment, she didn't understand. Without that prompt, she'd have been content to just passively feel, forever. But she put her hand into his. He guided it, holding it flat an inch above the bright crimson and mauve that dappled the skin of Nola's bottom. It was radiating a fierce heat.

'Hot, huh?' he asked.

A sadistic whim made Amanda clear her clogged throat and say, 'Give her some more. Make her naughty little bum even hotter.'

'What do you say to that, little pink Nola?' Trevor asked.

'Please? Please, no, I mean, I think, I mean . . .'

'You have to say, "Please no, Trevor," if you want me to stop,' he reminded her. This time, he'd made sure to give his victim a verbal way out, and he'd made her practise it several times. 'Say it if you want to.'

Nola twisted her tear-streaked face towards him and managed a brave grin. 'If you want me to say that, you're going to have to make me.'

'Saucy little bitch!' His hand drew back and descended again.

Nola yelped. Her head dropped back down, leaving a vision of her brimming eyes, her tear-wet cheeks and her slack slobbering mouth burning in Amanda's mind. At that moment, she couldn't imagine anything more beautiful – or desirable. She circled Trevor to kneel before Nola's head. Her hands cupped the girl's saturated cheeks and lifted her face. Amanda's tongue slavered over Nola's flushed cheeks. She lapped up bitter tears mixed with sweet saliva and found the cocktail intoxicatingly erotic. Inevitably, Amanda's serpentine tongue sought out Nola's parted lips and lanced into the girl's mouth.

Trevor congratulated them. 'You're perverted little sluts, one neither better nor worse than the other!' He accelerated his slaps.

Nola wrenched her mouth away from Amanda's. She gasped, 'Please no, Trevor! No more!'

The spanking stopped immediately. Trevor lifted Nola up into his arms with almost reverent gentleness. His left hand stroked her hair. His right cupped her blushing face. 'Good girl. You endured a lot. I'm so proud of you.'

Amanda felt a twinge of jealousy but dismissed it. He was praising the gift that she'd given him. His admiration for Nola was really praise for Amanda, exactly as if he was expressing his appreciation for a watch she'd given him for his birthday.

'She did very well,' Amanda said, to show them both that she wasn't suffering the least bit of envy. She was beyond such a trifling emotion.

'I think the little trollop has earned a reward, don't you, Amanda?'

Amanda felt that Nola had enjoyed quite enough rewards for now. After all, the little witch had climaxed at least three times while she was being spanked. Amanda's relationship with Trevor forbade her to complain or ask, though. She smiled her sweetest smile and asked, 'What would you like to do, or to have done to you, Nola?'

Despite how tender her bottom had to be, Nola bounced in Trevor's lap. 'Anything I like?'

'Subject to the usual rules,' Trevor told her. 'You know, safe, sane and consensual – on both sides, or on all three sides in our case.'

The girl's forehead creased in thought. 'I'm not used to having to choose, but I would love a taste of your cock, Trevor. It feels so good in my mouth. Oh, and your pussy, Ms Amanda. It's absolutely delicious! And I – damn it – I want everything

– to be fucked, both ways, you know what I mean, to have my nips pinched and twisted, and ... and anything but spanking. *That* I've had enough of, for now, thank you very much.' She smiled winningly at Trevor and Amanda. 'Mainly, what I like to do is to serve, to make my master and my mistress happy.' She paused. 'Use me any way you like, for your pleasure, both of you, any way you like. That's what I want the most.'

'Lovely answer!' Trevor nibbled on a shrimp as he considered. 'First, we should thank Amanda. She brought us three together. The best way to say "thank you" is with kisses, so ...' He lifted Nola off his lap and set her on her feet.

The girl swayed into Amanda's arms. Lips brushed lips like silk on satin. Between her and Nola, Amanda should have been the aggressor but Trevor was the puppeteer for now. Amanda allowed her softer sweeter side to emerge, as it had when she'd made love with Meg.

The partings of their lips were tentative, neither of them demanding, neither of them yielding, both of them melting. The taste of Nola's mouth was in Amanda's before their tongues met. Tip tapped tentative tip, became bolder, then began to dance the slow sinuous tango of the kiss.

Amanda was aware of Trevor's movements and the sounds of his clothes being cast aside, followed by the thump, pause, thump, of his shoes dropping to the floor. He was watching her and Nola, she was sure of that. It was for his amusement that she drew her lips back a little, so that the twin bridges of their writhing tongues were exposed to his view. Amanda's fingertips drifted down the slight outside curves of the girl's little breasts. The balls of Amanda's thumbs made circles that wobbled Nola's nipples by their peaks.

A sleek and slender thigh lifted between Amanda's. Amanda ground down on it and pushed her own right thigh forwards between Nola's. Each bore down on the other's leg and squirmed a soft mound on a hard flexed thigh.

Their tongues parted. They drew their heads back to glare ferocious lust into each other's eyes. Amanda's dominant side rose up in her. She felt a sudden urge to throw Nola down to the floor and simply take her. Perhaps Nola was able to feel Amanda's urge, for her body went limp. If Trevor hadn't wrapped his muscular arms around them both, Nola might have melted all the way down to Amanda's feet.

With no more effort than if they'd been a pair of Raggedy Ann dolls, he carried them bodily, breast pressed to breast and belly to belly, pubes crushed against pubes, thighs brushing thighs, feet dangling a foot above the floor, through to the living room and to Amanda's big leather sofa.

Trevor let Nola slither down to kneel on the carpet. He took Amanda by her hips and lifted her high. He sat on the sofa and deposited Amanda upright on his thighs.

'Oops!' he said. 'I forgot to bring the clarified butter. Go fetch, Nola.'

The girl scrambled to obey. Trevor sat back further and arranged Amanda on his lap, almost sitting on his flat lower belly, with both of their legs spread wide, hers overlapping his. Amanda looked down. His thick rod jutted up between her thighs, reminding her of the strap-on dildo she'd worn in her office.

Nola returned with a pot of melted butter.

'Set it aside, for now,' Trevor told her. 'You wanted to get your mouth on my cock and on Amanda's pussy? Here they are. Go right ahead. Enjoy.'

The girl knelt between their thighs. Her head tilted as she contemplated Trevor's thick staff, standing erect, almost as if it guarded Amanda's treasures. Nola's lips made an 'O'. She fitted them to Trevor's dome and opened her eyes wide, as if to ask how her tiny mouth could possibly accommodate so much manhood.

Trevor reached around Amanda, knotted his fist in Nola's hair, and pulled. His cock's head 'plopped' between Nola's lips and into her mouth. He pushed, plopping it out again. After a dozen short strokes, he lifted Nola's head higher. His forefinger eased his stiff shaft to one side so that it no longer blocked access to Amanda's glistening folds.

Nola said, 'Yummy.' Her tongue stretched out to its fullest before she buried it between Amanda's swollen lips.

Amanda closed her eyes and leant back against the broad expanse of Trevor's chest. Nola's tongue was lashing from side to side inside her, delving deeply and then curling up behind Amanda's pubic bone before resuming its lateral flickering. The sensations were more than pleasant, but they weren't 'tongue-on-clit'. She was starting to feel a need for it, but she willed herself to wait. In any case, whether Nola had noticed it or not, Trevor was in charge of the proceedings.

Trevor's free hand, the one that wasn't tangled in Nola's pink locks, played idly with Amanda's breasts, squeezing and releasing, rolling her nipples and flicker-fanning them into tiny tingling erections. He licked her ear and traced a line from it down her jawbone.

Hands and mouths moved on or in her body. The time had come, it occurred to Amanda, to participate, instead of just lolling and feeling and being done to. And so her first flicker of urgency unfolded and, with it, what little initiative Trevor would be willing to accept. She licked the palm of her hand and reached down to gloss it over the plum of Trevor's manhood.

Nola's cheek nudged Amanda's hand aside. The girl's mouth went from a suck on Trevor's knob to a squirm between Amanda's lips and back again. That was nice, but Amanda knew a better game. She lifted up. Her fingers guided Trevor's shaft. She sank down again, impaling herself slowly. Dear God, there was nothing better in the world than the sensation of a man sliding inside her; the bulk of it, the warmth of this hard living thing as it slowly inexorably filled her emptiest place. Now she and Trevor were one, a single sexual being for Nola to serve.

Trevor's hips moved, lifting Amanda a fraction and wriggling the cock that skewered her. Amanda sat up a bit to watch Nola at play and make it easier for Trevor. The girl's long pink tongue slavered up between Trevor's balls, along the two inches of his shaft that projected from Amanda's pussy, and up high, where the flesh was thin and pale, to flip up over Amanda's clit.

Mm! It was good. It was the sort of pleasure, or pleasures, that Amanda could have revelled in for hours. Nola's tongue's caresses were too widely spaced to drive Amanda to climax but close enough together to keep her very interested. Trevor's subtle movements reminded her that she was distended by a very thick and hard cock, and they did rub his cock on her G-spot a bit, but, again, not enough to take her all the way. Time was suspended. Amanda was afloat in a sea of bliss. Still no burning urgency. They had all evening, all night, all the next day. Amanda had climaxed once so far, from that obscene thing Trevor had done to her with the lobster tail. She'd climax again and again that evening, or that night, from things that either Trevor or Nola would do to her. She was in no rush.

But it seemed that Nola was. She was slobbering again now. Her mouth seemed frantic, gobbling on Trevor's scrotum and slavering its way up to Amanda's clit and down again.

Amanda craned her neck. Ah! That was why. The randy little slut, no doubt inspired by being allowed to service both of the dominants who were playing with her, had been fingering herself. She had to be close. 'You may climax now, Nola,' Amanda told her imperiously.

As if that was the signal, the pink-haired girl let out a choking sob, fell on to her back, jammed bunched fingers deep into herself, arched and screamed a long high scream.

'Some climax!' Trevor remarked into Amanda's ear.

'Spectacular,' she agreed. 'Would you like one – a climax, I mean?'

'I'm comfortable for now.'

'What if you don't have to move, not an inch, just lie there and let me take care of you?'

'That'd be nice.'

The stiff upper edge of her waspie bit into Amanda's flesh, just beneath her breasts, but she managed to lean far forwards and reach down to grip her own ankles. So, Nola had impressed Trevor with her convulsive orgasm, had she? She'd show them something, both of them. A rocking pull on her ankles raised her bum, slithering her pussy up Trevor's shaft till only its head was still between her lips. Amanda let herself fall again, impaling herself, and pulled again. She soon established a rhythm and syncopated it. Her hips rotated. She used Trevor's knob to masturbate her G-spot. She twitched, squirming on his rigid rod. The muscles in her tummy began to feel the strain, but that was good. Sweat beaded on Amanda's forehead and trickled between her bouncing breasts.

Nola, who had been watching Amanda's gyrations with admiration in her eyes, uncoiled from the floor and climbed up on to the sofa. Amanda couldn't see but she could hear the girl's wet kisses, likely on Trevor's chest as she knew he wouldn't favour the girl with his kisses unless he had used her as a bendy doll.

Spurred on, Amanda redoubled her efforts and contracted her internal muscles in an accelerating tempo. She gave no thought to her own pleasure. The entire focus of her being was on Trevor's climax. She compelled it to happen.

Strangely, her selfless efforts were rewarded with her own exquisitely tight little orgasm.

But, damm it, Trevor hadn't climaxed yet. And she was limp from her efforts. Amanda took a deep breath. She couldn't leave Trevor unsatisfied. Perhaps she had enough energy left to jerk and suck him off?

Before she could gather her energies, Trevor's broad hands took her by her hips and lifted her bodily. She just dangled, her head between his knees. His face worked from side to side between the cheeks of her bottom, spreading them. His strong tongue probed at the knot of her sphincter. He must have deliberately made saliva, because her ring felt a warm trickle.

Nola slid off the sofa and squatted below Amanda. She poured liquid butter on to her palm. Her arm reached between Amanda's dangling breasts to Trevor's rigid shaft, and slathered it with the warm grease.

Oh! So that's what he had in mind!

Nola held Trevor in place as he lowered Amanda. Her rear passage was wet and his shaft was buttered. And she was totally relaxed. There was hardly any resistance as his great knob eased its way into her, past her pursed opening and deep up the tight muscular channel of what had not so long ago been a forbidden place.

When she was snug on his lap, her tailbone pressed on to his pubic bone, he pulled her back to loll back against his chest. Trevor braced. His feet were flat on the floor. The back of his neck pressed against the back of the sofa. With just those contacts, he arched up, almost into a wrestler's bridge, and fucked up into Amanda's bottom.

Amanda bounced. Although she was being shaken, she could see that Trevor was pouring butter all over Nola's right hand. Why?

Oh! Was it possible? Trevor's cock filled her insides. It felt as if her organs had been nudged aside to accommodate its bulk. Surely he didn't expect her to take more distending than she was already enduring/enjoying?

But he did.

Nola stuck her tongue out so that each of Amanda's bounces flicked it over her mistress's clit. That was nice, but what concerned Amanda was the way Nola was fondling the lips of her pussy, spreading them wide and working two, or was it three, fingertips up into her.

Trevor stilled. Amanda was suspended, held up by his staff up her bum and his strong hands cupping her hips. Nola's fingers squirmed deep, then withdrew. When they pressed into Amanda again, she could tell that the thumb and little finger were tucked in, as Meg had taught her to do. Nola bore deeply, stretching Amanda as she had never been stretched before. The pressure became excruciating, in a way that was unbearable but simultaneously glorious. Amanda held her breath and tried to relax her internal muscles but she was afraid. If she hadn't been flattened by the invader that filled her back passage, she might have been able to bear the devastating sensations she was being forced to endure at Nola's hand.

Trevor's thrusts accelerated. He grunted. He was close.

Amanda closed her hand around Nola's wrist, stopping it from burrowing any deeper.

Trevor lifted his hips up, higher than before, and slammed back down on to the sofa. He erupted inside her, flooding Amanda's tunnel with his scalding essence. He let loose the bellow of a bull elephant in must, and slumped.

'Potato!' Amanda shouted immediately.

Trevor chuckled weakly.

'No more,' she amended for Nola's sake.

Nola drew her hand slowly out from inside Amanda. She

grinned at Amanda's sweat-streaked face. 'I think he's out of it,' she said.

Amanda managed a smile. She eased herself up off Trevor's softening cock and said, 'Yes. I think I'll just curl up here with Trevor for a bit.'

'What should I do?' Nola tilted her head in that way that Amanda always found endearing.

'Sweetie, how about you get us a throw? And a couple of pillows.'

'Sure! And then I'd like to tidy up while you sleep, if that's OK?'

'Silly thing,' Amanda muttered. She yawned and snuggled into Trevor's arms on the couch. Just before she drifted off she wondered if she'd been sleeping when first she'd dreamt up this eager, talented, energetic Girl Friday. If so, Nola was a pink-haired dream come true.

23

At seven after nine on a Monday morning, Eggerdon flustered into Amanda's office with an envelope in his quivering hand.

'What is it?' she asked.

He waved the envelope. 'Our Mrs Carrey – she's given us notice.'

'Oh? How long?'

'Two weeks, but not exactly.'

'But not "exactly"? What does that mean, exactly?'

'She's given two weeks' notice, but she's still due a week of this year's vacation time and she's taking it, so one week, really.'

'That's not much notice,' Amanda allowed. 'Who do we have to take over from her?'

'No one, and hiring someone new will take time, much more than a week.'

'What happened before, when she went on holiday?'

'We work a month in hand, so she did all the salaried people in advance before she left and had time to catch up on the hourly and part-timers when she got back, provided she took her holiday at the beginning of the month, which she was always meticulous about doing.'

'So we actually have a full month before disaster strikes.'

His eyes brightened. 'I suppose we do!'

Serendipity struck again. Only that morning, Amanda had read an article in *Financial News*, on outsourcing HR. She told Eggerdon, 'Outsource our payroll and HR. There are lots of companies that do that sort of thing. It should give our people better benefits packages, as outsource HR companies represent dozens of employers, not just one. I'll leave it up to you to investigate and organise.'

'I won't let you down, Ms Garland.'

'I know. Mr Eggerdon?'

'Yes?'

'Mrs Carrey must have known she'd be leaving us in the lurch. Why would she do that, do you think?'

He looked embarrassed. 'She – she and Sophie Sharpe got along very well.'

'Really? In that case, have Mrs Carrey escorted from the premises immediately. Arrange for a forensic audit of Mrs Carrey's books.'

Eggerdon looked shocked. 'You aren't suggesting ... ?'

'I'm suggesting nothing, but do it anyway.' She paused for thought. 'When you sign the outsourcing contract, bind us to it so that, if Sophie beats me and takes over, she won't be able to break it and rehire Mrs Carrey or, at least, she'll find it awkward to.'

'I understand. I'm behind you one hundred per cent,' he assured her.

'I know.' She patted his creased cheek. 'It's only just over a week until the shareholders' meeting, and then the suspense will be over, one way or another.'

He looked glum.

Amanda continued, 'Just in case, prepare a Letter of Intent for me to sign, would you? It should guarantee you your job, indexed with inflation protection, until you retire. Make it ironclad, so that any successor of mine, such as dear Sophie, couldn't possibly break it.'

'That's extremely generous of you.' He looked close to tears.

'It's nothing. You're a good man, Eggerdon. While I'm in charge, I want you working with me. If Sophie gets her way and takes over, at least you'll be protected against any repercussions for having supported me.'

Amanda followed Eggerdon out of her office. Nola was particularly outrageous today, in full *Harajuku* style. Her always wild hair was tied up in untidy bunches. She was dressed in a pervert's garish dream of a Japanese schoolgirl's outfit, with a floppy tie, a gauzy shirt that just hinted at the locations of her nipples, a pleated skirt that left six inches of her thighs bare above her red and white horizontally striped over-the-knee socks and flat buckle-up black patent shoes.

'That's quite the little outfit, miss. Find Rupert and Paul for me please; they're not in their office.'

The phone rang.

'Should I answer that before I go?' Nola was even more eager to please than she'd been before Amanda had presented her as a gift to Trevor.

'No, I'll get it.' Amanda shooed the girl from her office and picked up the receiver. 'Amanda Garland speaking.'

'Hi. Ms Garland, it's Meg.'

She'd have recognised Meg's voice anywhere. The sound of it made her tummy flutter. At the same time, Amanda felt a little guilty. 'I'm sorry I haven't been in touch, Meg. Things are pretty crazy around here.'

'That's OK. It's just that – well – Ms Sharpe came by this morning. She said she'd be back, at closing, to go through the books and such. I don't think she gets to do that, does she?'

'Certainly not. She's not in control of my company yet.'

'Well, she said it would go best for me to do as she says

and keep my mouth shut. But I thought it'd be best to call you.'

'Thank you for your loyalty, Meg. I'll come by after work and – or, no, I've a better idea. I'll ask the building security guard to come by. He'll make sure there's no trouble. His name is Trevor.'

'How will I know him?'

'Oh, you'll know him.'

Amanda placed a call to Trevor. From the background sounds, it was obvious he was in the middle of teaching a karate class, but he promised Amanda he'd be done in plenty of time to get to the store Meg managed by closing time.

'I'd really appreciate it if you'd protect Meg,' Amanda stressed, though she needn't have.

'Anything for you.' Trevor chuckled. 'How's that tasty pink-haired pet of yours?'

'More slavish than ever, thanks to you. Would you like her again?'

Trevor's answer surprised her. 'Not right away.'

'Oh?' Amanda was a little disappointed; it was if he'd made a fuss over a watch she'd picked out for him, but subsequently never worn it. 'Not your type?'

'All women are my type,' he replied. 'Some more than others, of course. It's just ...'

He was interrupted by a clipped shout, the word foreign, and delivered by a foreign tongue.

'I'm disrupting your class, Trevor. Sorry. Thank you for helping me.'

'My pleasure,' he replied, and hung up.

Nola came racing into her office, her ribbons askew. 'Oh. My. God.' She skidded to a stop at Amanda's desk.

'What's going on?' Amanda turned her attention away from

her conversation with Trevor and on to the flushed girl twisting to and fro in front of her.

'You know what, Ms Amanda. Whenever you're involved, there's always enough lust around for everyone to share.' She giggled. 'Like, you shared me with Trevor and you shared Rupert with me, and me and Paul and Rupert with you. I've been thinking about it. You're like a – a love-catalyst. You make everyone around you hotter without being changed yourself.'

Amanda didn't know about 'not being changed herself', but she said, 'I'll take that as a compliment, but what's going on? Is there something you want to tell me?'

Nola leant closer. 'Talking about people that you've brought together – guess why Paul and Rupert aren't answering their phone.'

'Do tell.' Again Amanda's tummy did a little flip.

'Well . . .' said Nola, obviously basking in the sun of Amanda's attention and eager to keep it for as long as possible. 'The storage room used to be part of Purchasing's main office. Then it got partitioned off, just a frame and wall-board, with cork tiles covering it on Purchasing's side.' Her voice dropped to a whisper. 'Only Paul and Rupert ever go in there any more. And there's a spot where you can see right through.'

'Go on.'

'When I saw they weren't where they were supposed to be, I peeped through the little peephole and sure enough Paul and Rupert are in there and they're – they're kissing.'

Amanda nodded. 'On company time.'

'Oh!' Nola's face fell. She'd been so sure Amanda would enjoy her story she hadn't thought it through.

'I'm not sure that's a very good idea. What else were they doing?'

'Nothing else. Nothing much. Oh, Ms Amanda, I didn't mean to get them in trouble.'

'We'll see,' said Amanda. She stood, smoothing her skirt down in front. 'I'll be right back. You get to work.'

With Nola's reluctant instructions, Amanda found the peephole with no problem. She peered into the darkness of the unlit storage room. Yes, there was Paul. He was the taller of the two, by a couple of inches. Now Rupert came into view. He was shaking his head. She couldn't hear what he was saying but, even though he seemed to be saying no, he just came closer until he was kissing Paul.

They stood like that, their arms at their sides, kissing hungrily. Amanda wondered how long they could continue ravishing each other's mouth without reaching out to touch.

Paul raised his hand first, to stroke Rupert's cheek. Rupert's entire body shuddered.

Then, surprisingly, his hands flew to Paul's belt and began flailing at it, clumsily trying to get it unbuckled.

God. Her first impulse had been irritation, but she already recognised it as jealousy. When she'd had them at her mercy, strapped into chairs and blindfolded, she'd purposely not made either boy actually perform any sort of sexual service on the other, though it might have been possible to substitute her dildo, or Nola's, with a real live cock. She'd held back for fear of pushing them into something they weren't ready for. And look at them. They were dying for it!

Paul stayed Rupert's hand. Instead, he stepped back and unbuckled his own pants, indicating that Rupert should do the same. Although their white shirts obscured the view, Amanda could tell that both boys were erect. Once again they stood, close but apart, facing each other, like opponents almost, equal opponents or, at least, equals.

This must be what it was like for the ancient Greeks, a sense of same-on-same being, not perverted or bad, just equal. Like her and Meg.

She blinked. Rupert and Paul were kissing again, as sweetly as girls. But their hands were on the move, each reaching for the waistband to the other's underwear, slipping inside now, grasping each other in a moment so tender, so private, that Amanda backed away from her spyhole.

How would she have liked it if someone had spied, unseen, while she and Meg had made love? And if that person had been her boss?

On her way back into her office, she beckoned to Nola to join her. It looked as if the silly girl had been crying.

'Stop snivelling. They're not in trouble.'

'Really? I thought you —'

'I'm not paying you to think,' said Amanda. She hastily amended the remark. 'Well, yes of course I pay you to think, but you needn't anticipate my actions. Those boys — those *young men* — work hard enough for me. If they want a couple of moments alone, so what.'

'That's what I thought. I mean — what I would've thought, if I were supposed to think.'

'You are supposed to think, Nola. I misspoke. Get back to work and don't say anything about this to either of them. If they want us to know about it, they'll tell us. OK?'

'Yes, Ms Amanda. I'm just a little surprised that Rupert never told me.'

'Oh? The two of you talk a lot, do you?'

'Uh huh. Some.' Nola started twisting in her skirts again, afraid she'd once more said too much. 'I'll go to my desk now.'

'You do that,' said Amanda. 'And shut the door behind you.'

When she was alone, Amanda gave herself a mental shake. What difference did it make how her young playmates interacted when she wasn't around? All three were hers for the taking. If she wanted something more, she always had Trevor, to take her, and Meg, to be her equal. Maybe everyone needed to be equal once in a while. It made sense. So why did it hurt?

24

All things considered, Amanda thought, everything was fitting together like the precision-made parts of a well-designed machine. Forsythe Footwear's shoe shop Number Twenty-two was performing the best in the drastic chain-wide sale. After just a couple of weeks, its manager had started to beg for more inventory, any inventory. The shop was blessed by being located in a rundown shopping precinct that was surrounded by towering blocks of cheap flats, with two hospitals plus an old people's retirement home close by.

Nurses from the hospitals came in droves for the cut-price duty shoes and often walked out with a couple of pairs of dress shoes as well, all for the price they usually paid for a single pair of flat duty whites. The old ladies from the home devoured every pair of the orthopaedic and 'sensible' styles and demanded more. Single moms from the flats were delighted to be able to buy 'for best' dress shoes at sneaker prices and, surprisingly at first, snatched up the sexier, more dressy, styles as well. It made sense, when Amanda thought about it. As a whole, the single young women with kids had more reason to want to look sexy and catch partners than the childless ones did.

When four more of their shops, one at a time, reduced their inventories to below thirty per cent, Amanda closed them, temporarily, as she would do all the shops when they got their stocks down to that level. The staff of each shop had stayed on for a couple of days to pack everything they had left into cartons and ship the stock en masse to Number Twenty-two. The full-time staff had then been given time off with pay until their shops were ready to be restocked and reopen.

Today, Meg's shop was scheduled to close temporarily. Amanda had intended to talk to her about it, make sure she was comfortable with the arrangement and that she'd be back when it was time to reopen for business. She hadn't heard a word from Meg since the girl had called for protection from Sophie Sharpe. But Amanda wasn't particularly worried – Trevor was more than a match for Sophie, even if she was a true battleaxe.

Amanda had tracked down some old friends from her amateur-theatrical days. She'd found an electrician and a set designer who were happy to work after their day jobs, fixing up the empty shops. She'd kept the costs down. Mainly, in the shops' interiors, she'd had them install rows of mirrors around the walls at ceiling height, to give the illusion that the premises were much bigger, and again at floor level, to encourage customers to concentrate on their feet and shoes. The tacky old backdrops in the windows were being ripped out and replaced with swathes of burgundy velveteen. The cheap fluorescent strip-lighting was being replaced by recessed spotlights and laser lights, for drama. The finished effects would be similar to club lighting. It was to wear in dance clubs and bars that young women bought their sexiest shoes, after all.

The first container of new styles would arrive in ten days. Paul had flown to Bonne and then on to Paris to oversee its packing so that a quarter of its cargo could be unloaded at each of the four shops that had been emptied, in order. More containers would follow, coordinated to supply the other shops as soon as they were ready.

There were still decisions to be made. Paul wanted the shops to start carrying hosiery at loss-leader prices, just to bring the young working women in. Amanda hadn't decided whether to close Number Twenty-two once everything was reorganised throughout the chain or to keep it open as their discount outlet.

Rupert wanted to open a speciality shop for more extreme styles, four-inch platforms and eight-inch heels, thigh-high skin-fit latex boots and kinky padlocked ankle strap pumps, for example, to cater to strippers and fetishists. If he could find a supplier or two, he'd like to add wider lasts in sizes up to fourteen, for transvestites and transsexuals. That would all be lots of fun, but it would have to make financial sense before Amanda gave his more extreme ideas green lights. The right location would be vital, and likely very expensive.

Of course, if Sophie Sharpe got her way at the shareholders' meeting, all this would be for nothing. Or would it? It would be small consolation, but Amanda had to smile at the thought of the nasty bitch finding herself dropped into the middle of a maelstrom of drastic changes, none of which she'd understand. Amanda was sure that the sour cow's first move, if she took over, would be to fire Rupert, Paul and Nola, thus ensuring that she'd have no one left to explain to her what was going on.

Amanda left her office and went to Nola's desk. 'It's time to make that special call,' she said. 'You've got everything straight?'

'Trust me,' Nola assured her. She picked up her phone and carefully punched each number. When the call was answered she said, 'Ms Sharpe? It's me, Nola, from Forsythe Footwear?' The girl gave Amanda a lop-sided grin. 'Nola the receptionist – you remember – pink hair, pretty, very short skirts that you didn't approve of?'

She nodded at Sophie's response. 'Your name isn't on the

list, Ms Sharpe, and it ought to be, oughtn't it?' She paused. 'What list? Oh, the one Ms Garland gave me to call everyone from.'

She frowned and rolled her eyes at Amanda. 'The list of shareholders, of course, Ms Sharpe.' Pause. 'What am I calling the shareholders for? Well, are you sure you should have been put on the list? I wouldn't want to . . .' She mouthed at Amanda, 'She's sure, fucking well sure, come to that.'

Amanda smiled and waited with Nola for Sophie's foul stream of invective to slow to a stop.

Nola continued, 'Well, about the shareholders' meeting, Ms Sharpe? The time's been, like, changed, and I'm supposed to tell everyone when it's been changed to. I can't think why your name isn't on the list. You being a major shareholder and all.'

She nodded and winked at Amanda. '*You* can think why? Really? Ms Amanda is a what?' Her eyebrows shot up. 'Well, if you're sure . . .' She mouthed at Amanda, 'Fucking well sure,' and almost laughed.

Amanda gave her a warning look.

Nola sat up straight. 'OK. Well, the meeting's in the same place, of course, but it's like, an hour earlier? One thirty instead of half-past two? No, I'm not asking you a question, I'm answering your question.' She rolled her eyes. 'Yes, I'm sure, oh, and, Ms Sharpe, may I say that it just hasn't been the same around here since you left us so very suddenly.'

Sophie Sharpe's hang-up was so violent that Amanda heard it and Nola winced.

'How did I do?' she asked.

'Perfectly,' Amanda congratulated her.

'It's the advantage of me being so young and looking sort of ditzy, right? No one suspects me when I'm being a bit crafty.'

'I'll never underestimate you, Nola,' Amanda promised her.

'No, you're good like that, sizing people up. That's what makes you such a great boss – that and how damn hot you are.' She licked her lips. 'Where's the party, after the shareholders' meeting?'

'I hadn't thought that far. Besides, you must prepare for the possibility that it won't be a party so much as a wake.'

'No chance of that,' Nola said. 'You're way too smart for that evil bitch, Ms Amanda.'

'Thanks. And now,' Amanda announced, 'I have some important calls of my own to make.'

So, on what might be her last night as President of Forsythe Footwear, Amanda Garland was once again alone and working late, scheming and dreaming, though more of the former than the latter for once.

Eventually, she packed up most of her desk, making sure to leave nothing that might be of use to Sophie Sharpe, should the latter be victorious the next day.

She hadn't consciously been waiting for Trevor but, when she heard the jangle of his keys as they bounced against his muscular thigh, her heart lifted and she realised she'd been dawdling so he'd come by before she left. There was no real need to see him as all their plans for the following day were made. But he'd been here the first night she stayed late, so it was only fitting he be here on what might be the last.

As soon as he responded to her greeting by entering her office, Amanda could see that something had changed. Trevor had changed, though she wasn't sure exactly how. His bulk, always so solid, seemed to be vibrating. His colour was high.

'What?' She grinned. She could always count on Trevor to amuse her.

'Thank you,' he said. 'I promised I wouldn't say anything

but I have to. Thank you.' Even his voice sounded different. Huskier than ever, yet sort of – lilting? If husky can be said to lilt.

'What for?' Amanda grinned again, eager to be in on any game, though 'the Gratitude Game' was one she was particularly fond of.

'For Meg, of course. My God, Amanda, she's just what I've been looking for. But then, you knew that.'

Amanda kept the smile pasted on her face, though her insides were turning upside down, her heart moving into the place where her stomach should be and her stomach up high, so high she couldn't breathe. 'Meg?' It was all she could manage to say but it was enough.

'She's fantastic, Amanda. Just perfect. The moment I laid eyes on her I knew, I just knew. I wasn't sure you understood just how ... how weary I was of ... playing games. But you did, and you did something about it. I'll never forget this.'

'And Meg?' She kept the rest of the sentence, 'the treacherous bitch', to herself.

'She feels the same. We just ... well first I got rid of Sophie Sharpe and then I helped her close and make the night deposit and then we literally fell into each other's arms. Holy Murphy, Amanda, we're in *love*.' He grinned at her, abashed.

Trevor, abashed? Fuck.

'Love?' She sounded like a parrot, or maybe one of those furry little animals that were so popular a few years back. A Furby. Yes. That's what she was. A funny little toy that had been all the rage for awhile and now lay discarded, untouched and unwanted, with dust balls matted in its once-glossy fur.

Tears prickled her eyes. She blinked fast to prevent them from falling. No one with a heart, not even a shrivelled black furbeest heart like hers, would mess with the joy that suffused the big man in front of her.

Amanda cast a protective shield, like invisible ice, around herself. That helped. Ice doesn't cry. Ice doesn't feel. Trevor, on the other hand, looked like he might start to jig any moment. Perhaps she should offer him a couch to jump on? Just keep it inside, she growled at herself. Don't let him know. Be frozen.

'Love! I haven't felt this way in years. I swore I never would again but here it is and goddam it all it feels good.' Trevor threw back his head and laughed.

Amanda realised she'd never really heard him laugh. What else had she missed? Plenty, it seemed. There was plenty about Trevor that she hadn't even noticed wasn't there, probably because it wasn't there in her, either. She'd been a playmate for him, and a damn good one, but nothing more. And what was he to me? A little voice inside her tried to be reasonable. He'd been *her* playmate and a damn good one. The best, actually, except maybe for Meg. The loss of both of them hurt, or would hurt, once she got this frozen face defrosted. God, he was still going on. His voice boomed in her ears, too loud, much too jubilant.

'... last-minute tickets to Jamaica. We've never been so it'll be an adventure for us both. I've resigned from the building and I'm taking my holidays in lieu of notice ...'

Her Meg? The willowy blonde with the wide-set grey eyes and the big grin. Clown-school Meg? Her angel-without-wings? She couldn't think which would be worse, to lose Trevor or to lose Meg. Losing both, to each other? No! Amanda's hands balled into fists but her face stayed frozen, smiling, her eyes glassy, her grin bordering on garish. Goddam it all to hell!

'... she wanted to wait until after the meeting but I knew as soon as I saw you that I had to thank you ...'

Hmm. Perhaps Meg had an inkling that Trevor's news

wouldn't be met with unbridled joy on Amanda's part? The conniving bitch. Had their entire evening together been a charade? Nothing more than a night of great sex?

'... understand why you said you wanted me to come to work for you and it didn't matter if our relationship changed. I understand everything now. You're tremendous, Amanda. All I can do is say thank you, over and over again, and promise to protect you forever, for the rest of my life. Me and Meg, both, we're committed to you. To Forsythe Footwear. Forever.'

She licked her dry lips. 'I may not be here when you get back from your honeymoon – I mean your holiday. Remember?'

'I have every confidence in the plan. I'll pick you up at one o'clock sharp. It's going to work. You're going to have everything you wanted, Amanda. Or should I say, Ms Garland, President and CEO of Forsythe Footwear. Everything you ever dreamt of.' Trevor circled her desk and swooped her up out of her chair to press her close to his massive rippled chest in a bear hug that crushed the protective ice shield she'd created and left her defenceless against her devastating loss. 'Hey. Are you all right?'

'Nervous about tomorrow but I'll be fine,' she managed to say. 'Go, do your rounds. I'll be gone by the time you're finished.'

'OK. See you tomorrow!' He dropped her back into her chair and was out of her office in three strides.

She managed to keep her silence until she heard the slam of a door that indicated he was out of earshot. Even then, she'd rather have kept the pain inside but it came creeping out her mouth in little muffled consonants, 'Nnnn. Ooww,' that hurt so much she had to open her mouth a little more and release the ragged sobs, and a little more, until she was half-howling from her loss.

Somehow she managed to stagger to her door and slam it shut. 'Everything you ever dreamt of.' The irony was murder. She flopped back into her chair and scrabbled at the locked drawer that held, among other things, the velvet bag. She dumped the bag in her lap. Her bracelet was a heap of buttercup gold amidst gleaming charms, old and new. The diamond silver anniversary charm captured plain office light in its microscopic heart and blazed it back through its facets to the surface, where it twinkled like a tiny constellation. Love light.

She'd loved Roger and he'd almost ruined her. Financially, well, that was one thing, that could happen to anyone. But emotionally. She'd loved him. She loved to make love with him; she loved to groom him and massage him and croon to him in the strange light of dawn when the horrors had him shouting in his sleep. She loved him.

The platinum watch was off her wrist in a trice. The gold was heavy in her hand when she picked up the bracelet. She wrapped it around her now bare wrist and closed the lobster claw. The weight felt briefly foreign, then deeply familiar. With it came back the memories of all that Mr and Mrs Garland had had and lost.

The charms chronicled a life, no, *her* life, as observed by her husband. She examined the bracelet more closely than she had since the day he'd given it to her. Over the years she'd received new charms to celebrate her achievements, which she'd considered modest but Roger had treated as momentous. A party hat and favour represented the fabulous New Year's Eve party she'd thrown for all of Forsythe Footwear, and a musical note with an emerald in it celebrated the day she'd received her Performance Diploma from the Royal School of Music. The globe was a tribute to the successful ball she'd held to solicit contributions to a charity for children, and a pair of comedy/tragedy masks marked her performance as Ophelia in a Little Theatre presentation of *Hamlet*. Every one of the charms was dated, so she'd always remember her successes, except for the heart with the ruby in the middle, which was simply inscribed 'Roger'.

Then there were the charms he'd purchased in advance, the ones he'd never had a chance to give to her. She'd only looked at the 25th anniversary charm and laughed at his optimism in thinking he'd live long enough for them to celebrate a date still seventeen years in the future. Now she spied among the other charms a baby rattle, no gem, just intricately engraved yellow gold. It too had no date.

This time she didn't laugh at his optimism; she wrapped herself in the cloak of it. They'd both wanted children but after many disappointments they'd endured an endless battery of tests, her dedicated to one thing only, having a baby, and Roger, just going along, always willing to give her what she wanted, always saying the same thing, 'If it's meant to happen it will, and in the meantime we always have each other.' When she'd finally given up and collapsed in his arms, bitter with disappointment, he'd crooned, 'It's you I want. Just you.' He'd always known how to soothe her.

Now Amanda looked at the bracelet in full. Though there were plenty of charms competing for attention, the initial fifteen still clearly spelled out their message. H-I-G-H M-A-I-N-T-E-N-A-N-C-E.

Her cheeks had flushed and she'd laughed so hard on their first anniversary. She'd covered Roger with kisses and repeated, 'You know me!' until he'd hushed her with his mouth. She'd been so delighted with all that gold, so amused by the message of the charms. So much in love.

All that happiness, gone.

Gone, gone, and she'd pushed away not one but two chances

at ever finding it again. Pushed 'em right into each other's arms.

The cloak of optimism she'd wrapped herself in fell away, but it had done its job. Amanda wasn't frozen any more, and all that melted ice turned into tears.

25

Amanda's cell phone was on four-way conference. She was wearing a big floppy blue felt hat and that short blue with white polka dots coat-dress that she loved, with sheer navy hose and matching four-inch stiletto-heeled pumps. There were no panties under her dress. Amanda had decided that 'going commando' felt empowering. Right now she was undercover but soon, soon she'd be face to face with the enemy. A shoot-out was imminent and not wearing panties made her feel like she'd be quicker on the draw.

That image, the one of the lone gunslinger, suited the alienation she'd been suffering from since the night before.

Amanda was seated behind a large potted fig tree with her back to the hotel's main entrance. It looked as if she was reading but her book concealed a good-sized mirror that she used to watch the entrance. She whispered, 'There's another crowd coming in through the revolving doors right now. Be ready!'

The first people through were a middle-aged couple in crumpled Hawaiian shirts and baggy shorts. They were followed by a tall thin fellow with bushy hair, then a stiffly erect army officer with red tabs, and right behind him came ...

'Sophie Sharpe's on her way. She'll be at the lifts in ten, nine ...'

Amanda swivelled round to bring the bank of lifts into her mirror's range. A pair of doors slid open. Rupert and Paul went into the cabin in a flash and turned their backs to study advertisements on opposite walls. Sophie Sharpe stepped in.

Something must have made her suspicious because she turned hurriedly, as if to leave – and was blocked by Trevor's massive bulk.

Paul stabbed at the buttons. The doors closed behind Trevor's back.

They had her, the bitch!

Amanda picked up her case and caught the next lift up to the tenth floor, one floor higher than the suite the shareholders' meeting was scheduled to be in. When she got to suite 1012, the tinted glass doors that led to most of the suite were firmly shut. Open double doors led to a boardroom, which was dominated by a big mahogany table at which a struggling Sophie Sharpe was seated, flanked by Paul and Rupert and pinned down by Trevor's huge paws on her shoulders. Her briefcase was on the floor beside her chair. Nola sat to one side, her neatly crossed legs exposed almost their full lovely length, far above the tops of her hose, practically to her lap, which was covered by a minuscule pleated skirt in Royal Hunting Stuart tartan. It occurred to Amanda that the girl could have sat in a muddy puddle without soiling its hem.

That morning, Amanda hadn't actually laid eyes on her three young employees. Everyone had had tasks to take care of and it looked like Paul, Rupert and Nola had performed theirs very well. The boys were holding their own. Rupert looked a bit grim, like it was hard for him to be there, but Paul, though pale, was staying the course. Nola seemed to regard it as a bit of fun but that was her speciality, wasn't it?

Sophie was struggling futilely, spluttering and screaming threats. 'Unlawful confinement! Kidnapping! Battery!' She paused to suck in a deep rattling breath before adding a triumphant shrill, 'Conspiracy!'

Amanda took off her floppy blue hat and let it sail across the room. She took a seat opposite the incensed woman.

'You think you can stop me like this?' Sophie demanded. 'You're burnt toast, all of you. The minute I get out of here, I'm calling the police *and* my lawyer. I'll have every penny you own, all of you, and see you doing hard time. I'll ...'

Trevor clamped a massive palm over the woman's mouth. 'Perhaps you should listen, Ms Sharpe, and find out what's going on?'

'That's a very good idea, Ms Sharpe,' Nola added. 'Listen to Ms Amanda. I always do.' She flashed Amanda her sunniest smile, the one that made her shine from the inside out.

Trevor lifted his palm.

Sophie looked daggers at Nola. 'You, you fucking little whore, you ...'

The palm descended.

'Thanks for the "little",' Nola commented complacently. 'All the men seem to like it that I'm petite.' She stretched her torso and smoothed her black skinny-fit jersey top down over her ribs, to emphasise her slenderness. 'It makes me easier to pick up.'

'A lot of women like it that you're small, too,' Amanda added, 'for the same reason.'

'Thank you, Ms Amanda.'

They exchanged grins.

Sophie shrieked, 'Perverts!' then Trevor's hand was over her mouth again.

Amanda levelled a calm look at Sophie. 'You're the pervert,' she hissed.

Not one pair of shocked eyes widened at her statement, but five. Sophie Sharpe stopped struggling.

'Look, Sophie, I have evidence that you have been engaged in unlawful activities while under the employment of Forsythe Footwear. Evidence that will put you in jail,' said Amanda.

Sophie shook her head furiously.

'I have evidence,' repeated Amanda, 'and lots of it. Now, I'm going to ask the rest of you to leave us alone.'

'You must be kidding,' said Trevor.

Paul and Rupert chimed in with similar exclamations.

Amanda waved her hand to Trevor, indicating that he should remove his hand from Sophie's mouth. 'I believe that some of the things that need to be discussed here today are between Sophie and me. Private matters. I'll give you one chance to agree, Ms Sharpe.'

Sophie shrugged. 'I'm not going to attack you or anything,' she muttered. She shoved Trevor's hand away and adjusted her suit jacket.

'That's the spirit,' said Amanda. 'Wait for us in the outer room, Trevor. Paul, Nola, Rupert – your work is done. Thank you. I'll see you at the office tomorrow.'

'If I hear any trouble ...' Trevor grumbled as he followed Nola out.

When they were alone, Amanda opened her case. 'I've got some things I'd like you to take a look at, Sophie, if you don't mind.' Amanda pushed a photocopy across the desk. 'Look at this.'

'What the fuck is it?'

'A copy of your last bank statement.'

'How the fuck did you get hold of that?'

'How I got it doesn't matter.' In fact, it was one of the few photos she'd managed to take the day she'd popped Tom Sharpe's cherry. The others were just as confidential, and as damning. 'Look at the items I've highlighted in yellow.'

Despite herself, Sophie looked. Her face drained of colour, except for two spots of blush that now looked clownish. 'What about them?' she bluffed.

'They're deposits,' Amanda explained. 'Large cheques from Ogilvy & Fitch, and from two other companies that just happen to be subsidiaries of Ogilvy and Fitch's, that also just happen to be major suppliers to Forsythe Footwear.'

'So what?'

'Kickbacks are illegal, Sophie.' Amanda spoke patiently, as if she was talking to a child, which was what Sophie deserved for her bluster. 'They constitute fraud. As several people had to be involved, it's also "conspiracy". We're talking about major jail time, here.'

'You can't ...'

'Yes, we can. Now take a look at these photos, please. I found them in my late husband's cell phone. Tsk tsk.' Amanda wagged a finger. 'Uncharacteristically sloppy of you, Ms Sharpe.' She pushed several eight-by-ten glossies across the table. 'Recognise my husband? The way he's dressed – or not dressed – just a dog collar and a leash?'

'So what?' The woman's face was white but her back remained ramrod straight.

'And this one, clearly you, in nothing but boots, carrying a riding crop?'

'That doesn't mean a fucking thing. What are you implying?

'Implying? My God, woman, you've got balls. I suppose that's what attracted him to you in the first place.'

'It's not like Roger and I are in the same picture.'

'You don't have to be. Look at the backgrounds. See that tacky picture on the wall, in both photographs? That locates them. That picture is on the wall of the motel room that Roger was found dead in. Roger's cell phone dates and times the pictures it takes. That proves that you were there with him the day he died. That's evidence, legal evidence.'

Sophie blinked. 'I never liked the idea of taking pictures.' She put her face in her hands. 'I didn't kill him. He had a heart attack.'

'That will be for a jury to decide.'

'Please. I can't stand trial. There's only me and my young son left of the family. He needs me. If I go to jail, what will become of him?'

Amanda shrugged. Sophie was obviously trying to portray Tom as younger than he really was. Perhaps it was a family trait? She suppressed a wry laugh. Still, Amanda had looked closely into the Sharpes' situation and it was quite true, there were only the two of them left.

'And the shame!' Sophie's voice broke. 'I couldn't bear it.'

'Oh, I know all about shame. Remember his funeral? Everyone knew just how he died, and where. I should have been the grieving widow. I should have been given solace, not pity.'

'That was never supposed to happen. No one was ever supposed to know. And anyway they didn't know just how he died. I – I took the collar off his body to preserve at least some of his dignity.' Sophie shuddered in spite of herself.

'How good of you to show such concern for his dignity. What about mine?' Amanda's voice broke. Her eyes met Sophie's and to her shock she felt them prickle as if they might tear up.

'Amanda,' Sophie began. 'We didn't mean – all I can say is that, once my dominant nature spoke to his submissive side, it was beyond our control to stop it. We tried, but we couldn't. However, we both worked very hard to keep it a secret.'

'Maybe if it was such a big secret you should've disposed of the body after you murdered him.'

'It's not so!' Sophie shrank into her chair. 'I didn't kill him!'

'Well, it'll all come out at the trial. Soon everyone is going to know everything.' Amanda gave Sophie a grim smile. Her blue eyes were once more bone dry.

'I swear to God in Heaven that Roger had a heart attack. You have to believe me.' Sophie's voice broke, to Amanda's immense satisfaction. Now they were even.

'Tell me exactly what happened,' demanded Amanda.

'I didn't even know he was gone! I was giving him a good whipping and he was thanking me for it. That's how it's done. In the BDSM world, the submissive thanks the domme for –'

'I get it,' interrupted Amanda. 'Go on.'

'He stopped thanking me, which I took as him pretending to misbehave in order to be punished more severely so I – oh, God, I admit I – I laid on a few more lashes, extra hard, but when he still failed to beg for mercy I – I stopped.'

'Any last words?'

Sophie shrugged. 'Um, "Thank you, mistress." I guess.'

Amanda frowned. 'Did he suffer?'

'I truly believe it was a massive heart attack. He was gone in an instant.'

Amanda sat back. That was the last information she needed about Roger's death. She had no more questions.

'I didn't fucking kill him. You have to believe me.' Sophie's desperation might have roused pity in Amanda had the future of Forsythe Footwear not been at stake.

'Even if you didn't kill him, even if it was his lifestyle that killed him –' Amanda allowed a bitter laugh '– you still left him there. You didn't call for help. That might be construed as manslaughter, or at least "criminal negligence contributing to death". I've asked around. It's true that you and Roger did an admirable job of hiding your S/M relationship. Right now, nobody knows.' She paused for effect. 'And nobody ever needs to know.'

Hope glimmered in Sophie Sharpe's eyes. 'What do you want?'

'You have the certificates to the shares Roger sold you, with you, ready for the shareholders' meeting.'

'Yes.'

'Simple. I want to buy them.'

Sophie brightened. 'Oh?'

'They amount to ten per cent of the company, correct?'

Sophie nodded.

'I'll give you a thousand dollars for them.'

Sophie sat back in her chair. 'That's ridiculous! I paid Roger a hundred times that.'

Amanda nodded. 'Is that all? You got them dirt cheap, but then you were his dominatrix, so he wouldn't have been hard to talk down.'

'You can't expect . . .'

Amanda shrugged. 'You used your power over him to influence his business decisions in a way that drastically affected me. I don't like that.'

Sophie frowned. 'There must be another way . . .'

'I could likely prove coercion, and that you paid Roger with funds you'd obtained either by fraud or by embezzlement, but all that would take time and be so boring and just add a few years to your jail sentence. Look at me, Sophie. I. Mean. Business.'

Sophie looked into Amanda's steely blue eyes for a second or two before she wilted. 'OK. I'll take the thousand, provided you don't press charges or ever make any of this public. And I get the hard copy.' Sophie picked up her briefcase and flipped it open. She reached for the pile of bank statements and X-rated glossies.

'Agreed.' Amanda let Sophie take the copies. They both knew Amanda could make more whenever she wanted. 'Don't think Ogilvy & Fitch are going to give you a job. I've already spoken to them. They've agreed to pay Forsythe Footwear considerable compensation in return for us not pressing charges against them. If it got out that they'd been bribing buyers, it'd finish them. You aren't very popular with that company any more.'

'Don't count me out,' Sophie said. Still, she was grim as she produced and signed over the stock certificates. Gleefully,

Amanda passed the woman a cheque for a thousand dollars. Done. And Sophie's reputation remained as pristine as her son Tom's. The Sharpe family was scandal-free.

The two women barely had time to freshen their faces before it was time to go down to the shareholders' meeting. It lasted a little more than twenty minutes.

Even with the proxies Sophie had gathered, without the ten per cent she'd coerced from Roger, Amanda retained control of the company. It was gratifying to Amanda to see how many investors had shown up in person, willing to give the widow Garland a chance to helm Forsythe Footwear rather than let it be scooped out from under her before she'd had a chance to show them what she could do. If there was any pity in the room, it was directed at Sophie, as Amanda accepted her resignation.

The meeting ended on a happy note. Amanda promised the shareholders that dividends would be paid at the end of the current financial year, for the first time in half a decade. They filed out rather jovially, each shaking her hand and wishing her the best of luck.

When the last one was gone, she sank back into her chair, grateful for support. It was over. She'd done it. She smiled. The future of her life as a businesswoman was downright rosy. Amanda's smile included the entire table, and then faded as she regarded the many empty chairs that surrounded it. She'd done it, all right.

26

Meg and Trevor were waiting for Amanda when she left the elevator in the lobby of the hotel. They were surrounded by luggage and Meg was wearing a straw hat, which suited her Tom Sawyer-like appeal tremendously, not that her appeal needed any help.

'What happened? I saw Sophie Sharpe leave a while back and she didn't look very happy,' said Trevor.

'The shareholders looked very happy, though,' said Meg. Her grey eyes were soft with concern.

Amanda didn't linger on Meg; she kept her eyes on Trevor as she delivered the good news.

He scooped her up in a big hug. 'Boss Lady!' Trevor spun round until Amanda was dizzy and pounding his shoulders to make him stop.

She refused to laugh. His new name for her hardly made up for not being his 'bendy doll' any more. Trevor put her down but kept his hand on her elbow until she was steady on her feet.

Meg stuck out her hand. 'Congratulations,' she said. 'Trevor tells me he already told you about us. I'd hoped to do it in person. But I'd like to thank you, too.'

Amanda focused her bright-blue eyes on Meg. If the younger woman saw some of the pain she felt at her loss, so be it. They'd been honest, the one night they'd had together, and she wasn't going to change that, too, now that everything else was changing. 'You're welcome, Meg,' she said. 'I'm happy for the two of you.'

Trevor caught her tone. He frowned, puzzled. 'You did set this up, right? Me and Meg? Or were you thinking me and Meg and ...'

'And me? Truthfully, I just wanted you to make sure nothing bad happened to Meg. But I'm glad you've found something in each other that, apparently ...' Amanda let the rest of the sentence hang, swallowing the urge to finish with '... neither of you saw in me'.

Trevor laughed. 'Silly!'

It was the last thing Amanda expected from him.

'You're just beginning to play!'

His infectious grin really made her want to smile. He always had a way of making her feel as flustered and giggly as a girl.

'True,' she conceded.

'I've been a player for a long time. And it was great, Amanda, especially with you. But I was at the end. I hadn't even kissed anyone for years until the night I kissed you. I was in danger of actually turning into a soulless sex machine.'

'I liked you as a sex machine,' grumbled Amanda.

Meg hugged her. 'That's why I wanted Trevor to wait until today. Just in case it wasn't the happy surprise he was sure it is. But Trevor's right, Amanda. We're looking for different things. I'm really lonely. I want to be with someone every night, not every so often. I want to be with Trevor.'

Amanda acquiesced. 'It's all good. Really. I'm fine.'

'We have a plane to catch,' said Trevor. 'And it's time for you to start celebrating your success.'

'I'm going home,' said Amanda.

'Home?'

Trevor and Meg exchanged worried looks.

Trevor said, 'What about your hat?'

'My hat?' Amanda gave him a blank look.

'That blue floppy thing you were wearing this morning. You

left it in the room we used for the shakedown of Sophie Sharpe.'

'I don't really care about my hat. To tell the truth I'm exhausted.'

Meg piped up. 'What about Paul and Rupert? They're a couple of handsome young stallions, hmm?'

'I guess.'

'That Nola's a bit of all right, too,' chimed in Trevor. 'Completely committed to Ms Garland's happiness.'

Amanda nodded.

'Go get your hat,' urged Trevor. 'You'll be glad you did.'

Again, she acquiesced. 'Fine, I'll go right now.'

'Great!' Trevor hoisted the luggage on to his back. 'When we return from our romp in the land of rum and reggae, we'll both report for work at Forsythe Footwear, Madam President.' He tried his best to give her his old two-fingered mock salute and only half-succeeded, laden down by luggage as he was. He leant in to kiss Amanda on the cheek.

'Enjoy monogamy,' whispered Amanda.

'I will,' he promised. 'I'll get us a cab,' he said to Meg, and was gone.

Meg and Amanda exchanged chaste kisses on the cheek.

'Enjoy monogamy,' Amanda whispered again.

'Manogama-huh? Whaddya mean?' Meg struck a 'Little Tramp' pose, her face a caricature of confusion. Then her guffaw resounded, which made Amanda laugh and caused most in the lobby to turn to look at its source and, when spotting Meg, to smile. 'We'll see about that, we will,' she said. Meg walked backwards, blowing kisses until she was out of sight.

27

The meeting room in 1012 was empty, suspiciously so. The suddenly important blue hat lay in the corner where it had landed when Amanda had sent it sailing across the room.

'Oh there's my hat!' She didn't bother actually picking it up.

A chorus of muffled giggles greeted her extra-loud exclamation.

'Hello?' she called out in her best 'I'm ready to be surprised' voice. 'Is that you, Nola?'

'In here,' Nola's voice sang out.

Amanda followed the sound through the slightly ajar glass doors into the main bedroom. It had been transformed into a scene out of *Arabian Nights*. Nola, resplendent in the garb of a belly dancer, gyrated in time with the exotic *afar* music that suddenly filled the air. She held a garish crown aloft.

Paul, draped only in a white sheet, lay on one of the double beds. His body gleamed as if it had been recently oiled. Rupert, also wrapped in a white sheet, duplicated Paul's pose.

All three called out together, 'Surprise!'

A big spangled sign was posted on the wall between the two beds. It read 'Congratulations, Ms Amanda, President of Forsythe Footwear and Our Sultana Forever!'

The coffee table was dominated by a big cake, as gaudy as the crown, which was surrounded by platters of food and a basket of fruit. Bottles of Dom Perignon '82, her favourite champagne in her favourite year, were crowded into ice buckets.

There were four champagne flutes waiting. Four. A nice number.

'Were you surprised?' Nola set the crown on Amanda's head.

'Oh yes!' Amanda clapped her hands. 'Completely! It's wonderful! I love it! Now let me see, Nola is my belly-dancing harem girl, but you two fine fellows, who are you?'

'Why, we are your sex slaves, Madam Ms President Amanda, Sultana forever,' said Paul, though the last word was a little strangled as he tried not to laugh.

'And we two slaves have a surprise for you,' said Rupert.

The young men stood facing each other. Their sheets dropped and Amanda saw that they were already both half-erect. Legs planted slightly apart, without moving their arms from their sides, Rupert and Paul leant forwards and kissed. It was a stunning tableau, made more so by the fact that, as the kiss lingered, both men's erections grew until their tips touched in the space between them.

'My beautiful boys.' Amanda's voice was husky.

'Think of the fun we can have now!' Nola exclaimed.

'Come, give me a hug and let's open the champagne.' Amanda's crown slid down over one eye and she adjusted it; garish though it might be, she quite liked it.

They surrounded her, kissing and hugging her until she was breathless. Paul broke away to pop the cork and serve the champagne. 'To Amanda,' he said as he handed her a glass. Amanda felt a frisson she hadn't experienced before with Paul. It wasn't like him to be careless, which meant he'd left the customary 'Ms' off the front of her name on purpose. Might he be a 'switch', like her, or perhaps moving in the direction of dominant? If so, eventually, she'd have to deal with being his boss but that was down the line. For now the possibility was exciting.

'To Ms Amanda,' chimed in Nola.

Amanda tilted her head to her Girl Friday. Nola was the perfect party girl, but eventually she'd tire of playing dumb, and her hair wasn't likely to stay pink forever. Then what?

'President and Sultana!' Rupert shouted.

And Rupert. What would he become as he matured? He seemed to have the nature of a true sybarite but would it be refined in the man Rupert was becoming, or would it become more extreme?

They clinked glasses.

Amanda started to tingle all over. Goddam! She hadn't lost her most interesting lovers; she'd simply lost the two oldest ones.

She sipped her champagne while the other three gulped half a glass each. Likely they'd never tasted anything as remotely delicious as the vintage Dom they were pouring down their throats. She suppressed a laugh as she imagined the bill she'd be presented with when they checked out. But that wouldn't be until tomorrow. They had a long lovely adventure ahead of them. It was time to take charge.

'You, slurping your champagne,' she said to Nola, 'you are more like a piglet than a pet.'

For a split second, Nola looked stricken, then she grinned and hung her head in mock-shame.

'You, my dear, shall have to be punished,' growled Amanda. 'Get on to that sofa and show me your greedy pussy.'

Nola hopped on to the sofa, hiked up her harem skirt and brazenly parted her knees to show off her naked not-so-private parts.

'You two, my adorable sex slaves, face each other again, as you did when you surprised me with your marvellous new deviance.'

The boys stood close, their hands at their sides and their feet planted as if for battle.

Pretending she didn't already know the answer, she asked, 'Are you willing to fondle each other?'

They nodded, a little shy but mostly pleased. Each reached to caress the other and both erections stiffened immediately.

Amanda's heart swelled with pride. Had they really done this, explored each other, for her? The idea thrilled her even though she doubted it was true. When she'd spied on them, she had seen an intimacy so profound it could only be born of true lust.

Amanda turned slowly on the spot. Life was such fun! Here she was, having defeated the Wicked Witch, surrounded by depraved young lovers, each of them toying proudly with their own or each other's sexual parts – at her command. Her heart swelled with pride. Two handsome cocks and a pretty pussy at her disposal. Anything she wanted, *anything*, was available. Where to start?

Nola. The girl was hardly moving. Just half the lengths of two fingers were buried between her neat, almost childish, nether lips. It was the play of the tendons on the back of her hand that told Amanda the girl was dabbling inside herself, stroking the intricate contours of her sex's lining.

'Show me your clit, Nola.'

Grinning, the girl pulled her fingers up and back, to spread her lips wide and expose the tiny pink polyp. Amanda wet a fingertip and gave the sensitive nub a delicate circular caress. Nola sucked in a gasp. Although she was pretending to be relaxed, Amanda could tell that the girl was seething with lust.

'Wait for it,' Amanda admonished.

'I'll try.' The muscles that ran up the insides of Nola's slender thighs twitched, further betraying her extreme arousal.

'Rupert, back on your bed, please,' she said. Amanda stripped off her coat-dress. She walked, bare but for hose, heels and crown, to Rupert's bed. Taking his firm young erection in hand, she gave it a few experimental strokes. Rupert's flesh was like velvet wrapped around stiff rope that was getting stiffer by the minute. She took his hand and put it around his rod. 'Keep stroking,' she told him.

'You too, sex slave number two,' she said. 'Up on your bed and stroking your cock, please.'

Paul did as he was bid.

Rupert truly was 'stroking'. His fingertips drifted up and down the length of his shaft, barely touching it. No doubt he was afraid that more vigorous caresses would take him over the edge. As his eyes wandered over Amanda's naked body, he bit his lower lip. Poor lad! It had to be absolute torture for him. Just to make it worse, Amanda bent over and planted a tiny soft kiss on his lop-sided arrowhead's wet eye. He groaned.

Amanda licked a dew-drop of his pre-come from her lips. 'Want me to suck you off?' she asked.

His legs doubled up. A strangled, 'Oh, fuck!' was his only reply.

'I'll take that as a "yes",' she teased before turning to Paul, on the other bed.

His fist was tightly wrapped around his shaft but pumping very slowly. Amanda tried to tousle his hair but on this occasion its spikes were too stiff for that. She trailed her fingertips down his gaunt ribcage and across the slight concavity of his tummy. As she neared his pubic mound, he tensed up and squeezed tighter. Her fingers tangled in his short hairs, which happily weren't styled into brittleness. As she tugged, she asked him, 'Wouldn't it be nice if that lovely thick cock of yours was deep inside my bum? Do you think you'd like to violate me like that? I could squeeze your cock as hard as your fingers are doing?'

He nodded violently.

Amanda turned to the entire room. 'Are you all ready to play "Everyone does Amanda"?'

Rupert nodded. Paul grunted.

Nola said, 'Yummy! Whenever you say, Ms Amanda, and *whatever* way you want us.'

Amanda ceremoniously removed her crown. 'I want you ... Yes, I promised you my bum, Paul, and you shall have it, but first ... Nola, come over here, on all fours, like the Sultana's pet pink pussy cat.'

Nola rolled off the sofa and crawled towards Amanda, hips swinging, making soft purring sounds in her throat. 'Meow?'

'Pussy likes pussy?' Amanda asked.

'Meow!'

'Then you shall have some.' Amanda perched on the edge of Paul's bed and spread her legs wide.

Nola crawled close. Her tongue flattened on Amanda's nylon-sheathed thigh, just above her knee, and rasped its way up to and over her mistress's lacy stocking top.

'Higher,' Amanda commanded.

'Meow.' The tongue glided over the glossy skin of Amanda's inner thigh.

Rupert blurted, 'Oh fuck! Lick her good, Nola!'

'You may finger her bum-hole while she licks me, Rupert.'

Nola's face nuzzled between Amanda's thighs. As Nola's tongue tantalised Amanda's engorged lips, Rupert wet a finger and touched it to the girl's tight little sphincter.

'I said, "finger", not tease,' Amanda told him.

Spurred by her order, he thrust and buried the full length of his finger into Nola's bottom. Nola wiggled her hips and humped back at him. Amanda took hold of Nola's nape and pulled her face in higher and closer.

Paul coughed. Amanda said, 'Patience, slave boy. I promised you a chance to please me and I always keep my promises.'

By then, Nola's tantalising tongue had teased Amanda's lips into parting so her liquid lust slicked her inner thighs and made them glisten.

'OK, everyone,' Amanda announced. 'It's time for you *all* to serve me. Give me room for a moment. Rupert, wriggle down the bed on your back a bit to give us space to play in.'

She stood up. Amanda nudged Rupert into position and climbed up astride him. 'Put his cock in my pussy, Nola,' Amanda said with deliberate crudeness.

Nola held Rupert in position while Amanda descended. The head nudged her nether lips. She wriggled, aiming for his shaft, and lowered herself with a series of little movements, skewering herself on his rigid pole until his pubes and her mound met.

Amanda bent forwards and looked into the boy's eyes. 'Tight enough for you, Rupert?'

He nodded.

'Well, it's going to get a lot tighter.' She turned her head. 'Lube my bum-hole, Nola.'

Without hesitating, Nola stretched over the bed and worked her face between the cheeks of Amanda's bottom. A slithery tongue probed. Amanda relaxed her sphincter to allow it access. Nola wet Amanda for a few enjoyable moments, and then withdrew. 'I think you're ready,' she said.

'Your turn, Paul. You know where to put your cock, don't you?'

'Yes.' He knelt up behind Amanda. It was Nola's hands that spread Amanda's cheeks as wide as she could. Paul's knob touched Amanda's pucker. He leant towards her and gripped her hips.

'Ready?' His voice held a commanding tone entirely appro-priate to the debasing act he was about to perform on her.

She nodded.

He surged into her. The first stroke was as sharp as the cut of a knife.

Rupert gasped. Amanda's inner walls were being squeezed flat with his rod resisting on all sides.

Amanda took a deep breath. 'Rupert, diddle me. Nola, kiss me.'

Nola's ripe mouth ravished Amanda's. Rupert rubbed her pink pearl and humped up into her pussy as best he could. Paul pumped down, into her bottom. The three-way assault was barely tolerable. Amanda's body was taut, too taut. With Trevor and Nola, this was where she'd had to stop, but this time she was determined to ride the sensation all the way. She willed herself to relax and take Paul a little deeper, bear down on Rupert a touch harder. For a few minutes the only noise was panting, kissing, and the harsh wet sound of pumping.

Amanda's toes curled.

'Do it,' she gasped, as much an invitation to them to climax with her if they were ready as it was an order to keep filling her with their hot young flesh. She groaned as the first of her contractions clamped on to not one but two plundering rods. The exquisite sensation made her spasm again, and that felt so fabulous it happened again, and so on and on she came. Slurping on Nola's tongue, garbling the words she used to articulate ecstasy, 'God' and 'Fuck' and 'Oh my God it's killing me' she rocked through half a dozen half-painful spasms, but no one stopped until Amanda went limp among them.

There would be time, for whoever hadn't come yet, to come, and for everyone else to come again. For the moment, Amanda was almost buried by lovers. Here in the harem they'd created for her amusement, sated by their sexual prowess, touched by their affection and respect, she felt surrounded by love, should she choose to look at it that way. Was it enough?

Slowly, Amanda untangled herself from the sweaty knot of limbs. 'Nola,' she said, 'dance for us, darling. Rupert, more wine? And, Paul, are those grapes I see? Come, my sweet sex slaves, feed me, amuse me and slake my thirst!'

It was enough, for now.

Visit the Black Lace website at
www.black-lace-books.com

FIND OUT THE LATEST INFORMATION AND TAKE ADVANTAGE OF OUR FANTASTIC FREE BOOK OFFER! ALSO VISIT THE SITE FOR ...

- All Black Lace titles currently available and how to order online
- Great new offers
- Writers' guidelines
- Author interviews
- An erotica newsletter
- Features
- Cool links

BLACK LACE – THE LEADING IMPRINT OF WOMEN'S SEXY FICTION

TAKING YOUR EROTIC READING PLEASURE TO NEW HORIZONS

LOOK OUT FOR THE ALL-NEW BLACK LACE BOOKS – AVAILABLE NOW!

All books priced £7.99 in the UK. Please note publication dates apply to the UK only. For other territories, please contact your retailer.

JULIET RISING

Cleo Cordell

ISBN 978 0 352 34192 1

Nothing is more important to Reynard than winning the favours of the bright and wilful Juliet, a pupil at Madame Nicol's exclusive but strict 18th century ladies' academy. Her captivating beauty tinged with a hint of cruelty soon has Reynard willing to do anything to win her approval. But Juliet's methods have little effect on Andreas, the real object of her lustful obsessions. Unable to bend him to her will, she is forced to watch him lavish his manly talents on her fellow pupils. That is, until she agrees to change her stuck-up, stubborn ways and become an eager erotic participant.

To be published in August 2008

WILDWOOD
Janine Ashbless
ISBN 978 0 352 34194 5

Avril Shearing is a landscape gardener brought in to reclaim an overgrown woodland for the handsome and manipulative Michael Deverick. But among the trees lurks a tribe of environmental activists determined to stop anyone getting in, led by the enigmatic Ash who regards Michael as his mortal enemy. Avril soon discovers that on the Kester Estate nothing is as it seems. Creatures that belong in dreams or in nightmares emerge after dark to prowl the grounds, and hidden in the heart of the wood is something so important that people will kill, or die for it. Ash and Michael become locked in a deadly battle for the Wildwood – and for Avril herself.

ODALISQUE
Fleur Reynolds
ISBN 978 0 352 34193 8

Set against a backdrop of sophisticated elegance, a tale of family intrigue, forbidden passions and depraved secrets unfolds. Beautiful but scheming, successful designer Auralie plots to bring about the downfall of her virtuous cousin, Jeanine. Recently widowed, but still young and glamorous, Jeanine finds her passions being rekindled by Auralie's husband. But she is playing into Auralie's hands – vindictive hands that drag Jeanine into a world of erotic depravity. Why are the cousins locked into this sexual feud? And what is the purpose of Jeanine's mysterious Confessor, and his sordid underground sect?

ENCHANTED
Janine Ashbless, Olivia Knight, Leonie Martel
ISBN 978 0 352 34195 2

Bear Skin
Hazel is whisked away from her tedious job and humdrum life by the mysterious
Arailt, to be his lover. The only problem is there is more to Arailt than meets the
eye – much more.
The Three Riddles
The elves, they say, know the secrets of events – but the queen has no time for
superstitions. As her kingdom crumbles, she longs for her lost love, but can she
risk her country on a whim?
The People in the Garden
Strange things are happening in the grounds of Count and Countess Malinovsky's
Gothic manor house. Local people tell of fairies, goblins and unnameable
creatures, and there are stories about a ghostly girl with an uncanny resemblance
to the decadent couple's beautiful servant Katia.

To be published in September 2008

THE STALLION
Georgina Brown
ISBN 978 0 352 34199 0

The world of showjumping is as steamy as it is competitive. Ambitious young rider
Penny Bennett enters into a wager with her oldest rival and friend, Ariadne. Penny
intends to gain the sponsorship and the very personal attention of showjumping's
biggest impresario, Alister Beaumont. The prize is Ariadne's thoroughbred stallion,
guaranteed to bring Penny money and success.
Beaumont's riding school is not all it seems, however. Firstly there's the weird relationship between Alister and his cigar-smoking sister. Then the bizarre clothes they
want Penny to wear. In an atmosphere of unbridled kinkiness, Penny is determined
to win the wager and discover the truth about Beaumont's strange hobbies.

IN TOO DEEP
Portia Da Costa
ISBN 978 0 352 34197 6

Librarian Gwendolyne Price finds indecent proposals and sexy stories in her sugges-
tion box every morning. Shocked that they seem to be tailored specifically to her
own deepest sexual fantasies, she begins a tantalising relationship with a man she's
never met. But pretty soon, erotic letters and toe-curlingly sensual emails just aren't
enough. She has to meet her mysterious correspondent in the flesh.

ALSO LOOK OUT FOR

THE NEW BLACK LACE BOOK OF WOMEN'S SEXUAL FANTASIES
Edited and compiled by Mitzi Szereto
ISBN 978 0 352 34172 3

The second anthology of detailed sexual fantasies contributed by women from all over the world. The book is a result of a year's research by an expert on erotic writing and gives a fascinating insight into the rich diversity of the female sexual imagination.

Black Lace Booklist

Information is correct at time of printing. To avoid disappointment, check availability before ordering. Go to www.black-lace-books.com.
All books are priced £7.99 unless another price is given.

BLACK LACE BOOKS WITH AN HISTORICAL SETTING

BLACK LACE BOOKS WITH A PARANORMAL THEME

❏ BRIGHT FIRE Maya Hess	ISBN 978 0 352 34104 4
❏ BURNING BRIGHT Janine Ashbless	ISBN 978 0 352 34085 6
❏ CRUEL ENCHANTMENT Janine Ashbless	ISBN 978 0 352 33483 1
❏ FLOOD Anna Clare	ISBN 978 0 352 34094 8
❏ GOTHIC BLUE Portia Da Costa	ISBN 978 0 352 33075 8
❏ THE PRIDE Edie Bingham	ISBN 978 0 352 33997 3
❏ THE SILVER COLLAR Mathilde Madden	ISBN 978 0 352 34141 9
❏ THE TEN VISIONS Olivia Knight	ISBN 978 0 352 34119 8

BLACK LACE ANTHOLOGIES

❏ BLACK LACE QUICKIES 1 Various	ISBN 978 0 352 34126 6	£2.99
❏ BLACK LACE QUICKIES 2 Various	ISBN 978 0 352 34127 3	£2.99
❏ BLACK LACE QUICKIES 3 Various	ISBN 978 0 352 34128 0	£2.99
❏ BLACK LACE QUICKIES 4 Various	ISBN 978 0 352 34129 7	£2.99
❏ BLACK LACE QUICKIES 5 Various	ISBN 978 0 352 34130 3	£2.99
❏ BLACK LACE QUICKIES 6 Various	ISBN 978 0 352 34133 4	£2.99
❏ BLACK LACE QUICKIES 7 Various	ISBN 978 0 352 34146 4	£2.99
❏ BLACK LACE QUICKIES 8 Various	ISBN 978 0 352 34147 1	£2.99
❏ BLACK LACE QUICKIES 9 Various	ISBN 978 0 352 34155 6	£2.99
❏ MORE WICKED WORDS Various	ISBN 978 0 352 33487 9	£6.99
❏ WICKED WORDS 3 Various	ISBN 978 0 352 33522 7	£6.99
❏ WICKED WORDS 4 Various	ISBN 978 0 352 33603 3	£6.99
❏ WICKED WORDS 5 Various	ISBN 978 0 352 33642 2	£6.99
❏ WICKED WORDS 6 Various	ISBN 978 0 352 33690 3	£6.99
❏ WICKED WORDS 7 Various	ISBN 978 0 352 33743 6	£6.99
❏ WICKED WORDS 8 Various	ISBN 978 0 352 33787 0	£6.99
❏ WICKED WORDS 9 Various	ISBN 978 0 352 33860 0	
❏ WICKED WORDS 10 Various	ISBN 978 0 352 33893 8	
❏ THE BEST OF BLACK LACE 2 Various	ISBN 978 0 352 33718 4	
❏ WICKED WORDS: SEX IN THE OFFICE Various	ISBN 978 0 352 33944 7	
❏ WICKED WORDS: SEX AT THE SPORTS CLUB Various	ISBN 978 0 352 33991 1	
❏ WICKED WORDS: SEX ON HOLIDAY Various	ISBN 978 0 352 33961 4	
❏ WICKED WORDS: SEX IN UNIFORM Various	ISBN 978 0 352 34002 3	
❏ WICKED WORDS: SEX IN THE KITCHEN Various	ISBN 978 0 352 34018 4	
❏ WICKED WORDS: SEX ON THE MOVE Various	ISBN 978 0 352 34034 4	
❏ WICKED WORDS: SEX AND MUSIC Various	ISBN 978 0 352 34061 0	

To find out the latest information about Black Lace titles, check out the website: www.black-lace-books.com or send for a booklist with complete synopses by writing to:

Black Lace Booklist, Virgin Books Ltd
Thames Wharf Studios
Rainville Road
London W6 9HA

Please include an SAE of decent size. Please note only British stamps are valid.

Our privacy policy
We will not disclose information you supply us to any other parties. We will not disclose any information which identifies you personally to any person without your express consent.

From time to time we may send out information about Black Lace books and special offers. Please tick here if you do <u>not</u> wish to receive Black Lace information.   ❏

Please send me the books I have ticked above.

Name ....

Address ....

....

....

....

Post Code ....

Send to: Virgin Books Cash Sales, Thames Wharf Studios, Rainville Road, London W6 9HA.

US customers: for prices and details of how to order books for delivery by mail, call 888-330-8477.

Please enclose a cheque or postal order, made payable to Virgin Books Ltd, to the value of the books you have ordered plus postage and packing costs as follows:

UK and BFPO – £1.00 for the first book, 50p for each subsequent book.

Overseas (including Republic of Ireland) – £2.00 for the first book, £1.00 for each subsequent book.

If you would prefer to pay by VISA, ACCESS/MASTERCARD, DINERS CLUB, AMEX or SWITCH, please write your card number and expiry date here: ....

....

Signature ....

Please allow up to 28 days for delivery.